THE
TRANSGRESSORS

STORY OF A GREAT SIN

A Political Novel of the Twentieth Century

FRANCIS A. ADAMS

1st WORLD
LIBRARY
Literary Society

The Transgressors

Francis A. Adams

© 1st World Library, 2006
PO Box 2211
Fairfield, IA 52556
www.1stworldlibrary.com
First Edition

LCCN: 2007920646

Softcover ISBN: 978-1-4218-3953-0
Hardcover ISBN: 978-1-4218-3853-3
eBook ISBN: 978-1-4218-4053-6

Purchase *"The Transgressors"*
as a traditional bound book at:
www.1stWorldLibrary.com/purchase.asp?ISBN=978-1-4218-3953-0

1st World Library is a literary, educational organization
dedicated to:

- Creating a free internet library of downloadable ebooks

- Hosting writing competitions and offering book
  publishing scholarships.

1ˢᵗ World Library Literary Society

Giving Back to the World

"If you want to work on the core problem, it's early school literacy."

- James Barksdale, former CEO of Netscape

"No skill is more crucial to the future of a child, or to a democratic and prosperous society, than literacy."

- Los Angeles Times

Literacy... means far more than learning how to read and write... The aim is to transmit... knowledge and promote social participation."

- UNESCO

"Literacy is not a luxury, it is a right and a responsibility. If our world is to meet the challenges of the twenty-first century we must harness the energy and creativity of all our citizens."

- President Bill Clinton

"Parents should be encouraged to read to their children, and teachers should be equipped with all available techniques for teaching literacy, so the varying needs and capacities of individual kids can be taken into account."

- Hugh Mackay

CONTENTS

BOOK I - HAIL TO THE SHERIFF OF LUZERNE

BOOK II - THE SYNDICATE INCORPORATES

BOOK III - THE SYNDICATE DECLARES A DIVIDEND

BOOK IV - IN FREEDOM'S NAME

BOOK I

HAIL TO THE SHERIFF
OF LUZERNE!

CHAPTER I

CLOUDS GATHER AT WILKES-BARRE

There are few valleys to compare with that of the Susquehanna. In point of picturesque scenery and modern alteration attained by the unceasing labor of man, the antithesis between the natural and the artificial is pronounced in many respects; especially at that place in the river where it runs through the steep banks on which is situated the thriving city of Wilkes-Barre. Here may be seen the majestic hills standing as sentinels over the marts of men that crowd the river edge. The verdure of these hills during the greater part of the year is the one sight that gladdens the eyes of the miners whose lives, for the most part, are spent in the coal pits.

The picture would be perfect were it not for the presence of the Coal-Breakers. These sombre, grizzly structures stand in a long line on the west bank of the river, and appear to the eye of one who knows their purpose, as the gibbets that dotted the shores of England and France must have loomed up before the mariners of the Channel during the Seventeenth Century, and when the supply of pirates exceeded the number of gibbets, large as this number was in both lands.

The breaker is a truly modern invention, which, had it existed in the days of the Spanish inquisition, would have placed in the hands of the malevolent fanatics an instrument of exquisite torture. It is constructed to effect a double purpose, the achievement of the maximum of production and the expenditure of the minimum of human effort. It is the acme of inventive genius. To work the breakers, a man need have no more intelligence than the tow-mule that plods a beaten path; and such a man is the ideal laborer from the standpoint of the owners of the breakers.

But such men are not indigenous to America; they must be imported, and that, too, from the most benighted lands of Europe.

What an incubator of warped humanity the breaker has become! It saps even the attenuated manhood of the aliens it attracts, and when they are rendered useless for its ends, emits them to be a scourge on the earth.

But the breakers are the monument of the civilization of the Nineteenth Century, which esteems commercial as superior to mental advancement.

As the drama to be unfolded will be enacted largely in this spot, which nature fashioned on its fairest pattern, and which man has seared with his cruel tool, a description of the town of Wilkes-Barre and its environs is essential. The town is the creation of the Mines. Coal abounds in the valley of the Susquehanna, and from the first impetus given the coal industry by the establishment of railroads, the mines at this place have been worked without intermission. The population of the town has been increasing steadily for the past thirty years, until to-day it reaches the proportions of a populous city. There is little variety in the citizens; but the contrast they present makes up for this deficiency. Broadly speaking there are but two classes, the magnates and their mercenaries. The former live in the mansions on the esplanade and constitute the governing minority. The coal miners and the workers on the breakers, who eke out their lives in slavery, and who sleep in quarters that make the huts of the peasants of Europe seem actually inviting, constitute the vast majority.

The most prosperous business of the town outside of the Coal

Francis A. Adams

industry, which is, of course, monopolized by the magnates, is the Undertaking business. There are almost as many establishments for the burial of man as there are saloons to cater to his cheer. In contradistinction to the custom in this country, the business has been taken up by others than the worthy order of sextons. That this condition should be, is accounted for by the fact that there is a paucity of churches in the town, and that the sextons were unable to accomplish the work that devolved upon their craft. Death is not attributable, in the main, to natural causes in Wilkes-Barre; it is brought about by the engines of destruction which the magnates are pleased to term, Modern Machinery.

Association makes the mind incapable of appreciating nice distinctions in regard to familiar objects or persons. Thus to the residents of the town there is nothing abnormal in their condition. It is only to the observer from without that the horrors of the Pennsylvania town are apparent. That such a spot should develop in a State high in rank, and among the oldest of those comprising the greatest republic, seems incomprehensible. In the very State where the Declaration of Independence was sent to the world, proclaiming that men are created free and equal, and that the right of the majority is the supreme law, how comes it that a settlement can be maintained where the rights of the majority can be ignored and suppressed at the point of the bayonet? For an answer to this question, comes the monosyllable—Trusts!

Wilkes-Barre is a typical specimen community which may be taken as the sample unit for a microscopic investigation of the conditions that have created the modern institution of *voluntary slavery*. The scrutiny of the specimen is given through the eyes of a resident of the town, and the observations are his.

"In a month then, they will shut down three of the mines, and will close the Jumbo Breaker. You know what that means. I have asked the men of Shaft Fifteen if they intend to starve, and they answered to a man that they would sooner be shot than starve like rats in their homes."

"What is that to me?" Am I to look after every man who has ever blasted a ton of coal in my pits or crushed in the breakers?

"You tell the men of Shaft Fifteen, and of every other shaft in the valley, that if they make a single move that threatens the property of the Paradise Coal Company I will see that they don't 'starve in their homes.'"

"Then you will not arbitrate?"

"There is nothing to arbitrate. I have no more work for the men. That settles it. The world is big, and if they can find no work in Wilkes-Barre, let them hunt for it elsewhere."

"Mr. Purdy, I give you ample warning. The miners will declare a general strike if you persist in locking out half of them now that the winter weather has set in. The pits and the breakers can stand idle while the demand for coal at an advanced price is created by an artificial coal famine; but the miners have to be fed. They work like machines; but as yet they have not learned the lesson of living without food."

"Metz, I have given you my final answer. The mines and breakers close on the day I stated."

Carl Metz is the foreman of the largest of the Paradise Company's Coal shafts, the "Big Horn." He is in consultation with Mr. Gorman Purdy, the president of the company. Their closing remarks as just quoted are uttered as they stand on the steps leading to the street from the offices on the main square of Wilkes-Barre.

The men nod to each other, and separate.

"What did he say?" a man demands of Metz, in a weak voice. The questioner is a typical miner. Death has placed its irrevocable stamp upon him; he has served his three years in the pits; has been transferred to the breakers when the signs of failing strength are perceived by the mine overseer. In another year he will be in the hands of the mortuary vulture; his last week's earnings will go to pay for the hard earned grave that is grudgingly given "A Miner."

"He says the mines will close."

"Yes, and we will starve. Well, you can tell him that we won't."

"I told him that the men were desperate."

"And he laughed at you. Why wouldn't he? We have threatened to strike for three years. It's getting to be an old story. This time it's our turn to laugh."

"What do you mean, Eric?" is the anxious query of Metz. He detects a hidden significance in the miner's words.

"Mean!" Why I mean that we are *going* to strike this time, and that it will be the biggest fight the coal region has ever seen.

"We can't get the mine owners to arbitrate, but we can get the coal miners to unite. If one man is shut out to starve we will all go out."

"And our places will be filled by imported miners," interjects the foreman.

"Not this time. We will have our pickets out in all directions, and every train will be boarded. The men the mine owners bring on will be told to keep away."

As the men speak they are unconscious of the approach of the Sheriff of Luzerne County. He has apparently been watching the movements of Metz. All the morning he has shadowed the mine foreman, now he steals up behind the two and stands within earshot. He overhears their words.

"Let me tell you one thing," he calls out in a shrill voice, as he steps up to them, "you don't want to forget that there is a Sheriff in Luzerne County when you count on winning out in this strike."

"We will do nothing that will require your attention," sententiously retorts the miner. "We have had one taste of Pennsylvania justice, at Homestead, and don't want another."

"I have my eye on you two, and if there is any trouble I'll know whom to hold responsible," continues the Sheriff. Then he walks on towards the office of the Paradise Coal Company. He enters the building and is soon in the private office of the President.

The miners walk on in silence towards their homes in the East End of the town across the Bridge. It is not a time to talk. These sturdy men have a reverence for words; they use them only when the occasion requires. At the door of the ramshackle hut that serves as the abode of Eric Neilson, the men halt.

"Eric!" says Metz, "I hope you will let me know of any steps that are to be taken by the miners in your section. I have been in this region for twenty years, and know where the rights of the miners end and the rights of the mine owners begin. To back our rights we have nothing but our bare fists; the mine owners have the city, state and Federal authorities."

"If there is anything to be done that will be of importance to us all, you will hear from me," are Eric's reassuring words.

Carl Metz knows the value of a promise from his fellow-workman. He is satisfied.

In the homely parlance of the mines, these men agreed "to keep tabs for each other on the square." They will let no event of importance go by without reporting it to each other, and in this way give each full particulars of the movements of the miners.

Metz turns back towards the centre of the city. He is bent on seeing Purdy again, and of appealing to him to reconsider his "shut down" orders.

Hardly has he reached Market Street when he runs across the Attorney of the Paradise Coal Company, a young and brilliant man who is one of the products of the town school and academy, Harvey Trueman.

"Good day, Mr. Trueman," is his salutation.

"How now, Metz?" responds the preoccupied lawyer. "Have you some trouble on your hands?"

"It's the same old story, sir, only this time the men are determined to strike." I have spoken to Mr. Purdy to-day. He refuses to yield a single inch.

"I thought it might be a wise thing to see him again and make the truth clear to him, that the men will unquestionably resort to violence if they are locked out at the opening of winter."

"You let this matter stand as it is. I shall see Mr. Purdy in an hour or so, and shall make it my duty to explain the situation. I know what the men are likely to do, and what concessions will satisfy them. Metz, I assure you we do not want trouble. If I have any influence with the Company, matters will be satisfactorily settled."

"When can the men have an answer?"

"Not for a day or two, I suppose."

"But they must know immediately, Mr. Trueman. You are aware that they are dependent upon the Company Stores for their food. Well, the notice has been posted that no more credit shall be extended after next Saturday. This means that, for the men who are laid off, there is nothing left but starvation."

Trueman is troubled at this statement. He has always been an opponent of the "Company Store" system; now he sees that it is likely to be the potent factor in exciting the miners to revolt.

"All I can promise you, is that I shall work in your interests and get as speedy a reply as possible," he repeats. "By the by," he adds, "will you come with me to my office now, I want you to go over some of the details of the 'Homestead Strike' with me. I want to see what lessons I can gather from it which will help me to advise Purdy in the present trouble. You were in the Homestead strike, were you not?"

By a nod of his head, Metz answers in the affirmative.

They are seated in the office of the young attorney for the next hour, during which period they review the events of the great iron strike of '92; the reasons that led to it, and the similarity of the conditions that exist in Wilkes-Barre.

Having given Trueman the details of the Homestead affair, Metz explains the existing grievances of the miners of Wilkes-Barre as follows:

"The question raised by the miners is not one for advanced wages; it is not one of reduced hours; it is not a demand for proper protection for themselves in the mines." These things they have asked for time and again—little enough for men who wear out their lives in the darkness and damp of the mines. But these things they have never been able to obtain.

"A bare living is all that the mine owners would concede to the miners." This living, meagre as it was, sufficed to keep life in the miners and their families.

"Now the miners are to be deprived of the crust of bread." You cannot snatch the bone from a hungry dog, without danger. Do you imagine that a man has less spirit than a beast?

"The whole trouble, Mr. Trueman, arises from the formation

of the Coal Trust." I have all the facts in regard to this matter. And so far as that goes, there is not a man in the labor organizations of this country who does not keep in touch with the events of the day. The education of the masses is a dangerous thing in a land that is ruled by force, fraud and finesse, as the United States is to-day.

"It is the Coal Trust that has brought on this threatened strike."

"When there were independent coal companies, the condition of the miners was better by far than it is to-day." The unrestricted operation of mines made it impossible for any two, or even a considerable number, of the mine owners to unite for the purpose of reducing the wages of the mine operatives, and of increasing the price of the coal to the consumer.

"But with the Trust in operation all restraints are removed."

"The illegal traffic rates that the Trust secures, make it impossible for any mine to be successfully worked that is out of the combine."

"The first step that the Coal Trust took was to limit the supply of coal at the height of the summer season, when big shipments are ordinarily made." This afforded a pretext for an advance in the retail price.

"To limit the supply, the Trust shut down work in half of the mines."

"For the past seven years this practice has been followed." Now the simple miners know what to expect. They have been submissive, because the suspension of work came in the summer time when they could live on little, and did not have to withstand the rigor of a Pennsylvania winter.

"Now the Paradise Coal Company announces that it will close down the work on three of the mines next Saturday. This throws the men out in the cold of November. If this plan is carried out it will bring on a long and bitter strike."

"I quite agree with you," assents Trueman. He puffs meditatively at a cigar.

"You are too young a man to remember the days of the Molly Maguires, those awful days when murderers lurked on every road in the anthracite coal field of this state." It was back in 1876 that the last of the Maguires was hunted down. Of course there is no excuse for murder; yet the Maguires were the result of a pernicious condition of wage depression and degradation of humanity.

"When the just demands of the miners were recognized the reign of terror ceased."

"But the Trusts have produced another organization of societies in this state, bent on murder and arson." The Irish, English and Welsh miners, who predominated in the region twenty years ago, are now supplanted by Poles, Hungarians, Italians and the worst types of Lithuanians and Slavs. These newcomers have brought with them the racial prejudices and institutions that caused them to be enemies in their native lands; they constitute a dangerous element in the population of this country. So long as they are able to get food they remain passive, except for the feuds they carry on amongst themselves. These immigrants are not inspired to come to this land by reason of an appreciation of the liberty that our Constitution vouchsafes to all mankind. They have been brought here by the agents of the Trusts, because they are willing to work for pauper wage.

"I can tell you, Mr. Trueman, that in the strike that I feel will follow the lock-out, there will be bloodshed. It may not be at the initiative of the miners. But the fear of the magnates is now aroused and they will not hesitate to employ force. Once the appeal to force is made, where is it to end?"

"All that you have told me, I shall report to Mr. Purdy,"

Trueman says, as he extends his hand to grasp that of the plain, earnest miner.

Metz departs, well satisfied with the progress he has made in advancing the cause of the miners.

Harvey Trueman goes at once to the private office of the President of the Paradise Coal Company.

He brings the strike matter up for consideration at once; and also the case of a widow who is bringing suit against the company for the recovery of damages for the loss of her husband who had been killed in the mines.

"You are to press the defence of this case for damages to a successful termination for the company," are Mr. Purdy's last words, supplemented by the remark, "I shall attend to the strike in person."

CHAPTER II

HARVEY TRUEMAN, ATTORNEY

Harvey Trueman steps from the County Clerk's office into the corridor, on the second floor of the Court House at Wilkes-Barre, with the absolute knowledge that the case in hand is won.

As he pushes his way down the stairway to the first floor where the courtroom is located, he elbows through a throng of rough dressed miners—Polaks, Magyars, and here and there a man of half-Irish parentage, whose Irish name is all that is left from the Molly Maguire days to indicate the one-time ascendency of that race in the lands of the coal region.

Certain victory within his grasp—a minor victory in the long line of legal fights he has conducted for the Paradise Coal Company—he does not smile. It is a cruel thing he is about to do. Cruel? He asks himself if the sanctity of the law does not make the contemplated move right. Harvey Trueman has a code of morals, an austere code, that has made him enemies even among the people whose champion he has grown to be in three years' practice of the law in Luzerne County, Pennsylvania.

He is a tall, slender, square-jawed man of thirty-six. His forehead is high and broad and his hair is worn longer than that of other young men—parted on the side and brushed back. He has thin lips and a mouth of unusual width. His

Francis A. Adams

mouth-line is as straight as a bowstring, and when he speaks, which is often, or smiles, which is not so frequent, he shows an even line of large white teeth.

There is something very earnest in the expression of Harvey Trueman's face—a soberness that is seldom found in men under fifty. A straight, strong nose, large nostrils and clean shaven upper lip that is abnormally long; cheek bones that stand out prominently; gray eyes set rather deep in his head for so young a man; a square chin protruding slightly; and wearing a frock coat that falls to his knees in limp folds, Trueman is a commanding figure, full of character.

He is an inch over six feet in height. Among the miners who look straight into the eye to read character, Harvey Trueman has been pronounced an unflinching tool of the coal barons—one whose unbending will means the ultimate accomplishment of any undertaking.

Not one of the miners employed by the Paradise Coal Company has ever known the young lawyer to take an unfair advantage. But he has upheld the law for the proprietors of the mines when the men have made a fight against the "company stores," where they are forced to spend the wages made by the sweat of their brows down in the mines or on the breakers.

Trueman is looked upon by all the miners of the region as a part and parcel of the law, and all law is regarded by them as a thing made to oppress the poor and aggrandize the wealthy.

A simple investigation on the eve of the present battle has placed in the hands of the young lawyer ammunition which will rout the enemy on the first volley.

But such an enemy! Above all things, Harvey Trueman is a magnanimous foe. Now that he has his case won, he feels half humiliated. In the court room, occupying a front seat while she awaits the arrival of her lawyer, sits the widow of Marcus Braun, the Magyar miner.

The miner was killed in Shaft Fifteen of the Paradise Company, which is three miles down the river from the wagon bridge at Wilkes-Barre. Standing at the bottom of the shaft when an elevator cage fell, upon which were two loaded coal cars, he was crushed to a pulp. His widow is suing for damages for the death of her husband. In the front seat with her, in the court room, is her five-year-old boy, whom she must support, perhaps by taking boarders at the mines, if the mine superintendent will permit her to go in debt for the rent of a house in case her litigation against the company is not successful.

True, the rope by which the cage had been lifted and lowered had worn thin, and the foreman had warned the superintendent the morning of the accident that a new one was needed. But the poor Magyar at the bottom of the shaft did not know it. He had in no way contributed to the negligence which brought about his death. He knew his work was perilous. In the law, it is a question whether or not the case can be successfully defended by the coal company.

Trueman's trip to the Clerk's office has been for the purpose of ascertaining the miner's standing with reference to his citizenship at the time of his death. With his experience in the practice, the lawyer surmised that the Magyar was never naturalized. If he was not naturalized, his widow has no standing in the court where the suit has been brought. In that case, it belongs to the Federal Court, and his widow and orphan, as well as the impecunious lawyer who has taken the widow's case on a contingent fee, will not have the means nor the fortitude to begin action in the higher court.

Trueman discovers after a few moments of investigation in the Clerk's office that his suspicion is well founded. The miner had never taken out naturalization papers.

Cruel? In the concrete, perhaps. The law is made for the multitude.

"It is a legitimate defense!" Trueman murmurs to himself, as he passes down the stairs. "The Magyar bore none of the burdens of citizenship. Neither should he or his, share in the protection which the State of Pennsylvania affords her citizens."

"Will the Magyar's widow get anything?" asks O'Connor, one of the half-Irish, half-Italian miners, whose elbow Trueman brushes as he walks towards the court room.

Trueman befriended O'Connor once in the matter of rent.

"No. He was not naturalized!"

"His blood be on old Purdy's head, then!" says O'Connor. "The mine boss has said he will put her out in the street. She's already months back in her rent."

Trueman passes on as if he has not heard O'Connor, who is at the Court House as one of the witnesses.

As the young lawyer pushes his way into the court room his quick glance catches the bent form of the woman in the front seat, clad in the cheapest of black, and the open-eyed boy at her side.

The proceedings are short. Trueman sits down at one of the tables inside the bar enclosure and hastily dashes off an affidavit containing the facts he has discovered, and a formal motion to dismiss. The Judge hears the motion, which is opposed to in a half-hearted way by the lawyer on the other side. The suit is dismissed.

When she is finally made to understand what has happened, the widow burst into tears. The boy, at sight of his mother's distress, sets up a wailing that echoes through the whole Court House. In the hallway, the bunch of miners from Shaft Fifteen gather about the weeping woman as she comes out. One more instance of the heartlessness of the law which is made by the men elected by the Coal Barons, is brought home to them.

To these ignorant men, to whom the first principle of self-preservation is that limit of erudition set by the coal barons themselves, whose first and last lessons in life are to read correctly the checks of the time-keeper and the figures on the "company store" checks which they receive in payment for their work, what difference does it make that the dead miner was a Magyar—not a full fledged American?

He lost his life down in a coal mine where he went to dig coal that some American, way off beyond the hills, might toast his toes on a winter's evening. His life's work was to help keep the American public warm. In return, all he asked was very poor food, a straw bed in a hovel, and a crust for his wife should he be killed in the undertaking.

There is much grumbling already on account of the company stores. The walking delegate of the miners' union has ordered a strike in Carbon County, adjoining, unless the Paradise Company shall reduce the price of blasting powder sold to the miners, fifteen cents a pound.

The miners leave the Court House grumbling. Soothing the Magyar's widow in their rough way, they form a grim procession and trudge back over the dusty road to the breaker and the row of hovels on either side of it.

Francis A. Adams

CHAPTER III

CONFLICTING OPINIONS

An hour afterward Trueman is seated in his office, in the Commerce building, on the public square of Wilkes-Barre, in the middle of which is situated the Court House. On the same floor with his office are the general offices of the Paradise Coal Company.

Besides giving him distinction as a "corporation lawyer," which has its effect in drawing outside clients, this proximity to the general offices of the Coal Barons' syndicate relieves the young lawyer from the payment of rent. For the convenience of having a shrewd attorney always at his beck and call, Gorman Purdy, president of the company, is willing that Trueman shall occupy the office rent free in addition to the liberal salary which is paid him.

While Trueman is successfully managing the legal affairs of the Paradise Coal Company and achieving a brilliant reputation at the bar of Pennsylvania, Gorman Purdy is "trying him out" with an entirely different object in view. He desires to test the young man's mettle as a man even more than as a lawyer. To accomplish this end it is most important that Trueman shall occupy the office next the suite of the great coal corporation.

Lying on the lawyer's desk is an open envelope, by the side of which is a check for one thousand dollars, being the amount of his salary from the coal company for two months. In his ears still ring the plaintive sobs of the Magyar's widow and the denunciation of O'Connor.

"The mine boss will put her in the street!"

In his mind's eye he pictures the dusty road separating the two rows of miners' huts, down around the bend in the Susquehanna. He sees the mountain beyond and the column of steam rising from a more distant breaker, half way up the slope—a beautiful vision from the distance, but how squalid in its dull gray misery to those who spend their lives in its midst.

At this moment the miners who were in attendance at court are trudging along this highway, chattering their grievances to one another. The widow and her boy bring up the rear, while the men march solemnly on ahead, talking of their right to live—just to live.

Across these mountains, in the city of Philadelphia, six score years and more ago a convention once uttered the identical sentiments being voiced by these serfs of the coal seams. Harvey Trueman has been a deep student of the teachings of that convention. On the shelves of his library are the well-thumbed writings of Washington and the Adamses and Thomas Jefferson. He is a firm believer of the doctrines enunciated at Faneuil Hall, and by Henry in Virginia.

To-morrow, perhaps to-night, the widow's paltry chattels will be set in the middle of that road by the sheriff. She will be dispossessed by the Paradise Coal Company. A frail woman, pale with poverty of the blood, shrinking with every breath she draws, because she knows the very air she breathes comes to her over the lands of the Coal Barons—a haggard widow of the mines will be deprived of her miserable shelter, not fit for a beast of burden, by the richest coal corporation on earth. Why? Because her abject misery is a lesson too graphic in its horrible details to be constantly before the miners. Allowed to remain there, the widow will breed trouble among the men who are all risking their lives every minute of every working day, even as her husband risked his. Dispossess proceedings do not come under the supervision of Harvey Trueman, but he has ever been observant. A blind man may not remain in ignorance of the human suffering in the coal regions of Pennsylvania. Men in the general offices of the Paradise Coal Company see only the papers and receive the returns. They ask not "Who put the widow of our latest victim in the street?"

The sheriff sees to the rest. All hail to the Sheriff of Luzerne! But Harvey Trueman knows of these things. He has a mind that pierces the thin walls of the miners' cabins and sees beyond the papers placed in the sheriff's hands.

"I suppose she will be hungry for three or four days," he tells himself, "except for the crusts the other women give her. But in a month she will be married again. If she had recovered a thousand dollars damages for the life of her husband, one of the other miners would have had it in a week."

He picks up the check and glances at it for the third time. Then he folds it and places it in his pocketbook.

"I am paid the thousand dollars," he continues, "for keeping her from getting it—for two months of my life spent in throwing up legal barricades to prevent the miners from approaching too near to the coffers of the Paradise Coal Company. If the Magyar's widow had collected damages for her husband's death, there would be twenty more suits filed in a fortnight."

And so he appeases his conscience. He tries to be flippant, as he has seen the officers of the great corporation flippant about such matters, but in spite of himself his heartstrings tighten. Harvey Trueman is acting a lie, and his heart knows it, though his brain has not yet found it out.

The office door swings open. A man of fifty-five enters—a short man with a stubby red beard, a round face, and hair well sprinkled with gray. He is dressed in a gray cutaway business suit and wears a silk hat. His neckscarf is of English make, his collar is of the thickest linen and neatest pattern, and his general appearance that of the aristocratic business man whose evenings in a provincial city are spent at a club, and in the metropolis at the opera.

It is Gorman Purdy. Trueman's fondest hope—next to the one that at some distant day, say ten or fifteen years in the future, he may sit in the United States Senate—is that this man's daughter, Ethel Purdy, renowned in more than one city for her beauty, may become his wife. Indeed, the hope of the Senate and of Ethel go hand in hand. With either, he would not know what to do without the other, and without the one he would not want the other.

"Trueman, we are going to have trouble with the men." Purdy draws a chair up to Trueman's desk.

"I've just been talking over the telephone to the mine boss at Harleigh." The men there and at Hazleton hold a meeting to-night to decide whether or not they will strike in sympathy with the Carbon County miners, because of the shut-down.

"Now, we've got to strike the first blow! The men over at Pittsfield and at the Woodward mines will join the strikers if the Harleigh and Hazleton men go out. We must get an injunction to prevent the committee from the affected mines from visiting the other men. If they come it is for the sole purpose of inducing the men to strike. Isn't that sufficient grounds for an injunction?"

"You can get your injunction, Mr. Purdy," Trueman replies, "but what effect will it have if you haven't a regiment to back it up?"

"We have the regiment! The Coal and Iron Police have been drilling in the Hazleton armory. We can put three hundred men in the field from the offices of the several works, armed with riot guns."

Francis A. Adams

"You may rely on me to get the injunction, Mr. Purdy," the younger man says, after a moment's pause, "but I would not advise calling out the Coal and Iron Police until some act of violence is committed by the miners themselves. It may lead to bloodshed, may it not?"

"Lead to bloodshed? Why not? For what have we been training the Coal and Iron Police? The miners of the Pennsylvania coal region need a wholesome lesson. They have no respect for property rights. Let them be incited to a strike by the walking delegates and their battle cry is 'Burn! Destroy!'"

"We want no repetition of the Homestead and Latimer riots." They were too costly to the employers! Coal breakers and company stores are no playthings for the whimsical notions of so-called labor leaders who do not know the conditions prevailing in this region. They are too expensive to be made the food of the strikers' torch.

"Stop the strikers before they have a chance to blacken Luzerne County with the charred ruins of the breakers! They'll be sacking our homes next." Already their attitude is almost insufferable. People beyond these hills do not understand the reign of terror under which these foreign-born men hold the Wyoming Valley!

"It has come a time when *we* must shoot first, if there is to be any shooting! I've had a talk to-day with Sheriff Marlin." It is fortunate that we have a sheriff who has the grit to stand his ground. He says a telegram or telephone message will summon him to Harleigh or Hazleton at a moment's notice, and he will swear our Coal and Iron Policemen in as deputies.

"Whatever they do then will be legal—*Understand?*"

Trueman looks straight at Purdy several seconds before he replies.

"No," he says, flushing, "not every thing they do. I do not set my judgment against yours, but I do counsel great caution in placing Sheriff Marlin in command of the Coal and Iron Police. While you may be correct in saying we must administer a quick and salutary lesson to the miners, as deputy sheriffs your men might be tempted to shoot too soon."

"Shoot too soon? If these men gather on mischief bent, we can't shoot too soon!"

Purdy in turn flushes, as he carefully scrutinizes Trueman's serious face, which has grown suddenly pale. It is the first time his talented young protege has ever shown the white feather.

"Oh, yes, yes, Mr. Purdy—they—they can shoot too soon. Even deputy sheriffs cannot commit murder with impunity. Fight these men with the law. It's all in your favor! Sheriff Marlin could not step out there in the street and shoot my fox terrier unless he could show someone's life was in danger."

With a show of impatience Gorman Purdy arises from his chair. He is displeased beyond measure with the attitude assumed by Trueman.

"Well, sir!" he says, "you should know there is a difference between Harvey Trueman's fox terrier, so long as you are general counsel for the Paradise Coal Company, and a man who marches along the highway with a revolver in one hand and a torch in the other, his cowardly heart filled with murder and arson! I am greatly disappointed with your views. Perhaps it were better that I place the injunction proceedings in other hands!"

A sharp retort is on Trueman's lips, words not sarcastic, but stinging in their earnest truthfulness, and wise beyond the years of the man about to utter them. Each man has discovered that which is repugnant to him in the other—that which has remained hidden through years of friendship.

The door of the office is unceremoniously opened, and a

girlish voice says:

"Ah, father—I thought you must be keeping Mr. Trueman. Don't you remember you promised me at breakfast you would not? Our ride was fixed for three o'clock. It is now nearly four. Why, you both look positively serious!"

Ethel Purdy, gowned in a black riding habit which displays a dainty, enamelled bootleg, and wearing a gray felt hat of the rough rider type, gracefully poised on one side of her head, smiles incredulously as she stands, one hand on the knob, looking in through the door at the two men.

CHAPTER IV

A QUIET AFTERNOON AT WOODWARD

Ethel enters Harvey's office just in time to avert a quarrel between the Coal King and his attorney. In her presence both men resume their normal reserve of manner.

"So you have come for your afternoon ride?" Purdy inquires, in a pleasant tone.

"Well, my dear, you shall not be disappointed. The matter Harvey and I were discussing can be deferred. Go and enjoy an hour's exercise. I shall be home when you arrive."

"Won't you go with us, papa?"

"Not to-day. I have a Board meeting to attend."

"I do wish you would pay as much attention to your health as you do to business. You are not looking well. Have you forgotten what the doctor told you about over-working?"

"No, my dear; I remember his advice; but he does not know what a responsibility rests upon me as the President of the Paradise Coal Company. If I did not attend to the details of this business, there would be a dozen competitors in the coal industry within a year. Even if I cannot go with you every day, you have Harvey as an escort. You two will not miss me. When I courted your mother, I should not have insisted upon a third party accompanying us on our rambles."

"Then we will join you at dinner," says Harvey, as he walks towards the door.

At the curb in front of the entrance of the office building, a groom stands holding the bridles of three magnificent hunters.

Harvey assists Ethel to her saddle and springs on to his horse. "Take Nero back to the stables," Harvey instructs the groom. "Mr. Purdy will not use him this afternoon."

The riders are soon out on the turnpike that leads to Woodward. For a November afternoon, the weather is delight-ful. The prospects of a bracing canter over the mountain roads could not be brighter. The high color on the cheeks of Harvey and Ethel show that they are not strangers to outdoor exercise. Indeed they are types of perfect physical condition.

Since the day Harvey Trueman became the attorney of the Paradise Coal Company, and the protege of Gorman Purdy, the young couple have been constant companions. They have been encouraged to seek each other's company by Mr. Purdy, who appreciated the worth of Harvey and who secretly hoped that the brilliant young lawyer would become one of his household.

"I have spoken to your father," Harvey says, as the horses climb slowly up one of the rough hills on the pike. "He has given his consent to our engagement."

"He's such a dear, good fellow, I knew he would not stand in the light of making me happy!" exclaims Ethel.

"Tell me all he said?" she inquires eagerly.

"He told me that he was glad you thought enough of me to wish to have me as your partner in life; that he had never had but one fear that you might fall in love with some worthless snob, who would make you unhappy and seek only the fortune which you would bring him."

"Your father was kind enough to say that he believed I would continue to be attentive to my business, and to his interests. What do you think he is going to give you as a marriage dot?"

"Don't make me guess. You know I am never able to guess a riddle."

"He is going to present you with his new villa at Newport."

"How could he have known that I was wishing for just that one thing? O, won't it be jolly to go there and spend our honeymoon," Ethel exclaims gleefully.

"We will make your father come there and spend the summer. He really must take better care of his health."

Discussing the details of their cloudless future, the lovers enter the dingy mining town of Woodward. The weather-beaten cottages, which never have known a coat of paint, do not attract their attention. The groups of ragged children playing in the dusty road, scurry out of the path of the horses. On the hillside to the left stands the Jumbo Breaker, the largest coal crusher in the world. Its rambling walls rise to a height of several hundred feet up a steep incline. The noise of the machinery within can be heard distinctly from the roadway. The grind, grind, grind of the mammoth crushers, which sound as a perpetual monotone to the townspeople, is lost on the ears of Ethel and Harvey.

Not until they reach the center of the town do they realize they are at the end of their ride.

"We never rode those five miles so quickly before," says Ethel.

"O, yes we have. Why, it has taken us longer to-day than ever," Harvey replies, as he looks at his watch.

"But of course it has not seemed long. We have had so much to talk about. We must make good time on the ride home or we will be late for dinner."

They turn their horses and are off at a brisk trot back toward Wilkes-Barre.

On passing through the upper end of Woodward they have not noticed a clump of men and women standing at the doorway of a miserable hovel, setting back from the road.

Now the men and women are in the road and block the way.

"I wonder what can have happened," exclaims Ethel.

"Another accident, I presume," is Harvey's answer. "It does seem as though the Jumbo Breaker injures more men than any other in the district. It's all through using the new crusher. It's dangerous. I said so from the moment I inspected the model. But it saves a hundred men's labor; the company will not abolish its use."

They are now so near the crowd that the horses have to be reigned in.

"Who's hurt?" Harvey asks of a miner.

"Nobody hurt, sir, only the Sheriff putting out Braun's widow."

The scene in the court room looms up before Harvey. He sees the bent form of the miners' widow as she had bent over her little boy, weeping at the decision of the Judge who had said that she could not claim damages for the killing of her husband. He thinks of the check that is in his pocket—the reward he has gained for winning the case for the Paradise Company. A blush comes to his cheeks; his inner conscience is awakened.

In the doorway of the hovel stands Sheriff Marlin. He is superintending the eviction.

There are several miners in the group who had been at the court house. They look at Harvey with glances which speak the thoughts they dare not utter.

Then, as a hunted fawn which will seek shelter of the huntsmen who are to slay her, the widow rushes from the house. She runs to the head of Ethel's horse and falls prostrate at the animal's feet.

"In mercy's name, don't let them put me out to freeze," she wails. "It is not for myself. I don't mind the cold; but little Eric, he will freeze to death.

"You give your horses shelter; will you let a child die on the roadside? It is not my fault that the rent is not paid. My husband never owed a cent in his life. He was killed in the mines, and the company will give me nothing—nothing. I won't ask for charity. All I ask for is a chance to work. I can break coal. I can dig it. I am willing to work even in the Jumbo, till it kills me. Anything to get food and a roof for my child."

This tragic scene is enacted, before Sheriff Marlin and his deputies grasp the situation. They do not long stand idly by and see the daughter of the great Purdy subjected to this annoyance. With a bound the sheriff, himself, is upon the woman.

"What do you mean by stopping this lady?" he shouts, at the same time grabbing the poor creature by the throat. "Back to your house and take out your goods, or I'll burn them on the road."

"Take your hands off that woman," cries Harvey. He stands in his saddle and waves his hand menacingly at the sheriff.

"Stop choking her! Do you hear!"

With savage energy Marlin hurls the widow to the ground.

"Do not be frightened, Miss Purdy," he says, in obsequious tone. "This woman will not annoy you again." "You must excuse me, Mr. Trueman," he adds, turning to Harvey. "But these mining folk cannot be handled like ordinary people."

The blush of shame has passed from Harvey's face; he is ashen.

"Are you evicting this woman for non-payment of rent?" he asks.

"She has not paid a cent since her husband's death, ten months ago. I received orders from the company to turn her out to-day. She has been making trouble here for the past month, and now that she has lost her suit it's time she got out."

"Mamma, mamma," cries the five year old boy, as he runs to his mother, laying prostrate in the weeds at the side of the road.

"Are you hurt, mamma, tell me?" and then he bursts into a flood of tears.

"Take that brat away," Sheriff Marlin says under his breath to a man. As the deputy starts to pick up the child, it utters a piercing shriek.

"Don't let them hurt the child!" cries Ethel, in utter horror. She has till now been a mute witness to the heartless acts of the agents of the law.

Harvey jumps from his saddle, and is at the deputy's side.

"Put that child down. I shall see that it is taken care of," he declares.

"Excuse me, Mr. Trueman," interposes Sheriff Marlin, "you must not interfere with us in the execution of our duty."

"Execution of your duty! You mean the execution of a woman and her child. I shall not stand by and see the law violated." You have authority to evict the widow for her debts; but you have no authority to assault her.

"How much does she owe?"

"Eighty dollars," is the surly reply.

"Here is the money," says Harvey, as he takes a roll of bills from his pocket.

"I cannot accept the money now," protests the sheriff.

Then stepping up to Harvey he says in an undertone:

"Mr. Trueman, the fact is, I have been told to put this woman out of town; she will cause trouble if she remains. The miners are all in sympathy with her because she lost the suit."

"Who gave you such orders?"

"Mr. Purdy."

"When?"

"This afternoon. I saw him just after you left the office. He told me to get the widow out of town this very day, so I took the switch engine and came out here."

"Well, you will let the matter stand as it is. I intend to pay the rent for the woman and see that she is placed back in the house."

"You will be opposing Mr. Purdy. He explained the case to me and asked my advice. We decided that with the widow in the

Francis A. Adams

town, the miners would be more likely to carry out their threat than with her out of sight. You had better let me carry out my orders."

"I have made up my mind to see the widow restored to her home," Harvey repeats. "Here is the rent money. I know the spirit of the miners better than either you or Mr. Purdy."

The sheriff takes the money reluctantly.

Widow Braun is now sitting up, vainly trying to comfort her child.

"You may go back to your home," says Trueman, as he bends over and helps her to arise. "I have paid your rent and here is some money for food, and for your next month's rent. I shall see that you get work."

"May God bless you," cries the widow, bursting into tears.

"You are my prisoner," Sheriff Marlin declares, as he places his hand on the trembling figure.

"On what charge," Trueman demands.

"For getting goods from the company's store on her husband's card when he was dead, and she had no money to pay for them," the sheriff asserts, triumphantly.

"But she has money to pay for the food she bought. And her husband's card is valid until cancelled. You had better take care that you do not overstep your authority. It is not the Widow Braun you have to deal with now. I am interested in this case. I am the widow's counsel. She has one thousand dollars to her credit on the books of the company's store."

Sheriff Marlin is in a fury. He realizes that he cannot serve two masters and he decides to be faithful to Gorman Purdy.

"It is not my will that you are opposing, Mr. Trueman," he says with emphasis. "It is your employer's."

The word "employer's" grates on Harvey's ears.

"Mr. Purdy is my employer, but he is not my master. I shall serve my conscience before I do any man. But I do not believe that Mr. Purdy would countenance this outrage."

"What do you mean by saying that the widow has a thousand dollars to her credit?" the sheriff asks.

"I mean that she has this thousand dollars," and Trueman drew the check from his pocket. "It is to be placed to her credit. I have something to say about the company stores."

"I shall take this business direct to Mr. Purdy," the sheriff threatens as he walks off.

The miners and their wives who have witnessed the quarrel between Trueman and Marlin give expression to their feelings in whispered words of praise for the young lawyer who bid defiance to the Sheriff of Luzerne County, the most dreaded man in that part of Pennsylvania.

The widow grasps Harvey's hand and before he can withdraw it she covers it with kisses. Her tears of gratitude fall on his hand. He appreciates that it is but tardy justice that he is doing to the poor woman.

"You need have no fear of being turned out of your home," he tells her. Then he springs back into the saddle.

"Come, Ethel, let us start for home."

The ride is finished in silence. Neither Harvey nor Ethel feels in the mood to talk. On reaching the Purdy mansion the riders dismount, and go at once to the library, where Gorman Purely is waiting for them.

Francis A. Adams

"Harvey, I am surprised that you should interfere with my orders," is Mr. Purdy's salutation. "Sheriff Marlin has just telephoned me. He tells me that you opposed his evicting the widow, and that the miners are now likely to make serious trouble. This is the second time to-day you have attempted to defeat my plans. I cannot understand what object you have in antagonizing me."

"You certainly misunderstand my motives," replies Trueman. "It is because I have your interests at heart that I cannot see you pursue a course that will lead to disastrous consequences."

"Do you put your judgment above mine?" asks the Coal King, sarcastically.

"In ordinary business matters, in affairs of finance and in the conduct of the mines I should not presume to dispute your judgment. But on the propriety of assembling the Coal and Iron Police and of evicting a woman who has the sympathy of the entire mining district I believe that I am better able to judge of the effect these acts will have than you are, for I come into close contact with the people."

"The sheriff tells me you have placed a thousand dollars to the credit of the widow at the Company's store. Is this so?"

"I intend to do so."

"It shall not be done, sir, not if I have the power to prevent it," declares the Coal King emphatically, rising and pacing the floor. "You must be out of your mind to make such a move, now, of all times, to offer encouragement to the lawless element."

"He did nothing wrong," interposes Ethel. "He prevented the sheriff and his men from injuring the woman and her child."

"Not another word!" Gorman Purdy speaks in a tone he has never employed when addressing his daughter.

"This matter must be settled, once and for all," he continues, addressing Harvey. "There can be but one head of the Paradise Coal Company. I wish to know if you will cease interfering with my orders?"

"I have never objected to carrying out any order of yours that was legal. As long as I am in your employ I shall continue to do as I have done. But to tell you that I will do your bidding, whether legal or not, that is something I cannot bring myself to do," Trueman replies, looking the Coal King squarely in the eye.

"I shall have no one in my employ who cannot obey me," Purdy says. He then rehearses what he has done for Trueman; how he has advanced him to the position of counsel to the company. "And all the thanks I receive is your opposition, now that I need your support," he states, and without waiting for a reply hurries from the room.

When Ethel and Harvey go to the dining room they find that the irate Coal King has gone to his private apartment, where his dinner is being served.

Harvey spends the evening at the mansion.

As he and Ethel sit in the drawing room they discussed the events of the day, and speculate on the result that will follow the quarrel with her father.

"My father will regret his hasty words," Ethel says. "He admires you and places absolute confidence in you. Only yesterday he told me that there was not another man in the world to whom he would confide his business secrets as he has done to you."

The lovers go to the music room. Harvey's voice is a remarkably rich baritone. At Ethel's request he sings a ballad which he has recently composed.

Standing at her side as she plays the accompaniment, he sings.

"THE SEA OF DREAMS

"Sing me of love and dear days gone;
Sing me of joys that are fled;
Strike no chord of the now forlorn;
None of the future dread,

Ah, let thy music ring with tone
That speaks the budding year;
The Winter's blast too soon will moan
Through the forest bleak and drear.

Then sing but a line from the dear old days
We sang 'neath the moon's soft beams,
When we were young, in those gladsome days,
While we sailed on the sea of dreams.

There are no songs that reach the heart,
Like those sung long ago.
New singers and their songs depart;
The old ones ne'er shall go.

Nor is it strange that they should be
As balm to the sad heart;
They tell of love when it was young,
And all its joys impart."

At eleven o'clock Trueman leaves the Purdy mansion and goes
to his hotel. To him it is clear that an irreparable breach has
been made in the relations between himself and Gorman
Purdy. He knows the unrelenting character of the President of
the Paradise Coal Company.

"It was a question of right and wrong," he muses. "I could not
see a woman and her child thrown out in the highway, when I
knew that it was through my skill as a lawyer that just damages
were kept from them." The law was on the side of the
company; but justice was certainly on the side of the widow.

"Every day I have some nasty work of this kind to perform. It is making a heartless wretch of me. A man can make money sometimes that comes too dear."

The next day, at the office, Purdy and Trueman have a long talk. It results in Trueman withdrawing his objections to the assembling of the Coal and Iron Police. As to the widow, a compromise is effected. She is to be set up in business in a neighboring town where her case is unknown.

The thought that to break with Purely would mean to lose Ethel, turns Harvey's decision when the moment comes to choose between duty and policy.

The work of preparing to defeat the pending strike is at once taken up, Purdy and Trueman working in perfect accord.

CHAPTER V

AN UNQUIET DAY AT HAZLETON

Nearly two months have passed, and a mantle of snow covers the ground. The rigorous December weather has come and is causing widespread distress among the mining population of Pennsylvania. Forty per cent of the operatives of the Paradise Coal Company have been laid off, as Purdy declared they would be. This means that starvation is the grim spectre in six thousand homes.

The anomaly of miners in one town working at full time, and those of an adjacent town shut out, must be explained as one of the insidious methods of the Trust to create an artificial coal famine.

Gorman Purdy, whose word is law in the Paradise Company, had determined to exact an advance of twenty-five cents a ton from the retail coal dealers. To do this he had to make it appear that the supply of coal was scarce. This led him to close the mines in Hazleton. The miners in the town sought to force the opening of the mines by bringing about a sympathetic strike in the neighboring towns. To prevent this, the Coal and Iron Police have been brought to Hazleton to intimidate the miners and to suppress them by force if they make any concerted move looking toward bringing on a strike.

Preliminary to enforcing the order that debars such an army of men of the means of support, the Coal Magnates, at Purdy's suggestion, have massed three hundred of the Coal and Iron Police in the town of Hazleton. This mercenary force occupies the armory, built two years before by the benevolent multimillionaire Iron King of Pennsylvania, whose immense mills and foundries are situated some two hundred miles distant.

Sheriff Marlin is in command of the Coal and Iron Police. He has sworn them in as deputies, and each bears on his breast the badge of authority.

The propinquity of Woodward and the other small towns to Wilkes-Barre saved them from suffering the effects of a close-down. The Magnates did not desire to have the scenes of distress brought too near their own homes. So Hazleton and the outlying districts were selected to be sacrificed to the arbitrary coal famine. Day after day the idle miners congregate in the Town Hall to discuss their situation and to devise some means of relieving the starving families. These meetings are under the strict surveillance of Sheriff Marlin. Every letter that is sent from the hall is subjected to his scrutiny.

There will be no incendiary appeals addressed to the miners of other districts.

The newspaper correspondents, though they send accurate stories of the awful condition of the miners and their families, are disappointed to receive copies of their respective papers with their articles revamped, and the essential points expurgated, to meet the approval of the "conservative reader."

"The committee on rations reports that the allowance for each miner and his family must henceforth be reduced to two loaves of black bread a day. As some of the miners have eight and ten children, an idea of the actual need of relief from some source may be formed."

Paragraphs like the above never reach the printed page of a newspaper that has sworn allegiance to or is bound to support the Magnates.

It is now December twentieth. The miners resolve to make a final appeal to the Paradise Coal Company to at least start the mines on half time. If the company grants this appeal, there will be joy in the miners' homes for Christmas.

Christmas is no more to the Magnates than any other calender day. The necessary time for the creation of the coal famine has not elapsed, and until it has there will not be another ton of coal taken from the pits.

Harvey Trueman is expected to confer with the leaders in the afternoon. He will deliver the appeal to the company, and the following day, Sunday, the miners will know if they are to go back to work.

"In the event of Purdy, the final arbiter, refusing to start up on half time," says Metz, who is now the leader of the Miner's Union, "we can go to Latimer and Harleigh, to-morrow. The mines will be closed; they are only working them six days a week now. We will appeal to the men to quit work unless the Paradise Company gives us a chance to earn our bread."

"If the Harleigh men won't go out, they will at least give us some food for a Christmas dinner," says a miner whose hollow cheeks tell of long fasting.

"Peter Gick died last night," a miner states as he enters the hall. "He went to the ash dumps to pick a basket of *cinders*; on his way back to his house he fell. He was so weak that he could not get up. The snow is two feet deep on the road, and it was drifting then; it soon covered him up. This morning his son, Ernst, found him. Of course he was frozen stiff."

"Where is his body?" Metz asks.

"Sheriff ordered it buried by the police."

"A public funeral might prove dangerous to the Magnates," observes Metz.

"Our modern rulers have profited by the experience of the ancients."

Promptly at two o'clock Trueman arrives at the hall.

The committee on resolutions present him with their petition.

"I shall do all that I can to make the Company appreciate the condition in which you are placed. You may depend upon it, there will be work for you before Christmas," Trueman assures them at parting.

"We shall want an answer by to-morrow morning at ten o'clock," the miners urge in chorus.

Harvey Trueman leaves for Wilkes-Barre on the mission of appealing to the humanity of the Coal Magnates.

Miners' wives and children stream to the Town Hall, to receive their bread and rations.

It is at such times as these, where the miners are ruthlessly shut out of the mines, that the highest value of the Miner's Union is demonstrated. From the slender treasury, which is enriched only by the pennies of the miners during their weeks of employment, the money is drawn to purchase the rations that must be had to keep the miners and their families from actually starving when they can no longer buy from the company store.

To supplement the rations distributed by the Union, the Hazleton miners have a small supply of medicine. This is as important as food. The medicine chest was given them by Sister Martha, the ministering angel of the mines.

Martha Densmore was the daughter of Hiram Densmore, who had owned great tracts of the coal lands. He had been forced out of the industry by refusing to enter the combine which resulted in the formation of the Coal Trust. At the time of his death, of all his fortune there remained but a small part. Mrs. Densmore had not survived her husband a year. Martha was left an orphan.

She has an income of $6000, and could live a life of idleness did she so desire. But it was her purpose from girlhood to be always on missions of charity. She had loved Harvey Trueman. They had been schoolmates, and would undoubtedly have wed had not the wreck of Densmore's fortune been accomplished just as Trueman was leaving college. Gorman Purdy had been quick to perceive the calibre of the young man and had brought him into the Paradise Company. With father and mother dead, and with her heart's longing unappeased, Martha determined to join a sisterhood, and devote her entire time to ministering to the poor and the sick.

The suffering of the miners of Hazleton attracts her sympathy and she has come to the town from Wilkes-Barre.

It is her presence in the town hall that makes even Sheriff Marlin curb his blasphemous tongue.

Her calm face, which wears an expression of contentment, if not of happiness, is a solace to the miserable men and women who come to ask for medicine. She always has a word of cheer.

The life she has led for eight years has not aged her, and to judge from her manner she would not be taken for a woman more than thirty. She is, however, six and thirty; her natal day being in the month of March, the same as Trueman's. And they are both the same age. In the school days they celebrated their birthdays together.

There is not a miner or one of his family who would not give up their life, if such a sacrifice were necessary, to keep Sister Martha from being injured. They have seen her enter a mine where an explosion had occurred, when even the bravest of the rescuing party hesitated. They have seen her in their own hovels, bending over the forms of their sick and dying children. The yellow flag of pestilence never makes her hesitate.

By her practical acts of charity and humanity, she has come to exert a wonderful influence over the humble citizens of Luzerne County. In this present crisis Sister Martha is the central figure.

In the Armory the Coal and Iron Police are playing cards and enjoying themselves as men always can in comfortable barracks.

So the winter night closes. The hearths of the miners are cold, their larders empty; but the armory is warm, the police are well fed.

"The Company refused to open the mines. They will, however, send thirty barrels of flour to be distributed for Christmas." This is the message returned by Trueman, on Sunday morning.

There are sixty miners in the Hall. They decide to go at once to Harleigh, to exert "moral suasion" on their fellow miners there.

They start from the Hall unarmed, walking two by two. At the head of the line of sixty men, one carries the Stars and Stripes; another a white flag. There is nothing revolutionary about the procession. It is a sharp contrast to the armed force of the Culpepper Minute Men, who, under the leadership of Patrick Henry, marched to Williamsburg, Virginia, to demand instant restoration of powder to an old magazine, or payment for it by the Colonial Governor, Dunmore. The Minute Men carried as their standard a flag bearing the celebrated rattlesnake, and the inscription "Liberty or Death: Don't tread on me."

The route to Harleigh is in an opposite direction to the armory. The little column passes out of the town of Hazleton and is a mile distant when the Coal and Iron Police learn of their departure.

Instantly there is a bustle in the armory.

"Form your company, Captain Grout," the sheriff orders.

"Give each man twenty rounds. Tell them not to fire until I give the order. When they do open fire, have them shoot to kill."

The company is formed on the floor of the armory. It receives the orders; one-third of the force is left to guard the armory.

In column of fours the main body marches out, Captain Grout and Sheriff Marlin in the lead.

To catch up with the miners the column marches in route step.

"We will head them off at the cross roads this side of Harleigh," the sheriff explains. "There is a cut in the road there, and we can put our men on either side. When the miners come within range I shall challenge them. If they do not turn back, it will be your duty to compel them to do so."

Unconscious of the approach of the sheriff and his posse, the miners march on. The road is heavy and they are so much run down by long weeks of short rations that they cannot make rapid headway.

Sheriff Marlin and his men are now at the cut near the cross roads.

Captain Grout stations his men to command either side of the road. The banks of the cut are fringed with brush, which affords a complete cover for the men.

"You keep out of sight, too, Captain," Sheriff Marlin orders. "I will stop the miners. If they see you and the Coal and Iron

Police they may scatter, and some of them reach Harleigh."

The ambuscade is complete. Five minutes passes. There is no sign of the miners.

"Can they have been told of our plan to head them off?" asks the sheriff.

At this moment the head of the procession of miners turns the corner of the road. The American Flag and the White Flag are still in the van.

The sheriff takes up a position on the side of the road. As the miners come up to him, he calls them to "halt."

"Where are you going?" he demands.

"To Harleigh," replies Metz.

"Who gave you permission to parade?"

"We are exercising our rights as freemen."

"Well, you cannot march in a body on the highways of Pennsylvania."

"Then we can break up our procession and walk individually."

"*In the direction of Hazelton*," Sheriff Marlin says, significantly. "I know what you are up to; do you think that I am going to let you cause a sympathetic strike in Harleigh because you are locked out? Not if I know myself."

When the miners come to a halt, the men in advance cluster about Metz and the sheriff.

Now thirty men surround the sheriff.

Some of them are, of course, in advance of him.

"Get back to Hazleton," Sheriff Marlin cries, at the same time raising his arms above his head and waving them.

He pushes his way through the crowd of miners to the edge of the road.

Off comes his hat

It is the signal which Captain Grout has been expecting.

"Company, attention!"

Two hundred Coal and Iron Police jump to their feet.

"Get back to Hazleton or I'll take you prisoners," shouts the sheriff.

But his words are lost. The miners are terror-stricken. The sight of the police, armed with deadly rifles, has made the miners insensible to every thought and impulse but that of self-preservation.

They scatter up and down the road.

"Don't let them escape to Harleigh," shouts the sheriff. Taking this as an order, the police open fire on the men who have passed the sheriff.

Crack! crack! go the rifles.

Each shot fells a miner. They are practically at the muzzles of the weapons.

A miner rushes up the bank on the left to get out of the range of the police on that side. He is riddled by the bullets from the opposite side.

Another dives into a snow bank; it affords him no protection. "Pot that woodchuck," shouts Captain Grout to one of his men.

A bullet is sent into the hole. The miner springs to his feet; then drops dead.

The line of carnage is now stretched out for two hundred yards.

There is no return fire. So the armed police come out from cover and pursue their victims.

The police have lost all self-control. Each man is acting on his own responsibility.

Of the ten miners who run toward Harleigh, not one is spared. Three lie in the road; the snow about them tinged with their life's blood. Another is clinging with a death grip to a stunted tree, which he caught as he staggered forward, with three bullets in the back.

"Mercy! mercy!" cry several of the miners. But their wail is lost on the ears of the Coal and Iron Police. The police are there to kill, not to grant mercy.

Now a miner falls on his knees and prays to God for protection.

This attitude of submission is not heeded; a bullet topples him over.

With their hands above their head, some of the men walk deliberately toward the deputies. Indians will recognize this as the sign of surrender, and will give quarter. But the deputies, with unerring aim, shoot down the voluntary captive.

It would not be so terrible if the miners were returning the fire, if they were offering any resistance. But they are absolutely unarmed. Their mission has been to present a petition to the miners of Harleigh. The slaves of the South had enjoyed the

Francis A. Adams

right of petition. How could these twentieth century miners anticipate that the sheriff would massacre them on the highway for seeking to present a petition?

"Have you shot any one?" asks one of the deputies of his nearest companion.

"Shot any one! Well, I should think I had. I've seen four drop. Here goes a fifth."

To stand, to run, to fall to the ground, all are equally futile as means of escape. Extermination is all that will stay the fire of the police.

Sheriff Marlin and Captain Grout stand in the middle of the road. Metz, O'Connor, and Nevins, a mine foreman, are standing beside them.

O'Connor carries the white flag; Nevins the National emblem.

"Disarm those men," Marlin directs the Captain.

"Disarm them?" Captain Grout repeats, inquiringly.

"Certainly. They have sticks in their hands."

Two deputies, who have exhausted their supply of cartridges in their magazine rifles, stop reloading and rush upon Nevins. They beat him over the head with their rifle butts. The flag is snatched out of his hands.

O'Connor is dealt a blow an instant later.

The subjugation of the unarmed miners is accomplished.

One by one the Coal and Iron Police return.

Some of them bring in captives who have escaped death, but who still have felt the sting of the bullets.

Of the sixty miners, twenty-three are killed outright; ten are mortally wounded; twenty-one have less serious wounds.

Six have run the gauntlet and are fleeing back to Hazleton.

The triumphant march of the police to Hazleton is begun.

"We will carry the wounded," says the sheriff. "They might get through to Harleigh and Latimer."

"We will round up the six who escaped," Captain Grout assures the sheriff. He then details ten men to run down the miners who have eluded capture.

This is an easy matter, as the footprints of the miners are perfectly distinct in the soft snow. On the six trails the men set off, as a pack of hounds on the scent of game.

This man-hunt results in an addition of *six* to the list of the slain.

Gorman Purdy's orders have been carried out.

His police have been sworn in as deputies; they have met the miners and have "fired first."

The sanctity of the law enveloped their act. They shot as *Deputies*.

They dispersed a band of miners who were on the highway, armed, according to the sheriff's version, "with sticks," and bent on creating trouble in Harleigh.

Did it matter that the "sticks" were flag staffs on which were displayed the White Flag of truce, and the Emblem of Liberty?

CHAPTER VI

A STAND FOR CONSCIENCE SAKE

News of the massacre on the highway can not be suppressed. A wave of indignation sweeps over the country. Newspapers, clergymen, statesmen, ordinary citizens are of one opinion, that the sheriff and his deputies should be made to suffer for their dastardly acts. The result of the agitation is a call for trial for a case of murder. The Grand Jury of Luzerne County find an indictment against Sheriff Marlin and Captain Grout. These men are placed on trial.

Gorman Purdy at first is highly elated over the result of the sheriff's summary action against the miners. "It has taught the miners a good lesson," he asserts openly.

The morning after the Grand Jury returns its indictment, Purdy enters Harvey Trueman's office.

The relationship between Purdy and Trueman is no longer strained. In three months time Harvey will marry Ethel. He is to live at the Purdy mansion until his own house can be built.

"You have read the papers this morning?" Purdy asks.

"Yes. It begins to look serious for the sheriff and Grout. I understand that they are to be imprisoned to-day."

"Now I want to have a talk with you about defending them."

"Defending them!" exclaims Trueman. "You want me to defend them?"

"It was in our interests that they acted," says Purdy, "and the least we can do is to defend them."

"It was not in my interests, nor was it at my suggestion that the Coal and Iron Police were sent to Hazleton. You must remember that I deprecated that step."

"Well, we won't go over that matter anew, Harvey; the defense of the Sheriff and Captain Grout is essential to the interests of the Paradise Coal Company. You are the chief counsel of the Company, and I look to you to secure their acquittal."

"But you cannot want me to defend two men who are guilty of cold blooded murder," protests Trueman. "I am the last man in the world to ignore the sanctity of the law. When I see the highest law of the land trodden under foot by an ignorant and arrogant sheriff, I wish to see the law enforced against him as it should be against the commonest offender."

"It's all very well to have high ideals of law and justice," Purdy observes, with a cynical smile, "but you cannot be guided by them when a commercial interest is involved. The conviction of the sheriff would lay us open to the violence of the mob."

"You can find a more capable man than I to defend the prisoners."

"There is no one who is as familiar with the mining life as you are; I have thought the matter over carefully before broaching it to you. There is no way out of it, Harvey, you must take the case in hand. It is not the company's request. I make it personal. I want you to do your best to get these men off."

"Mr. Purdy, I cannot comply with your request."

"You refuse to oblige me?"

"I refuse to defend men who I believe have committed murder."

"I am an older man than you, Harvey Trueman, and I caution you to think twice before you refuse to obey the request of the man who has made you what you are." Purdy is white with rage, for he feels that Trueman will remain obdurate.

"It may seem an act of ingratitude, but I cannot suffer my conscience to be outraged by defending the perpetrators of an atrocious crime."

"Your conscience will cost you dear. If you do not defend this case you may consider your connection with the Paradise Coal Company at an end. You sever all bonds that have united us, and your marriage to my daughter will be impossible. Is the gratification of a supersensitive conscience to be bought at such a price?"

"There must be something back of your demand," Trueman declares.

"There is only the just claim that I have on you to work for my interests."

"Mr. Purdy, I was a man before I met you. I am indebted to you for my present position; yet I am not willing to pay for its retention by forfeiting my honor. If you insist on me defending the case, I tell you I would sooner pay the penalty you name."

Trueman's voice is tremulous. He realizes that his decision has cost him not alone a position of great value, but all chance of wedding Ethel Purdy.

"You will live to regret this day, Harvey Trueman," Purdy cries menacingly. "Whatever is due you from the Paradise Coal Company will be paid you to-day. Henceforth you will find office room elsewhere. Remember, sir, I forbid you to have any communication with my daughter."

With these words Purdy walks out of Trueman's office.

"It may be better for me to get out of this damnable atmosphere while I still have a spark of manhood left," Trueman muses, as he sits at his desk. "If I remained here many years more I should be as heartless as Purdy himself.

"I wonder how Ethel will act in this crisis? She loves me, that I would swear to with my life, but can she sacrifice her fortune to marry me? I cannot expect her to do so. No, it would be too much. I have money enough to live but I could not support her in the style to which she has been accustomed from her birth."

For an hour he sits intently thinking. He reviews the past. At the recollection of his school days and the first love he had experienced for Martha Densmore, a sigh escapes his lips.

"I might have been happy, had I married her," he says to himself.

"But then I should not have become a lawyer." What good have I done in the law? I have been the buffer for a heartless corporation. The president of the corporation demands of me to do an act that is against my manhood. I refuse and I am turned out like a worthless old horse.

"I shall henceforth use my talents to some good. The Paradise Coal Company and every other concern that is waxing rich at the expense of the people will find that I can be as formidable an antagonist as I have been defender. How could I have been blind to my duty so long?"

Trueman arises and walks from his office. A thought is forming in his mind.

"I'll do it," he says aloud, as he reaches the elevator.

"The miners have no one who is capable of prosecuting the case of the people. The District Attorney and his staff have been bought off. Any one of the injured miners has standing in the court, and can be represented by counsel. Yes, there is O'Connor, I shall be his counsel."

Trueman hurries to the east side of the town and hunts up the quarters of Patrick O'Connor. The miner is still in bed; the fractured skull he had received by the blow from the rifle barrel nearly proved fatal.

In a few words Trueman explains how he had been driven to leave the Paradise Coal Company; and how he is now determined to be the champion of the people.

"I believe you, sir," says O'Connor, feebly, "for you have always been kind to me. But the rest of the miners think you are to blame for all of their troubles; especially when they face you in court."

"You will tell them to put faith in me, won't you, O'Connor?"

"Indeed I will, sir."

The door opens to admit Sister Martha.

Harvey Trueman has not been face to face with Martha for eight years.

"You here, Martha!" he exclaims.

"I am here every day. My duty brings me among the sick."

The two playmates of the happy school days walk over to the window and talk in low tones for half an hour. Trueman tells of his determination to be an antagonist of the Magnates, one of whom has attempted to buy his soul for the sordid interests of a corporation.

"You may be sure I shall be pleased to help you all I can," Sister Martha assures him. "And I have many friends among the miners. It will be some time before they will accept your protestations in good faith. You must know that your masterful knowledge of the law has kept many of them from winning their suit for damages against the Paradise Company. If you do something to prove your sincerity it will win you many friends."

"If I appear as the counsel of one of the miners and prosecute the Sheriff of Luzerne County, will that be sufficient to demonstrate my sincerity?" Trueman asks.

"It will make you their champion."

"Well, you may tell the miners of Wilkes-Barre that I am to appear as counsel for Patrick O'Connor in the coming trial. We will meet often now, I hope?" Harvey asks as he leaves the room.

"Whenever you come to this quarter of the city you will be able to find me," Sister Martha responds.

Events move rapidly. The trial is set for February first. Between the day Harvey Trueman left the employ of the Paradise Company and the opening of the trial he wins the name of "Miner's Friend." Eight damage suits against the Paradise Coal Company are won for miners by his sagacity and eloquence.

He has been able to learn of the effect of the break in the friendship between the Purdy's and himself. Ethel had been prostrated by the event. For many days she had been actually ill. As soon as her health permitted she had been sent abroad. She is now in the south of France.

At the trial of Sheriff Marlin and his lieutenants, Trueman distinguishes himself by the searching line of questions he puts to the sheriff's deputies and two lieutenants, who are placed on the witness stand. In cross-examination he succeeds in eliciting the fact that the only "weapons" carried by the miners were the two flag staffs.

He brings to court as witnesses men who had been shot in the back as they had run to escape the deadly fire of the deputies.

One of these men, carried to the court room on a cot, testifies that he ran up the embankment and had fallen at the feet of one of the deputies.

"I begged of him to spare my life; that I had a wife and six children. He stepped back a pace and pointing his rifle at my head, fired. The bullet grazed my temple. I rolled over. He thought I was dead. I lay there motionless for several minutes. Then I was struck in the shoulder by another bullet."

This testimony causes a tremendous sensation.

The defendants counsel asks for the recall of the witness the following day. He is brought to court and answers two questions. Then with a groan he turns on his side and dies in the presence of the crowded court and before the very eyes of his assassin.

The trial is a travesty on justice. The jury is composed of men known to be in sympathy with the prisoners. The deputies are in court each day fully armed. They make no pretext to conceal their pistols. This is done to influence the jury to believe that the deputies had shot in self-defense. Both Sheriff Marlin and Captain Grout are acquitted; but they are not vindicated in the eyes of the people of the United States or of Wilkes-Barre.

Trueman emerges from the trial as the recognized champion of the people.

It has taken twelve weeks to try the case. The cost of this victory for the Coal Barons is one hundred and twenty thousand dollars.

Sister Martha and Harvey meet frequently. She is a great aid to him in getting information from the miners. She is inspired by the grand results that Trueman realizes for the poor miners whose cases he handles. She hears him mentioned as the candidate for some office, and asks him if he would accept it.

"I do not wish to mix in local politics," Trueman tells her. "I might accept the office of Congressman; but it is impossible to elect a candidate of the miners in Pennsylvania."

Early in May a call is sent out through the several States for delegates to attend an Anti-Trust Conference in Chicago. This Conference is deemed urgent as the outgrowth of an atrocious move on the part of the Magnates who seek to vitiate the laws of the United States as applied to capital.

Martha asks Trueman if he will accept the appointment as a delegate from the State of Pennsylvania. He signifies his willingness to do so; but doubts if the miners outside of Wilkes-Barre hold him in high enough esteem to so honor him.

"I have not done enough yet to redeem myself for the years that I stood as the barrier to the poor getting their deserts," he declares.

But the election shows that he is recognized as a faithful friend of the people. At the Conference it is believed he will win recognition for the claims of the miners, for justice, and for the Federal enforcement of the laws of common safety in the mines.

The ten months that have passed since the afternoon he won the case against the Magyar's widow, have been the most momentous in his life. They have taken him out of the service of a soulless Company and put him in the position of leader of a million miners.

BOOK II

THE SYNDICATE
INCORPORATES

CHAPTER VII

AN ANTI-TRUST CONFERENCE

From the hour that Trueman was selected as a delegate to the great Anti-Trust Conference to convene in the city of Chicago, he has devoted his hours, day and night, to study. In making his advent in the conference, he enters the arena of national politics; he means to go prepared. Martha has prevailed upon him to accept the nomination as a candidate for the State of Pennsylvania, and he has been elected by the unanimous vote of the Unions. This exhibition of confidence on the part of the toilers of the state has made a deep impression on him, and has fixed his resolve to do something that will be worthy of his constituents.

The sudden transition he has undergone from being the staunch supporter of the coal barons, to becoming their bitterest opponent, has left many of the opinion that he is working some deep scheme for the undoing of the unionists. Nor is this opinion confined to any small number. "He changed his views too quickly," is the general sentiment in the ranks of the small unions where Trueman is not personally known. This lurking suspicion was what had operated strongly at first against securing Trueman's consent to be a candidate. Martha has worked quietly, assiduously, among the men she knew, and who placed absolute faith in her advice. She has been the direct means of bringing about his election.

Now he is to leave her, and must face the supreme opportunity of his life.

It is not without a pang that he bids her farewell. She has come to be a source of great comfort to him since his enlistment in the ranks of the humble. The schoolday acquaintance has been renewed. He has learned to appreciate the fact that he was the cause of her having donned the dress of the sisterhood. His ambition to rise in the world made it impossible for him to yield to the dictates of his heart and the mental vista that opened before him at the close of his college course, did not have her in it. The woman he saw there must be the favorite of fortune. He had selfishly abandoned certain love for possible fortune and in the active life to which he was at once introduced, all thoughts of Martha had been driven from his mind.

But Martha had had no counteractant to soften or obliterate the thoughts of her blasted hopes. The refuge of the convent appealed to her as the one remaining avenue by which she might escape from her youth and its recollections.

It is impossible for Trueman and Martha Densmore to ever again be lovers; the inexorable ban of the church is between them. Yet they can be friends. And Trueman feels that in Martha he has found his firmest friend and advisor.

"You will hear from me from time to time," she says as they part. "I am confident that you will do your duty; that you will awaken the finer instincts in the delegates. With the scenes that have surrounded you in Wilkes-Barre, you cannot be an advocate of violence as a means of settling the struggle for the restoration of the rights of the people."

"It shall be my untiring labor to avert the adoption of any measure that entails an appeal to force," Trueman assures her.

On his arrival at Chicago he finds the convention already in session. An hour in the hall convinces him that the result will be nugatory. The radicals are in the majority and the proposals they make are temporary expedients that look only to appeasing the demand of the masses for action against the usurpers of the public rights.

With a view to defeating the objects of the conference, the Magnates have contrived to send a number of their hirelings as delegates. These are among the loudest in demanding impossible remedies. It is not long before Trueman discovers who these spies are, and he loses no time in exposing them in open conference.

This action brings him into prominence.

"Who is this delegate from Pennsylvania?" asks Professor Talbot, a venerable scholar sent by the Governor of Missouri to represent that state, of Nevins, a neighboring delegate.

"He is a convert to the cause of the people," comes the quick reply.

"A tool of the Coal Barons, you mean," observes a New Yorker. "I knew him three years ago when he was the attorney for the Paradise Coal Company," he continues, "and a more relentless man to the miners never was known in Pennsylvania."

"Yes, I know. He was once a counsel for the Paradise Company," assents the champion of Trueman. "I know his record from A to Z. You can't find a straighter man in this conference. He has come out for the people and I believe he is sincere."

"Whoever he is, or whatever he has been," says the Professor, "it is evident that he has the power of reading character. He was not here two hours before he detected the presence of the goats in our fold."

"Would you like to meet him?" asks Nevins.

"Indeed, I should be pleased to do so."

Professor Talbot and the friendly delegate approach Trueman.

For an hour or more the three are engrossed in animated conversation. Professor Talbot is delighted to find that Trueman is conversant with the most complex questions of the hour.

"I shall make it a point to have the chairman call upon you for an address," he assures Trueman at parting.

For three days the sessions of the conference are devoted to partisan discourses. There seems to be no hope of reaching middle ground. The newspapers ridicule the utterances of the speakers as the vaporings of demagogues. And they are little else.

On the fourth day, true to his promise, Professor Talbot gets the chairman to call upon Trueman for a fifteen-minute speech.

From his first words Trueman wins the attention of the audience. His voice is full and far-reaching; his language simple, and it is possible for every one to grasp his meaning instantly. He chooses to win the delegates to his way of reasoning by force of the truth he utters rather than by appealing to their senses by a display of forensic and oratorical ability.

In the few minutes allotted to him, he reviews the industrial conditions of a decade and shows where the insidious principle of class legislation has undermined the prosperity of the people to bestow it upon the few. In an unanswerable argument he pleads for the restoration of the rights of the majority; by a rapid review of the causes that have led to the downfall of the nations of the past, he shows that the unjust distribution of the fruits of labor must inevitably lead to the disintegration of the state.

His peroration is a fervent appeal to the delegates to reaffirm the equality of man; it calls upon them to adopt resolutions advocating the government control of all avenues of transportation and communication, and for the strict regulation of all industries that affect the common necessities of life.

"There is no law above that of the Creator. He did not fashion some of his children to be damned with the brand of perpetual servitude; He did not anoint some with omnipotence to place them as rulers over the many. When He made mankind in His image, it was to have them live in fraternal relationship. There should be no competition for the mere right to live. Until God's design is declared to be wrong, I shall never cease to counsel my brothers to live true to the Divine principles of liberty, equality and fraternity."

With these words he closes his address.

There is no means for measuring the exact effect of his words. The plaudits of an audience are an uncertain criterion.

In the final vote that is taken, after three other delegates have spoken, a resolution is adopted calling for the appointment of a standing committee of three to continue the investigation of the Trust question until another year.

This result is not satisfactory to the radicals, yet they make no open objection. To Trueman it is a source of gratification to know that the heretical proposals of some of the delegates have been voted down.

The conference is on the point of closing when Delegate William Nevins moves that the chairman of the special committee be empowered to increase the number of the committee to forty at his own discretion. This motion is adopted.

The conference ends. It has exemplified the old adage of the convention of the mice to discuss the advisability of putting a bell on the cat. All agreed that it would be for the good of micedom; yet no mouse had a feasible method to advance for affixing the bell. The papers in every city tell of the failure of the Anti-Trust conference to agree upon a plan of action.

The millions of toilers bend lower under their burdens; the Magnates tighten their grasp on the throat of labor.

In all the United States there is but one man who holds a solution of the problem of emancipating mankind from commercial servitude. This man has been a delegate. He has spoken but a few words; he has been present as an auditor.

His hour for action is soon to come.

Francis A. Adams

CHAPTER VIII

A STARTLING PROPOSAL

The special committee has been directed to hold meetings at intervals of a month and to have a report ready by the first of the following January. Thirty-seven of the most intelligent and earnest of the Anti-Trust members have been placed on this committee by its chairman. The meetings are now secret.

The first meeting is held in the hall that had been used for the big meetings of the conference. After this the meetings are clandestine.

The comment that was provoked by the conference of the radical leaders of the Trust opposition died out in the usual way, and then the interest in the efforts of the special committee was confined to the few people who realized the earnestness of the men who had decided to take the Trust problem up and bring it to a speedy settlement.

Day by day the members of the committee met to discuss the phases of the all absorbing question.

The managers of some of the largest corporations are warned of these secret deliberations and institute a vigorous investigation. The aid of the police is secured, and the officers of a dozen of the shrewdest private detective bureaus are put in possession of the few facts that have been ascertained. In a hundred directions public and private sleuths are set in motion. But their untiring efforts are unavailing. They have to combat a more adroit, more nervy and more intelligent force than they have ever before been brought in contact with.

The Committee of Forty has its ever watchful sentinels on guard, and every move of the detectives is anticipated and provided against.

Thus matters progress until on the night of June tenth a startling climax is brought about by the report of the secretary of the committee.

At this memorable meeting there is a full attendance. The chairman, in his call for the meeting, has intimated that very important business will be transacted. He has in mind the discussion of a plan for awakening the interest of the wage-earners in the effete Eastern States, and the reading of a report.

What actually transpires is a surprise to him, as it is to all but three of the committee.

When the routine of business has been gone through with, the chairman announces that the meeting will proceed to the consideration of new business, if there is any.

William Nevins, the man who had carried the Stars and Stripes at Hazleton, now a committeeman who has always taken a subordinate part in the work, asks to be heard.

Supposing that he is to speak on the one subject uppermost in the minds of the committee, the chair recognizes him. Rising from his seat in the back of the room Nevins walks to the front of the hall, and standing before the chairman, half turns so as to face the men in the assembly.

From his first words it is apparent that he has a matter of grave concern to impart. The attention of all is engaged.

"Mr. Chairman," he begins, "I am unaccustomed to speech-making; yet on this occasion I feel that I am capable of expressing myself in a manner that will be clear and forceful. I am to tell you a few truths, and in uttering the truth there is no need of depending on rhetoric or oratory."

"As you all know, I am a poor man." How I came to be reduced to a position little better than beggary is not known by any of you, for I have studiously avoided airing my troubles to any one. To-day I intend to tell the story. It will cast some light on the subject that we will be called upon to discuss later.

"We have no time to hear the life-story of any one," sententiously observes a man in the front seat.

"But you will have to take time to hear me," retorts Nevins, and he continues.

"I was a graduate of Yale, in the class of 1884. My name was not Nevins, then." After a year spent in travel in Europe I returned to the United States and began to practice my profession of a civil engineer, in the city of New York. My father had died when I was a child and had left my mother a fortune of about $40,000. From this sum she derived an income of $2000 a year. She gave me an allowance of $800 up to the time that I began to work as an engineer.

"Two years after I had entered the office of a leading railroad I planned an extensive change in the working of the road and submitted it to the president." He approved of the suggested changes and put the matter before the board of directors. Shortly afterward I was informed that I could proceed with the work. The work was accomplished and the officials were more than pleased. They made me chief engineer of the road and a stockholder. I soon had a considerable block of stock. Then a great Magnate looked at the road with covetous eyes, and ruin came upon us.

"The stock of the road was depreciated and borne down on the

Exchange until the road became insolvent." All my money was in the road, and when the crisis came I found myself stranded. The King of the Rail Road Trust, Jacob L. Vosbeck, bought up the stock and then raised it to even a higher figure than it had ever before attained.

"Ill-luck followed me and I have gone down, down, until I can scarce make a living as a draughtsman in a shop." The curse of monopoly has caused my ruin. I did not succumb to fair competition. I am now enlisted in a fight against the usurpers of the free rights of the people, and I declare to you all, that I am in this fight in dead earnest. By an appeal to justice we can gain nothing.

"I was one of the sixty miners who were attacked on the highway at Hazleton by the High Sheriff of Luzerne County." I witnessed the mock trial in Wilkes-Barre. I have thought of all the possible means the Trusts have left to us, and find that there is but one available.

"They have all the money and all the agencies of the law; they have intimidated the humble and ignorant workingmen until these poor creatures are no better than serfs, and to be assured of bread, they work as voluntary slaves."

"What is there for us to do but to fight the magnates with their own weapons?" Intimidation is their deadliest method. The horrible picture of a starving family is held up before the wage-earner, and he is asked if he will vote to put his wife and children on the street. He is told that if he will accept starvation wages, the Trust will let him make such wages. In desperation he accepts the terms.

"What I propose is to intimidate the criminal aggressors so that they will fear to make their fortunes at the expense of the honest, hard working and credulous people."

"How shall it be done? Ah! it is a simple matter."

Francis A. Adams

Here the voice of the speaker becomes husky, and he turns to face the chairman of the committee. In almost a whisper he exclaims: "I propose to give them an object lesson. They have given many to us." Again he resumes his normal voice.

"Have you not seen mills closed before election time so as to coerce men to vote as the mill owners directed?" Has not this suspension of work brought distress, starvation, death, to thousands of homes? Is it not murder for men of wealth to resort to such means to win an election in a free country?

"Well, I now propose to form a syndicate—a Syndicate of Annihilation!"

"Mr. Chairman," cry half a dozen voices. "Mr. Chairman, Point of order! Point of order!"

Before the chair can recognize any of the speakers a general commotion ensues. Men begin discussing with one another excitedly; there is a perfect bedlam.

All the while Nevins remains standing as if awaiting an opportunity to resume his speech.

At the expiration of some minutes order is restored so that his voice can be heard. "Permit me to explain," he cries.

The committeemen, as if acting by a common impulse, cease to squabble, and are attentive again.

"I propose to hear the circumstances under which each of you has been brought to the condition that leads you to combine against the Trust; and if there is sufficient ground for belief that you will be zealous workers in my syndicate, I will admit you to membership. No man who has not had a more serious grievance against the Robber Barons than I have outlined, will be eligible. *I have told you but one incident of my case.*

"The work that I shall outline to you after hearing your stories, will require stout hearts to carry it into execution.1"

"It cannot be accomplished by fanatics. It requires the concerted efforts of men of sound judgment; men of courage. The assassin is a coward at heart—the political martyr must be valiant."

The novelty of the suggestion that has just been made is the first thing that appeals to the minds of the committee. They begin to realize the horrid character of the proposition. Much discussion follows. Men want to know what Nevins means by a Syndicate of Annihilation. Whom does he intend to murder? Annihilation and murder are considered synonymous.

To all questions Nevins replies that the details will be given as soon as the men recite their grievances.

Professor Talbot and Hendrick Stahl, the two men who are in the secret with Nevins, advise the members of the committee to comply with the demands.

Then begins the strange, startling recital of the stories of human distress. Of the forty men of varying professions and trades, there are those who tell of their efforts to stand up under the weight of the yoke of commercial despotism. Each man is of impressing character and strong individuality.

The chairman, Albert Chadwick, is the first to tell his story. It is the prelude to the concerted cry of the oppressed—the cry which has sounded through the ages as the one never varying note in the music of the universe; the dread inharmonic monotone that marks the limitation of humanity, exhibiting man's inability to convert the world into a paradise.

CHAPTER IX

ARRAIGNMENT OF THE TRANSGRESSORS

Standing upon the little platform which serves as a rostrum, Chadwick, a man of fifty, seared and bent, lifts his hand to command the attention of the committee.

He is a figure that would do credit to the brush of a great artist. His appearance is that of a man who has been deprived of the power of looking at the world as a place of rest; he is a bundle of nerves, and at the slightest provocation bursts into a storm of irascibility. A tortured spirit lurks in his soul and is visible in his stern, tense features.

As he begins the recital of his grievances against the Trust, it is apparent that he means to give the audience an embittered story. So the attention of all is centered upon him.

"Human liberty is the boon which man has sought since the dawn of creation; it has furnished the incentive for his struggle to reclaim the earth from the domination of brute force; it is the inherent idea that the founders of this Republic sought to embody in the Constitution. But Liberty must have as a complement unhampered opportunity," are his opening words.

"The man who is dependent upon another for his livelihood is not capable of enjoying real liberty, or of attaining happiness." When the men of a nation are debased to a position of minor importance, where they can only act as servants, they lose the stamina necessary to make them good citizens. This condition now prevails in the United States.

"My own experience will exemplify this statement."

"Forty years ago I attained my majority." I was a citizen of the state of Pennsylvania, and considered that I was a freeman. By the death of my father I had come into a fortune of fifty thousand dollars. I lived in the oil region, and sought to engage in the oil industry. To this end I purchased land contiguous to a railroad. On my holdings a well was located which yielded three hundred barrels of oil a day.

"No sooner had I begun to operate my well than the agents of the Oil Trust, which had then but recently sprung into existence as a menace to individual refining, came to me with a proposition to incorporate my well in the Trust's system." The well was capable of earning a net profit of seventy thousand dollars a year. The Trust offered me a paltry two hundred and thirty thousand dollars for my plant. This I refused to accept, for the actual value was one million dollars.

"Then by crafty insinuation the agents of the Trust intimated that unless I sold my property and accepted inflated stock in the Trust and allowed my well to be absorbed in the system, I would find myself opposed by the mighty consolidation." Still I refused to abrogate my right to conduct an independent business.

"Failing to allure me by their offers, which would have proved valueless in the end; or of intimidating me by their threats, the agents reported to the office of the Trust that I was obdurate and must be disciplined."

"Accordingly pressure was brought to bear on the railroad over which I sent my product to a market." The railroad discriminated against me; it gave the Trust a rebate on all oil shipped over the road and made me pay the full schedule rates. Even against this detrimental condition I was able to sell my oil at a small profit.

"I might have survived the unequal struggle had not the 'pipe line' system been introduced." By this the Oil Trust transports its oil to the sea-board at a cost that enables it to undersell all competitors. And for a time the price of oil was reduced, and all the minor competitors were driven into bankruptcy or forced to sell out to the Trust at a ridiculously low figure.

"Owing to my well being centrally located I was able to hold out longer than many others."

"John D. Savage, the Oil King, realized that some more potent means had to be devised to crush me. This means was found in the expedient of 'Sacrifice' sales." At every depot where I sold, the agents of the Trust offered to sell oil at figures lower than I could possibly sell it. I lost my trade. In an effort to retrench, my fortune was consumed, and from a position of affluence I descended to beggary, and had to join the ranks as an employee. So bitter was the animosity of the Trust that it sought to rob me even of the opportunity to earn a living. I have been hounded from post to pillar; my life has been made miserable. I have seen my family want for bread.

"And all because I withstood the assault of the Oil King."

"As an American I protest against the existence of a corporation that can set at naught the mandates of the law; a corporation that can, with utter impunity, resort to arson as a final means of gaining its illegal end, as the oil Trust has done, again and again."

"I thank God that I still possess my fore-fathers' spirit of resistance against oppression." There are few men who are in want, or in actual dread of being thrown out of employment, however unremunerative, who will assert their right. A nation composed of such men is not free, no matter what its form of government may be.

"I am ready to do anything that will restore the right to the individual citizen to engage in business; I am ready to make a stand against the few plutocrats who now usurp the avenues of human activity; and I believe that we will be able to enlist men in support of the idea that the rights of the majority transcend the aggressions of the oligarchy of American capitalists."

As Chadwick concludes his statement, Hiram Goodel, a delegate from New Hampshire, obtains the floor.

"Coercion is the word that epitomizes my grievance against the Trusts," he begins. "It was by the exercise of coercion that I was driven out of business." I conducted a retail tobacco store in Concord, in my native state. My business sufficed to insure me a decent living, and a comfortable margin to be husbanded as a safeguard for my declining years. I had a wife and three sons. My sons were all under age, and I kept them at school to provide them with good educations.

"There was competition in my business; such natural competition as is met with in all pursuits." It did not, however, prevent my making a success of my business.

"Then came the Tobacco Trust." It set out to control the retail trade. This was to be effected by the inauguration of a system of "consigning" goods to the retail stores with strict provisos that the retailer would not handle the product of any concern out of the Tobacco Combine. In order to ingratiate themselves with the store-keepers, the Trust managers at first offered terms that were so far below the current prices that a majority of the stores bound themselves to handle the Trust goods exclusively.

"Three years passed, in which the independent tobacco manufacturers strove to hold out against the ring. Then came a crash."

"I had opposed the innovation of binding myself to buy from one concern; for I felt intuitively that as soon as the Trust was

Francis A. Adams

all-powerful it would begin to exercise dictatorial sway over the retailer."

"My fears were soon justified."

"The Trust advanced the price of its goods to the retailer, and compelled the trade to sell at the same retail figures."

"When this system of extortion was successfully launched the Trust determined to reward its patrons, as a means of pacifying them for reduced profits."

"The reward came in the shape of discriminating against the store-keepers who still handled the goods made by the fast vanishing opposition concerns."

"I was informed that unless I signed an agreement to use only the Trust brands of cigarettes and tobacco no more goods would be sold to me." As the Trust embraced all of the leading brands, that meant that I must go out of business.

"My puritan blood boiled at the thought that I must submit to the tyranny of a band of robbers." I determined to fight to the last. Four years of business at a net loss, drove me into insolvency; then a mortgage was placed upon my freehold, to be followed by foreclosure. I still struggled on, under the delusion that I was in a free land and that the Trust iniquities would not be permitted to crush the individual citizen forever. The decision of the courts of the several states where the Tobacco Trust was arraigned, upholding the Trust, disillusioned me. But it was too late, I was a ruined man.

"My sons were forced to work in the cigar factory of the local branch of the Trust; and I was obliged to apply for a patrimony from the Government, as a veteran of the war for the emancipation of man from slavery. On this slender pension I now live."

"Can anyone blame me for being a volunteer in the crusade

against the most insidious and dangerous foe that has ever assailed a land; a foe that seeks to entrench itself by emasculating the citizens and degrading them to a position of servants of mighty and intolerant masters?"

There is a pause. The aged speaker trembles with emotion.

"I am an old man, over seventy years of age, yet whatever vigor remains in me will be expended in my last battle with the destroyers of free government."

"What right has Amos Tweed, the Tobacco King, to tax me?"

"I was born a free man; I fought to free an inferior race. Alas, I have lived to see the shackles placed upon the wrists of my own sons. So help me God, I shall strike a blow to make them free once more."

Overcome with the exertion of delivering his fervent speech, Hiram Goodel totters. He would fall, did not the strong arms of Carl Metz support him.

"Where is the man who can view this picture of patriarchal devotion, and hesitate to give significance to the prayer that freedom may again be the inheritance of the youth of America," demands Nevins in thrilling tones.

It is apparent that the recital of the grievances of the members of the committee is making a deep impression on every man.

Horace Turner, a farmer from Wisconsin, who had migrated to that state when it was in its infancy, preferring its fertile plains to the rocky hillside homestead in Vermont, is the next to speak. He is sixty years of age, well preserved, temperate and fairly well educated.

"I can quote no higher authority than the Holy Bible," are his opening words. "If in that book we can find authority for complaining against tyrants; if we can find a prayer that has come down from age to age, shall we not be justified in uttering it?

"Are these words from the Psalms meaningless? 'Deliver me from the oppression of Man; so will I keep thy precepts.'"

"There is vitality in this cry from the oppressed; because the oppressor exists. You and I are both victims of oppression."

"I am a producer of wheat, the great staple of this country." You are all consumers of my product. When I cannot make a living by producing wheat, and you cannot purchase it without paying tribute to a band of speculators, there must be in operation a damnable system of oppression to bring about this condition, for it is not natural.

"The Wheat Trust determines what price I shall receive for my wheat; it sets the price at which you shall buy it in the form of bread."

"Whether there is a bounteous crop or a short one, the Trust still controls the wheat and flour and arbitrarily fixes their price."

"When the newspapers assert that the farmers enjoy the advance of the price of a season's crop, they state an absolute falsehood."

"By the system that prevails in this country to-day, as a result of the Wheat Trust, crops are sold a year in advance. There are never two years of exceptionally large crops; so the benefit of the advance of one year does not go over to the next."

"The farmers of this country are compelled, by the present system, to pledge their next year's crop to the local wheat factors who control the elevators. The purchase price is determined by the factor. The farmer receives a certain number of bushels of 'seed' wheat from the factor, agreeing to repay him with two or two and a half bushels of the coming crop; a large percentage of the remainder of the crop is pledged to the local store-keeper for the goods that the farmer must have to do his work and to live upon."

"Wheat is the medium of exchange." The Trust's price is the measure of value. Why? Because the farmer cannot sell to any one except to an agent of the Trusts, as the Trust has arranged traffic rates with every railroad; and the wheat, if bought by any one outside of the Trust, could not be transported to a market and sold at a profit. This statement is indisputable.

"The Wheat King, David Leach, depresses the market when the crop is to be sold, and so gives a semblance of reason for the inadequate price he allows the farmer."

"It is the farmer who does the planting; he has to run the risk of the loss of the crop by drought, or excessive rain; he has to do the harvesting. Yet he does not share in the just profits of the sale of his product."

"And the consumer is made to pay exorbitantly for the bread that keeps life in his body."

"If there were no Wheat Trust, no speculation in wheat and no discriminating traffic rates, bread could be sold at a fair profit for three cents a loaf, and the farmer would still be able to get a higher price than he averages now."

"I have toiled as a farmer for two score years, and all I have in this world is a farm of two hundred acres, valued at thirty-six hundred dollars, on which there is a two thousand dollar mortgage at six per cent." When the interest is paid and my yearly expenses are defrayed, I am lucky to have one hundred dollars to my credit in the bank. For the past six years I have been obliged to send whatever I had remaining to my son, who has married and who is struggling to live in Milwaukee. He is engaged as a brakeman on the railroad that exacts thirty per cent. of the value of every bushel of wheat I raise.

"I am not one of the discontented, homeless vagabonds who the Plutocrats declare are alone demanding the destruction of Monopoly. I am a citizen who can foresee the inevitable result that will come from a perpetuation of Commercial Despotism. I am not afraid to assert my opinions, nor will I fear to act on any suggestion, that will insure independence to the farmer and to all the citizens of the Republic."

Donald Harrington, a delegate accredited to Maryland, now begins his arraignment:

"It will not be necessary for me to take the story of my ruin back to the beginning; you are interested only in that part which has to do with the effect of the Trusts upon me."

"I could say that they were the sole cause of my downfall, but in this statement I should be doing the Trusts an injustice." I felt the first downward impulse given me when I was a lad of sixteen. I had entered the employ of a banking house and was a clerk in their counting room. It was my especial duty to see that the books of the company were put in the safes at night. This duty I faithfully performed for more than three years.

"One day I was tempted to steal."

"It was an easy matter for me to take a sum of money from the drawer and make away with it." I was not detected in the first peculation; this encouraged me to take more. So matters went on until I was guilty of having stolen a sum aggregating ten thousand dollars. I knew that I could not keep the game up much longer, for the annual accounting would disclose the deficit.

"Of the sums I had taken, I had less than half saved. I did not know how I was to get out of the position in which I was placed." Then the idea struck me that I might make the entire sum good if I could make a successful turn on the Exchange.

"This I determined to try."

"From the first I was successful." Soon I had three times the sum required to make up my peculations.

"I restored the money to the safe and breathed easily."

"This was my first venture in dealing with other peoples' money."

"The experience led to my entering upon a career as a banker and broker."

"For eight years I was actively engaged in rolling up a fortune. I was sought out by the Magnates of many of the largest Trusts, and they extended me unlimited credit."

"When the country was precipitated into a panic in 1893, I was not one of the sufferers; I was one of the scoundrels active in bringing the distress upon the people. I aided in the establishment of the all-powerful Money Trust."

"Later I was interested in a big mining scheme." It appeared to me to be one of the best things in which to invest money. I put the bulk of my fortune in the mining stocks, and lost.

"In attempting to retrieve my losses I dissipated my fortune to the last cent."

"The whole of my career as a banker was of a criminal nature." Nearly everything I had touched was a speculative venture. The cursed practice of watering stocks to three and four times their actual value was the common work of my days.

"At the end I was caught in the net which I had so often thrown out to ensnare others." My former partner, James Golding, the Napoleon of Finance, wrought my undoing.

"All of this leads to this conclusion:"

"I am an enemy of the Trusts now, because I know their

methods; I know the results that follow the practice of fictitious speculation. Before you all I acknowledge that my past has been of the darkest and most disreputable nature."

"I also wish to state that I have experienced a change of heart." It has not come upon me solely because I have lost my fortune; I have felt it creeping upon me for the past three years. In my inmost heart I feel a beating that will not be stilled unless I am engaged in the work of destroying the power of the accursed Trusts.

"That there is a chance on earth for a man to redeem himself, I am confident. I have heard the call and have responded to it." I am resolved to use the rest of my strength in battling with the enemies of the people. And I am the more in earnest since I can never forget that I am personally responsible for the distress of hundreds. Widows and orphans, young and old, all have been my victims.

"What object Nevins may have in getting us to recount our grievances, I do not know; but if it will lead to any good result, he may depend upon me to give my untiring aid."

"I have but a word to add. Since my ruin, I have seen my wife and only child, a daughter of twenty, languish and die before my very eyes. This has embittered me against the men who have worked the ruin of the masses more than anything else. I have pledged myself to avenge the sufferings of humanity. I shall be doing something for the good of the race; something to atone for the evil deeds I myself have done."

There is nothing in the recital of Harrington's life's history that is of an exceptional nature. True, no one present is aware that he had at one time been the head of the great bond issue plot.

But the delegates are looking for something of a far different tone than a mere recital of crime and a fall from affluence to penury. Several of the committeemen are on their feet demanding the floor.

Cyrus Fielding, the delegate representing the federation of stone masons, is recognized by the chair.

Fielding is a man of short stature, his eyes betray a lacklustre that might be the result of over-indulgence in liquor or want of rest; he is thin and poorly clad, his face is cleanly shaven. At every pause in his speech he runs his fingers through his thick dishevelled black hair, and finishes this mannerism with wiping his forehead with the back of his hand. His delivery is awkward and these repeated movements intensify this awkwardness.

"I have a grievance against the Trusts that dates back as far as my birth." I never had a fair start. My father was a victim of the power of gold and I inherited his misfortune.

"My first work was as a helper in the great Pennsylvania Iron Trust's works that are owned by that old man, the self-styled philanthropist, Ephraim Barnaby, a hypocrite of the first water, who goes about the world asking people how he can best dispose of his fabulous fortune."

"From the rank of helper I soon rose to the position of foreman of the moulding shop." This was a most important place and I felt proud that I had attained it in so short a period as three years.

"It was my ambition to learn all I could relating to the work in the iron industry." Toward this end I spent four hours every night in reading and experimenting. At the end of another three years I had a fund of knowledge that put me in the front rank as a constructing engineer.

"But I was not a graduate of a college of engineering, so I could not get the degree." The opportunity of utilizing my practical knowledge by forming a competing company was closed by the bar of traffic rates.

Francis A. Adams

"My employers advanced me to the rank of superintendent of the shops in the largest iron manufacturing city in the state. I had to be satisfied with a position under the iron masters."

"Then came the memorable strike that led to the killing of the men by the paid detectives of the Iron Masters."

"The claims of the men were just, and as a man I could not side against them. I put my fortune in with them." The details of the strike are known to you all. The story of the shooting of unarmed mill hands at the instance of the mill owners will never be forgotten; it has marked an era in the history of this country.

"Well, I was a conspicuous figure in those days." The strikers hailed me as a champion; the mill owners first sought to win me over; then they contrived to do away with me. Three times I was assaulted by murderous men who had been hired to kill me.

"When their schemes of violence failed they resorted to the most effective method of destroying me." They discharged me and refused to let me return after the strike was declared off. Not satisfied with having turned me away from their mills they dogged my every step. Since that day I have been unable to get employment in any mill in this country.

"As I am acquainted with the methods of the iron trade I have been able to give the trade Union many valuable points. It was upon my suggestion that the amalgamation of the unions was effected."

"From my intimate knowledge of the manufacture of iron I know that the item of wage is less than fifteen per cent. of the cost of the completed casting, yet the tariff on manufactured iron is on the average thirty per cent." Where does the additional fifteen per cent. go? To fatten the pockets of the favored manufacturer. But that is only half the story. The fifteen per cent. that is supposed to protect the American laborer, does it go for this end? Not at all. All of you are familiar with the wage schedules in the iron industry. They have not been advanced five per cent. since the imposition of the high tariff. So the manufacturer gobbles more than ninety per cent. of the tariff bounty.

"It is because I keep telling the iron workers this truth that I am hounded by the minions of the Trusts."

"We have allowed ourselves to be robbed long enough." I am an American to the back-bone, and I propose to fight the men who have disputed this country till I die.

"Let me say that to whatever Nevins may propose I am willing to lend my support, provided the ends he seeks to obtain are honorable and the means reasonable."

"As I am talking I cannot keep out of my mind the home which the Iron Masters destroyed." I had a wife and two children who loved me and were the idols of my heart. I saw this home destroyed. I saw my children turned adrift and their mother forced to work to support them; for during the first three years after the strike I could get nothing to do.

"With these memories which had as a climax the deaths of two nearest and dearest to me, I have nothing left to live for but the fulfillment of my resolve to break the power of the Monopolists who have control of this country."

"This meeting will be protracted to the middle of next week if we all take a half hour or more to tell our tale of woe," observes one of the committee who cannot foresee the end of the discussion.

The chairman asks if the members wish to limit the time of the speakers to five minutes, and this proposition meets with the approval of all.

So the remaining stories are told in short intensive sentences which describe the heart-breaking history of men who have been trodden down under the heel of monopoly.

There are examples of every type that can be imagined. Men who have been defrauded of their ideas and patents; others who have been the victims of unjust legislation, the dupes of the speculator, the betrayed friends of men who have ridden to fortune on the backs of those who gave them their first start.

Under the new ruling, the first man to be recognized is Herman Nettinger, a man known to all the assemblage as an anarchist. He had been admitted to the councils on the supposition that the best way to pacify and placate the Anarchistic element was to offer them full representation in the work of regenerating the government.

Nettinger had been one of the few men who succeeded in eluding the police during the days of the reign of anarchy in Chicago in 1885.

He is a man of gigantic build, and of imperturbable placidity. When a soldier in the German army had provoked him to the point where he had to fight, this modern Titan had seized his tormenter and without apparent effort had dashed the man's brains out by butting him against the wall of the barracks. For this episode Nettinger had been compelled to serve eleven years in the military prison.

During these years he had familiarized himself with the teachings of the socialists, for his companions were, many of them, students of sociology. Upon his release he had come to this country. He invented a compressed air motor, but the American Motor Trust robbed him of his patents.

In the space of five minutes Nettinger strives to defend the theory of anarchy. He denounces all government as a makeshift, and asserts that man should accordingly dispense with the forms of government and depend upon animal instinct to regulate the social community. He names Samuel L. Bell, chairman of the International Patent Commission, as the man who contrived to rob him of his patent rights.

The meeting adjourns at the conclusion of this harangue.

In the hour that has passed the elements for a political revolution have been brought together and combined by a master mind.

CHAPTER X

THE SECRET SESSION

It is apparent that the views of the men who have the most serious grievances against the Trusts are yet to be heard. Most of the members are glad that the meeting of the previous night had adjourned so as to afford time for them to consider the salient points of the remarkable proposal that had been sprung by Nevins.

One of the members, who was conspicuous at all of the meetings, a man of pinched features and diminutive form, a veritable Pope Leo, as it were, makes a motion, as soon as the meeting opens, that three of the members be heard, and if their stories in any way coincide with the general views of the others, the pledge of the remaining men, that they hold equally strong opinions, be sufficient to admit them to the standing necessary for the exposition of the plan.

As a means of expediting matters, the committee adopts this resolution and the three men who are to tell their life's history are chosen. The first of these is a man of the world, a fallen idol of society, who had lately joined the ranks of the oppressed as a consequence of dire financial difficulties.

When he made his advent in the company of the desperate men of Chicago, he had adopted the name of Stephen Marlow.

This name is sufficient, for the men with whom he comes in contact are not occupied in searching genealogies. They are working for results. Marlow is in every sense of the word a leader. He has the grace of manner and the personal charm that at once attracts men. His physical development makes him the envy of the male sex and the idol of the feminine. In stature he is slightly under six feet, with broad shoulders and a fullness of figure that impresses one with the fact that he is a good liver, yet withall muscular.

A pale complexion, strongly marked features and high forehead, with dark brown hair and clear brown eyes, make him a conspicuous figure in any assemblage.

As he rises to address his fellow-committeemen on this momentous occasion, a flush of excitement adds to his attractiveness. He is a man of thirty-five, with the experience of a man of fifty.

"Were I to take the course pursued by those who have already spoken to you," he begins, "I might take you back to the scenes of my childhood and portray pictures of affluence and luxury that few of you could quite appreciate." But the days of my childhood are gone; I am a man and have to fight the battles of men, so I shall limit myself to the few facts that are pertinent to the discussion before us.

"In the past six months I have made the sudden transition from the highest stratum of society to the one in which I am to-day." We cannot, and do not desire to pose as contented men, or as men who are looking for mild solutions of the problems that are now pressing for settlement. I cannot, therefore, affront you when I say that by being among you I prove that I am a radical reformer.

"What you will be interested in learning will be the reasons that impelled me to come here."

"There is not a single thing to be hidden from you." I am here for the purpose of satisfying a revenge.

"My every fibre is quickened by the desire to see the men who caused my downfall brought to my level."

"I am selfish in my purpose; so deeply rooted are my resolves to be avenged that I here and now state to you that any thing radical that may be proposed by this committee shall receive my full support."

"And do you blame me?" Listen to my reasons:

"Six years ago I entered the employ of Stephen Steel, the New York banker." He is a man whom the people of the city and the country at large look upon as a paragon. His words are constantly quoted in the papers; his advice is sought by men of affairs.

"My friends told me I was indeed fortunate to be associated with such a prominent man."

"Well, he was a schemer." At every turn he was on the lookout for a chance to get at the wealth of others. I had not been in his employ more than a month when I discovered that he was at the bottom of a plot to loot the treasuries of three of the largest banks. His scheme was diabolical. It would have entailed the loss of the savings of thousands of small depositors.

"With this knowledge in my possession, I did not know just what my duty was. To shut my eyes to the affair and let it culminate in disaster to innocent thousands, would have been a simple matter. For several days I was in a quandary, but my conscience at length conquered. I mustered up courage enough to speak to my employer. I chose for my time the hour after his return from church on Sunday. He had passed the plate with the unction of a saint. Men and women had looked at him and inwardly said: 'What a fine man Mr. Steel is; if there were only more like him.'"

"At the first intimation I gave him that I looked upon his plans as illegal and immoral, if not absolutely criminal, he attempted to prove to me in a plausible argument that bankers have a right to look out for themselves, no matter who it hits."

"'This plan of mine,' he said, 'is just a stroke of financiering; it is what any man would do if put in my place.'"

"This did not satisfy me, and the expression of scorn that came over my face did not escape him."

"From attempting to prove the righteousness of the case, he then took to berating me for interfering with his business." Had I not enough to do to attend to my affairs in his office, without prying into his outside dealing? Was it a matter that he must lay before his manager? These were the questions he put to me in sharp tones.

"I saw that it would be useless to argue with him so I arose and said:"

"'As you will not listen to reason, as you are a hypocrite and a villain, I shall be compelled to quit your employ. But I wish to inform you that I shall expose this diabolical plan. It shall not be carried out if I can prevent it, and you know that I am in possession of the facts.'"

"At this statement his anger knew no bounds." He railed at me as a trickster. He charged me with wishing to blackmail him. Then seeing that this was not the way to gain his point, he adroitly shifted his lines.

"Would I not take a share in the profits that were to be made?" Did I not see that banking was a business in which every advantage was to be seized and worked for all that was in it? At length he offered to let me in his firm as a partner. This last offer was one that a man would have been more than human to set aside without weighing.

Francis A. Adams

"He saw me hesitate." It was not the hesitation that comes as a forerunner of surrender; it was the pause that a man will make when he has to confront a momentous problem that is to have an effect on his after-life. I did not intend to accept his alluring terms; it had been my resolve at the outset to leave his employ should he refuse to abandon his scheme of loot.

"In the few seconds that I stood facing him, the light of lust came in his eyes, he became the incarnation of greed." A snake that sees its quarry edging inch by inch toward the fangs of death could not have had a more exultant, triumphant look shoot from its treacherous eyes.

"'You will be a man,' said he; 'you will listen to reason.' He uttered these words not as a query, but as an assertion of fact."

"'I shall do as I have said,' was my reply, and I walked toward the door."

"'But you do not mean to say that you refuse to become a partner?' he ejaculated in amazement."

"'That is just what I mean. I tell you once for all that I will not be a party to such crimes as you propose to commit.' 'Then I warn you, young man,' he thundered, losing his self control, 'that if you attempt to thwart me in my business I shall make it uncomfortable for you in this city.'"

"'Yes, I tell you now once for all, that you will find me the most unmerciful enemy that was ever known. I have too much at stake to let a fool of a man upset me."

"Do you think that the world will credit the utterances of a nobody as against mine?" Why, you will be lodged in an insane asylum. I shall have that matter fixed at once.

"By the way, where are the bonds that I entrusted to your care last week?"

"'What bonds?' I demanded hotly." For even then I saw the purport of the question.

"What bonds? Ah, that will not satisfy a jury."

"And the banker chuckled at the thought that he had struck upon the proper weapon with which to crush me."

"In the confidence of his own power, and no doubt as a means of avoiding publicity, he thought that the affair had gone to a point where he might appear magnanimous. 'I do not hold any ill will toward you,' he continued, 'it is as a friend that I speak.' You are suffering from a sensitive conscience, which is out of place in this age and generation."

"I can pity you, but of course it would be impossible for me to allow sentiment to rule me in business."

"We will let this evening pass out of our minds. You will return to your duties, and in the future let my outside matters be distinct from your work and concern. But remember, not a word of this to any one."

"As the last few words were spoken we walked as if by common impulse toward the door."

"I bade him good-night, and the next minute I found myself on the sidewalk." It was winter, and the cold bracing air soon made me alive to the events that had occurred in such quick succession in the banker's parlor.

"My mind was in a flurry." What was I now to do? Did my silence at parting indicate that I had accepted his offer to return to work as his clerk?

"With a muddled brain I walked on and on until I found I had reached the entrance of the Park at Fifty-ninth street and Fifth avenue." I entered the park and sank exhausted upon a bench.

"Then I began to review the words of our interview."

"It all became clear to me." I was in the power of an unscrupulous man. He could throw me into prison at a word; if this was not to be desired he could have me declared insane and put in an insane asylum. My word was as naught against his. So I determined to work in his bank until I could get the evidence that I needed to prove my case.

"I had misjudged my man, for a week later he called me into his private office and informed me that he had no further use for me."

"*His bank wrecking scheme was successfully carried out.*"

"In vain I sought to awaken the interest of the press." The story I told was not credited. I lacked documentary proof. When the crash came the editors realized that I had told the truth. But it was too late.

"When I began to look for employment, I found that my name had been blacklisted." Wherever I go, from Maine to California, I am confronted by an agent of my arch enemy. I cannot even hold a position as a day laborer.

"The damning brand of the magnate is on me, and employers are warned against me. And all because I possess a conscience that would not stoop to crime. I have stood out against retaliating as long as I can. Now my vow is given to be avenged on Steel and his ilk."

Of all the committeemen none has a more distinguished bearing than Professor Herbert Talbot. He is a scion of an honorable New England family; the advantages of refined home surroundings and a college education have combined to give him a polish that should win him the respect and admiration of all who know him.

From the day of his graduation from one of the leading

universities he had begun to teach his favorite study, political economy. At fifty years of age he found himself the recognized authority on economics, a professor in his alma mater, and the recipient of honors at home and abroad.

That was in 1894. What a difference a few years has wrought. Now he is an outcast, driven from his position in the faculty by the order of Rufus Vanpeldt, the Woolen King, the patron of the university. Talbot is reviled by his fellow-collegians, and ostracized from the society in which he had always been a leader; and all because he has had the manliness to express the truth on the political conditions of the country.

He has advocated the reduction of the tariff to a reasonable point; he has been a staunch supporter of the income tax; his views on the money question are deemed heretical and he is dismissed from the circles of learning.

From being the submissive hireling and servitor of the educational institution, he entered the political field as their most powerful adversary. He is one of the leaders of the Anti-Trust movement. When the committee of Forty was organized, he had been one of the first selected.

Many of the committee await his speech with lively interest. Whatever view he takes of the proposition they determine to adopt. He is the next member to be called upon.

In an impressive, convincing argument he approves of the proposition. Not that it is faultless, but because it offers the only remedy for the vicious condition of the country's social condition.

In presenting the arguments in favor of the adoption of the proposition, Professor Talbot demonstrates that the centralization of capital in the hands of a few men is the gravest mistake that a republic can permit to occur. It creates an oligarchy that is more pernicious than one of class distinction, since such a one can be coped with, while an oligarchy of wealth possesses so many ramifications that it is practically unassailable except by direct and physical means.

"It is the common belief that labor-saving inventions are accountable for much of the distress that exists in this country," he says, "but this is not so in so far as the inventions themselves are concerned."

"The evils that have followed the introduction of labor-saving machinery are the results of capitalists seeking to squeeze the last cent of profit out of their enterprises."

"When an inventor produces any improvement in manufacture he does the world a good; when the manufacturer who adopts this invention, at the same time discharges his adult male operatives and substitutes child labor, he vitiates the good that has been done and works a great harm to society."

"The crying evil of to-day is *child labor*, and the labor of women in trades and at work that is manifestly fit only for men."

"I shall make no lengthy appeal to you to adopt a direct means of securing your rights." I shall set you an example by announcing that I pledge my support to Mr. Nevins in anything that he may do that has for its object the emancipation of the women, children and men of this country from industrial slavery.

"There is a living to be had for every inhabitant on the earth if he will work. We in America should guarantee more than subsistence to our citizens. A life of plenty is here for all if the social conditions can be readjusted."

Peter Bergen, a socialist who represents Kansas, is the last to speak. His views are those of the radical. Nothing but instant centralization of all the land and property of the country to be owned and operated by the people as a whole, appear to him to offer an adequate solution of the social problem. He is ready to aid in any movement that is calculated to bring this condition about. He rails against the tyranny of landlordism.

"What justification is there to the laws that will permit an alien to hold land idle in this country until American energy improves the surrounding property?" What justification is there in permitting an alien to withdraw rents from this country without paying a tax toward the support of the Federal government?

"I have fought for this country; I have paid a land tax on my farm and a tax on everything I consume." What does the alien land-holder pay? Nothing.

"I am ready to defend my home and country now." I will ever be loyal to it, for it is the best in the world.

"Its government is not perfect; it is our duty to make it so."

"Let us confiscate the lands of expatriated Americans as an initial step."

"The man who will not contribute to the support of the government does not deserve its protection." His words are uttered with vehemence.

When he concludes this recital of personal grievances against the Trusts, the chairman announces that at the next meeting the members will be given full particulars of the purpose of the syndicate.

The forty men separate, each carrying with him the conviction that at length the time has come when something definite is to be decided upon in the war against Trusts.

Francis A. Adams

CHAPTER XI

MARTHA'S PREMONITION

Trueman remains in Chicago after the close of the Anti-Trust conference so as to be present at the National convention of the Independence party. He is one of the delegates at large to this convention, and hopes to be able to exert an influence over its deliberations, now that he has won some renown as a speaker.

In the rush of the sessions of the Anti-Trust conference he had had no time to keep his promise to Martha. Once only had he sent her a note telling her of his safe arrival in the city. It had not occurred to him that she would be anxiously awaiting a letter from him containing his views on the results of the conference. Why should a woman be interested in such matters?

It is with unbounded surprise therefore that he receives the following letter from her:

WILKES-BARRE, JUNE 13.
My Dear Friend:

It has been so long since I have heard from you that I take the initiative and write to ask you to forward to me as soon as possible, an article embodying your views on the recent Anti-Trust conference. I have a special reason for wishing this before the assembling of the Independence convention.

To be frank with you, I have a premonition that you will be honored with the nomination for the Vice-presidency. Your friends in Pennsylvania, and in the other Eastern states, are working for you. I am handicapped by being a woman, yet in some ways it has proven advantageous to me.

By my peculiar intimacy with the families of this district, I became acquainted with the fact that your name is being mentioned as a possible candidate for the office. As soon as I learned this, I set to work to 'boom,' as the politicians would say, the incipient movement. Last night I was assured by O'Connor, the local leader, that you were sure of the support of the delegations of Pennsylvania and New York. For this reason I can wait no longer for a letter from you.

Let me know at once if you look favorably on the proposition of being a candidate for the high office.

Are you a member of the Committee of Forty? And what is this body?

As ever your friend,

MARTHA.

Here is a revelation.

Unknown to him, his friends, and especially Martha, are at work planning for his nomination as a candidate for the office of Vice-president. The idea of his achieving such a success has never entered his mind.

How can an unknown delegate hope to receive the support of the convention. It seems unreasonable, and he is on the point of writing to Martha that the effort could not help but end in a ridiculous farce, when an interruption prevents him from doing so. A card is brought to his room. It bears the simple inscription:

A FRIEND

"Invite the person up," Trueman tells the servant.

The apartments he occupies are in a quiet boarding house on Lincoln Avenue. He has been in the house six weeks, during which time no one has ever called to see him.

A minute passes in which he ransacks his mind in an attempt to think who can have any business with him. It is half-past eight at night.

A loud rap at the door announces the visitor.

"Come in," calls Trueman.

"Good evening, Mr. Trueman." It is William Nevins who speaks.

"O, it is you, Mr. Nevins," exclaims Trueman.

"I owe you an apology," he continues, "for being surprised at seeing you; but the fact is I am a stranger in Chicago and have had no visitors. When your card came I could not imagine who could wish to see me."

"I am well aware that you are a stranger in this city," Nevins replies. "And as I am little better off I thought that I would drop in to have a chat with you."

"We were delegates at the Anti-Trust Conference and will have much to discuss," says Trueman, in his most affable manner. "I certainly am glad you thought of me. Take a seat, and make yourself as comfortable as the quarters will permit."

They seat themselves near the table. A pipe and a jar of tobacco lie on the table.

"Will you smoke?"

Nevins shakes his head negatively, saying as he does so:

"I cannot talk and smoke at the same time. To-night I want to talk."

"The fact is I have become interested in you since your speech at the close of the conference."

"You will remember it was I who suggested that the committee appointed to investigate the Trust question be increased to forty."

"When I made that motion I had an object in view. I was anxious to have you become one of the committeemen."

"Then the full committee has been appointed?" Trueman asks.

"The forty committeemen have been named. You are not among them, and the reason is that the chairman is jealous of you."

"He can have no reason to be jealous of me."

"The fact remains that he is." I strove to get him to appoint you. He flatly refused to do so. I could get no reason from him. So I concluded that he fears you would outshine him in the work that the committee contemplates doing. Your speech was masterly. I am not given to flattery. I say candidly that it was the best delivered at the conference.

"Since I failed to get you on the committee of forty, I come to see if you will aid me in a project that will make the committee superfluous; I have an idea that the trust question, monopoly and the other social problems can be speedily solved."

"You did not speak at the conference; that was the place to propound such an idea," interposes Trueman.

"Quite true." But I held my peace there, because it was not a place to bring forth the plan that I have evolved. You will agree with me if you will hear me through.

"My plan requires in the first place the services of an honest man—one who is proof against the blandishments of the Plutocrats—who will spurn the offers of gold and office that will be tendered him by the men of wealth when they perceive that he is on the eve of winning the popular support."

"Such a man is hard to find in this age of commercialism which has all but quenched the spark of true patriotism in the hearts of the people. I have sought for the ideal leader in all the States and was on the point of giving up the quest in despair when I suddenly came upon him. Once I determined that the man had been found, I set about learning his record. It appears that he is the product of evolution. From the servant of the Plutocrats he has come to be their most powerful adversary. In him the people will recognize the long-looked-for deliverer."

Here Nevins pauses for a moment to let his words sink into the mind of his interested listener.

"Mr. Trueman," he resumes, "I have decided that you are the man to lead the people out of their bondage."

"I certainly feel complimented at your estimate of my integrity," Trueman replies, "but you greatly overestimate my ability and the hold which I have upon the people."

"It was by the merest chance that I was elected to the position of delegate to the conference. I have really little influence with the men of my own State. This you must know if you have made a careful investigation."

"I know why you are not the recipient of the full support of the men of Pennsylvania." They cannot conceive of a man changing his views so thoroughly as you have. But this lack of perception they will overcome.

"I want you to assure me that you will become the leader of the Independence Party." If you do this I, in turn, will assure you of the nomination for the Presidency.

"That I am not speaking of impossibilities you will be able to understand when I show you the proof of the power I hold to elect the man I decide upon."

"If I am not mistaken, you are opposed to violence as a means of rectifying the social conditions of the people of this country."

"It has been my purpose to defeat every proposition that advised force," comes the quick response. "I am too vividly acquainted with the horrid results that follow an appeal to force."

"My hope is that the people will regain their rights by the proper exercise of the ballot."

"If they discard their all-powerful weapon to take up the sword or the torch, the end must be the destruction of popular government."

"Were you in the position of the chief executive you would follow this view? You would be as determined in suppressing violence as you were in preventing crime of any other sort? Your gratitude to the people for electing you would not blind you to your duty in preventing them from instituting a reign of anarchy? I am correct in this supposition?"

Nevins looks Trueman in the eyes with a glance that seems intent on reading his inmost thoughts.

"I should do my full duty under the constitution," Trueman declares emphatically.

"But, really," he adds, "I cannot appreciate this situation. It is inexplicable why you should interest yourself in my behalf to the extent of seeking to bring about my nomination for the Presidency."

"My reason is not hard to divine." It is not you whom I am working for; it is the people.

"In you I find the proper agent to fulfil the mission of a leader in an hour of grave importance."

"Older men lack the power of attracting the masses." Of the young men whom I have studied, none has the ability, the needed environment that you have.

"Men are creatures of circumstances only when they permit themselves to drift." If one cannot propel himself to a given haven of success he should at least anchor in a place of safety.

"With you it is only necessary that you give me the sign, and you will become the master of circumstances. You will be the man to lead the people to the plane of high civilization that their government makes it possible for them to attain."

For three hours Nevins continues to unfold in detail the plan he has for accomplishing the nomination of Trueman at the coming convention. He shows his prospective candidate letters pledging the support of a majority of the State delegations to the man whom he should designate. In explanation of his power as a leader Nevins states that he has been the secret agent of the Allied Unions for three years, that he has been deputized to select a man to be presented to the convention as a possible candidate. If the man proves acceptable the delegates representing the unions will support him.

"The Committee of Forty is working for you," he says in conclusion. "Their work will bring them in all sections of the country and they will be able to influence a great number of the people."

He gives no hint of the true mission of the committee. He

knows that Trueman would repudiate the party that would resort to so drastic a means of rescuing the people.

"Have I your consent to bring about your nomination?" he asks.

"I shall have to give this matter much thought." You shall have my answer—

"To-morrow night," Nevins interjects. "Delays are dangerous. The convention meets in two weeks time."

"To-morrow night, then," assents Trueman.

Nevins leaves abruptly. He does not wish to weaken the effect he has produced on Trueman by further discussion.

When he finds himself alone Trueman walks back and forth in the cramped room. He is weighing a question that has never before been put to a man.

There is no doubt in his mind as to the sincerity of Nevins. It is clear that this strange man, who, in a matter-of-fact way, asserts that he holds the power of a great convention in his grasp, could have used it for base ends; he could have chosen a man of less inflexible character than Trueman.

"If I can bring myself to believe that it is because of my honesty that Nevins has selected me, I shall give him my consent."

Trueman makes this mental reservation, then turns to the table and writes a long letter to Martha. He sets the matter before her, tells her he will enter politics, and asks for her advice. Regarding the Committee of Forty, he tells her all he knows, which is to the effect that it has been appointed to investigate the work of the Trusts and to make a full report at the next Anti-Trust Conference.

He then goes to his bed. It is daylight before his mind has exhausted itself. He sleeps until midday. On awakening he renews the consideration of Nevins' proposal. At eight o'clock in the evening Nevins arrives.

Where Nevins had been the one to speak the night before, Trueman now enters upon an exhaustive interrogatory. He asks for the most minute particulars of the events that have brought him to the notice of Nevins. To all his questions there is an instant reply. At the conclusion of three hours Trueman definitely makes up his mind to try for the candidacy.

"You may work for my nomination," he says, "and be assured if I am nominated I shall strive to be elected."

"If it is the will of the people to elect me I shall be faithful to the high duties of the office."

Nevins bids his protege good night, assuring him that they will keep in constant communication.

The Committee of Forty, which is in session in a hall on the outskirts of the city in the vicinity of the stock yards, is surprised when, at midnight, Nevins appears before them to announce that he has selected Harvey Trueman to be the candidate for the Presidency on the Independence ticket.

CHAPTER XII

TAKING THE SECRET OATH

Eternal vigilance is the policy of the Magnates in keeping their sleuths ever on the alert for the unearthing of the plans of the anti-trust advocates. In every city detectives are untiring in their efforts to discover the work of the Committee of Forty. It is suspected that the committee is to obtain damaging evidence against some of the most oppressive of the monopolies and bring the full story of the wholesale robbery of the people out as a climax in the coming campaign.

By diligent investigation the detectives learn the names of the thirty-seven men who have been added to the committee by the appointive power of the chairman. It is also ascertained that the forty men are still in the city of Chicago.

This fact is open to several interpretations. It may indicate that the committee has determined to work from a central office; or that the committee is a blind, intended to mislead the detectives into watching it while another agency is at work. The importance of discovering the true mission of the committee is therefore most urgent.

To inspire the detectives to solve the question, the Plutocratic National Committee secretly offers a reward of $5000 to the man who will obtain the desired information.

In holding their daily meetings the Forty observe the greatest caution. Each member goes to the appointed place alone, avoiding as much as possible attracting the attention of the detectives whom they know are on the lookout. It is not their intention to have any mystery connected with their existence, yet they wish to work unhampered by the servants of the Magnates.

For its semi-monthly conference the committee meets at Drover's hall. The deliberations are not open to the public; still, no attempt is made to conceal the fact that there is a meeting.

Nevins and the other leading members decide that the secret meeting at which he is to develop his plan shall be held in a place where there will be no possible way for a spy to creep in.

They select a deserted rolling mill on the edge of the river in North Chicago. This mill was one of the most prosperous in the city prior to the consolidation of the iron industries. Immediately following the combine the mill had been closed and the work that should have gone to it was transferred to the Trust's great plant in Pittsburg.

For eight years the fires in the furnaces have been extinguished; the incompleted iron work that lies about the ground has been given over to the ravages of rust; desolation is the master of the mill.

The spot is an ideal one for a secret meeting place. The police never enter the grounds except at long intervals, when the inspector of the precinct is on his rounds. This official makes a perfunctory survey of the mausoleum of dead industry. In his report the entry, "Iron works vacant," sufficiently describes the place.

On the night of the secret meeting the members arrive at the mill by various routes. There are three entrances on land and a wharf extends along the eastern limit of the enclosure. Five of the delegates cross the river in a skiff.

At nine o'clock all the men are present. They gather on the second floor of the storage shed, a brick structure one hundred by one hundred and fifty feet in area, and three stories high. There are no windows in its bleak walls. On each floor in the wall that faces the interior court of the mill enclosure are two corrugated iron doors. These doors are closed, and effectually exclude the light from without, as well as any light that might be made within. On the floor where the committee meet there is a rough plank table that was used by the machinists of the mill.

At this improvised tribunal the Forty meet to discuss the regeneration of the nation.

Two candles at either end of the ten foot table serve to reveal the dense darkness rather than to dispel it. The flickering-lights fall on the faces of the men as they sit on the floor in a semi-circle. Their eyes are alone perceptible, and the several members are unable to distinguish one another.

The voice of one speaker after another issues from the darkness, producing a supernatural effect upon the assemblage. The nerves of even the most intrepid are at a high tension.

A gust of wind rattling the iron doors causes the men to start; the lowest whisper is intensified to what seems a sonorous shout. In this strange theatre, the actors in what is to be the greatest world-drama, wait to be assigned their parts and to play the first act.

Nevins is the stage manager; he has chosen the settings; has assembled the caste. Now it is his duty to give the signal for the curtain to rise. As with the dramatists of old, he decides to introduce his production with a prologue.

Advancing to the centre of the semi-circle he begins the explanation of his plan of salvation.

Is it destined to end as many thousands have done, in

miserable failure?

"What I propose will strike you as the ravings of a man who has lost his last grain of sense," he begins. "Yet I am prepared to demonstrate that the plan is not only feasible, but that it is the only one which can be put into execution and carried through to a successful issue. The greed and the power of the Trust Magnates is insatiable. They will not make the least concession to the people. The day for arbitration is at an end; the time for the people to act is at hand.

"Every means of defence against the Trusts has been absorbed by them." What are we to do, surrender meekly, or fight?

"History shows us how terrible a thing war is—especially revolutionary war." Now, I have thought out a plan by which war and its attendant calamity can be averted and the people be reinstated in their power.

"There is not a man here who would not enlist to-day at the call for troops." Many of you have already proven yourselves patriots by your service in the field and on the ships of the United States.

"Now, it is not always necessary to be on a battlefield in order to show courage. Men can be heroes in the humble walks of life."

"What I want of you is a pledge that you will stand by me to put out of existence the deadly foes of this country. I want you to swear that you will not flinch when the moment comes for you to fight, even to the death."

"Are any of you unwilling to swear that you would fight the foes of our country to the bitter end?"

No one speaks. The excited condition of the speaker impresses the men strangely. They do not know just how to take him.

"I shall at the next meeting name forty men, each of whom has been an enemy of the United States; each of whom has seen the growth of his private fortune built upon the ruin of homes; each of whom has opposed every measure for the alleviation of the condition of the masses of the people."

"Many of them are known to you as offenders of national notoriety." You have mentioned them in your recital of grievances.

"You all know of the bloody history of the Czar of the Lakes, Anthony Marcus." The graves of the murdered sailors and long-shoremen are a sufficient indictment against him.

"Need I tell you of the horrors that have been daily perpetrated by the ruthless oil magnate, Savage, in my own State of Pennsylvania?"

"Is the right to check competition by the use of the torch to be conceded to him? Is murder for the sake of commercial advantage to be sanctioned as our national policy?"

"The ancients were never so free or so powerful as when their citizens exercised the right to proscribe unworthy citizens."

"Let us constitute this meeting into a forum and issue our list of the proscribed." When the list is read I shall be glad to substitute others for the names I have selected.

"The people are too subservient to aid us in carrying out the edict; so I propose that we each select a man from this list of forty, and that we then see that the edict is enforced. *We shall thus rid the earth of its chief transgressors.*"

"When the French revolution was brought on, the world knew nothing of the possibilities of combined wealth as an agency for the improvement of the condition of the human race. Now we are familiar with all of the wonders that can be accomplished by the combining of money into corporate form."

Francis A. Adams

"We also know that at the present time all of the combined capital of the world is held in the hands of a mighty ring of magnates." The civilized world's billion of people slave for the benefit of a few thousands, who have usurped the prerogatives and the rights of the whole. Nowhere is this condition more aggravated than in this country. We were all born freemen and we find ourselves to-day at the mercy of a few thousand plutocrats. The advantage of improved production is being kept from the people. We are denied our heritage.

"We cannot fight the magnates in the open, for they have attained control of the army and the judicial forces of the government." We face the alternative of submission or revolution.

"What does it avail if we send Representatives to Congress who are tools of the magnates? What does it avail if Congress enacts laws which the executive refuses to enforce?"

"The ballot has become a weapon to destroy those it should protect. Elections ruled by coercion are a mockery."

"I am in favor of inaugurating a scientific revolution." There is no need to raise a guillotine in the city's square and drag to their death those who are living upon the life's blood of the many. This is the crude way to reach a desired end.

"The world is never lastingly horrified and deterred from evil by the mere letting of blood. Crime can be obliterated only by reformation of the criminal element of society. Condemnation of individuals who are caught is productive of little good."

"The destruction even of an army momentarily shocks; but in the one breath the people will cry, 'war is hell; let us have war, for peace sake.' And when war comes it never affects the cowards, the usurers, the rogues; they stay at a safe distance from the scenes of action, and, with the instinct of the hyena, they profit on the nation's calamity. Our trusts are the result of the jobbing that was started during the Civil War, and which has never lagged since."

"The fight that I would have you make is against forty cowards and scoundrels who are sucking the very life out of the country—the forty who represent the high council of the magnates. Let it be a personal fight, a tourney; you the Knights Errant who ride against the dragons."

"When the world awakens some morning and reads that at a given hour the forty Robbers of America were sent to their eternal resting place with their crimes on their heads, the shock will not pass away in a day. It will be far different from reading of a battle fought six thousand miles from Washington. Then will be the time for the men who have the good of the people at heart to reestablish them in their rights."

"Money is the god that the Nation is asked to worship. It makes fools of the majority and knaves of the rest."

"It will take some unprecedented occurrence to stir the masses. The firing on Fort Sumter shook the Nation more than the carnage of Gettysburg." The Nation has come to be apathetic on a vital question; even more so than in the ante-bellum days. The dry-rot of Commercialism is consuming us. We are governed by dividend worshipers. We must act, if our manifest destiny to be a lasting republic is to be fulfilled.

"If the taking off of the forty men would do the work that I wish to see done I would be glad; but it will require a sacrifice on our part of more than our prejudice against taking of life. We shall each have to kill our man, and then commit suicide."

"What!" ejaculate several.

"We shall be obliged to commit suicide. There is no other course open for us, for if, on the announcement that the forty men have been murdered, there is not the still more surprising statement that the murderer of each is found dead beside the slain, the effect will be common-place, and everyone will say it is a cowardly plot to kill forty of the 'best citizens.' There is no way out of it. You would all gladly fight with an enemy of the country to the death. To rescue the flag from the enemy you would face a hail of lead."

"This flag of Freedom is defiled to-day by the Magnates." You are asked to rescue it. It was snatched from my hands on the highway as I went to present a petition to my fellow citizens.

"When each of us has been allotted his man we will work to the accomplishment of the plan at the given time." On each there will be found a letter explaining what led to the killing of the public enemy. These forty letters will appear in the papers throughout the land; they will be compared and found to be counterparts; then the public mind will grasp the significance of the seeming murders. It will then be regarded as an act of deliverance. In place of being regarded as murderers we shall be recognized as men whose love of country impelled us to sacrifice our lives unhesitatingly.

"By the blotting out of forty of the chief despots, and the publication of the reasons; and by the announcement that the people are determined to regain their rights, the road to National Ownership and Control of Public Utilities, and the regulation of the finances and commerce by the government, will be materially cleared."

"In fact, I am confident that the next election after this object lesson will find the robbers ready to sell at a just price and the people eager to come into possession of their own?"

"We will time the execution of our design so that it shall occur on the 13th of October, four weeks before the National election." The Independence Party will have as its candidate a man who is known for his honesty and ability; who is an avowed opponent to force either by the magnates or the people. The people will be eager to entrust their safety in his hands.

"The dread of a repetition of the edict of Proscription will cause even the supporters of the Robber Barons to prefer the election of the people's candidates, than to face the results of the election of a Plutocrat."

The Chairman interrupts the speaker: "We will not take a vote on this question to-night, so I should suggest that the meeting be brought to a close. This will afford us all time to further consider the proposition."

The meeting closes in silence. There is a stern anxious look on the faces of many of the men; others look as if they are on the point of fainting. They reach the court-yard and seem relieved to get a breath of fresh air.

The two members who represent the Anarchistic element are the most depressed. They speak to several of the men from the socialistic orders and try to get at the reason why they shall have to commit suicide for doing what they believe to be the best thing for the world. No one is able to give any very good reason, so the two anarchists go to their homes in any thing but a serene frame of mind.

At the meeting held the following night, the members discuss the momentous proposition in all its details, the result being that they all agree to pledge themselves to the carrying out of the edict of annihilation.

Without unnecessary ceremony each member of the committee takes the preliminary oath that Nevins demands. The reading of the list of the proscribed is postponed for a week.

From the time the committee decides to take the serious step, there is a decided change in the attitude of many of them toward William Nevins. Some of the men have a vague notion that he is not sincere; that he is an agent of the Magnates.

Not that he has said a word that would lend color to this

belief, for, on the contrary, it was he who expressed his views freely as originator of the drastic plan. It comes rather as the result of his being superior to his colleagues in many ways. His reserve of manner, his invariable good judgment and the exhibition of his erudition, instead of endearing him to the members, make them distrustful of him.

A free expression of the feeling that exists is not made, however, until the evening of the allotment. This is the occasion which the men who hold Nevins in disfavor have determined shall be made the moment for his dismissal from the council and for a change in his plan, if not a total rejection of it.

Before the appointed hour of the meeting, these skeptics meet in secret conclave.

"It will be our duty to-night to decide upon the means by which the plan we have been considering may be carried into execution, or abandoned," states the chairman of this impromptu meeting in a perfunctory tone. "If there is any preliminary matter to be discussed, I am ready to entertain it."

This brings three of the men to their feet.

Coleman, the delegate from California, is recognized.

"Mr. Chairman, I am opposed to allowing any man to take part in this work who is not in thorough sympathy with the rest of the committee." It would be a manifest impossibility for this very dangerous and unprecedented undertaking to be launched with the possible danger of there being a spy in our company.

"I am not prepared to say that there is such a spy here, yet until it is satisfactorily demonstrated that we are all of us true friends of the laboring men of the country, I shall be against proceeding to the further outlining of the plan."

"It is not enough that a man profess friendship. He must be able to show by his acts that he has done something for his fellow-men besides theorize."

These views are quickly seconded. Then follows a talk among the men as to what each of them has done to establish a record as a friend of the masses. From the statements and the corroborating testimony of dissenters, all of the members, with the exception of Nevins, pass satisfactorily. He has no acts to his credit. No one admits knowing of him outside of his work as a committeeman. Not one of those in attendance at this special meeting will speak a word in his behalf.

At this juncture, when it looks as though he is to be ruled out of the committee and his plan repudiated, Hendrick Stahl asks to be heard.

As Stahl is a member of high standing and the leader of a strong labor party in Minnesota, he is permitted to speak. In a few forceful words he denounces the men for their ungenerous suspicion; he tells them that he has known Nevins as a friend and co-worker for years.

Not without a visible degree of dissatisfaction the objecting members accept the situation and agree to attend the meeting to hear the reading of the list of proscribed. The men present do not know that Nevins had planned the seeming rebellion to test the sincerity of the men whom he is to take into his full confidence; that he has Professor Talbot and Hendrick Stahl working as his lieutenants.

Nothing now standing in the way of the plan, the men await the hour for the night session. They are eager to hear the reading of the list.

CHAPTER XIII

THE LIST OF TRANSGRESSORS

At length the hour arrives in which the men are to be given the names of the transgressors. It would be disastrous to have any knowledge of the affair fall into the possession of the sleuths of the Trusts; so every precaution for secrecy is observed. The loft of the deserted mill is again chosen as the place of meeting. A thorough search of the storehouse is made, and then the committee assembles in the narrow semi-circle.

After the meeting is called to order, there is an apparent apathy on the part of a number of the Eastern members. When questioned they freely admit that they do not believe their constituents would sanction the drastic measure.

Nevins is absent on his visit to Trueman. He has arranged with Professor Talbot and Stahl to delay the meeting and put the members through another test.

The proposition is argued anew.

It is explained that each man is called upon to make an equal sacrifice; that there is no difference in declaring one's patriotism by enlisting in the army or navy to fight a common foe, or in being one of a numerically small and intrinsically strong army of forty. The Trusts and Monopolies have proven a menace to the people, and can consequently be looked upon as a foe to the government, to be dealt with accordingly.

A unanimous decision to carry out the plan is reached.

At this juncture Nevins appears.

He asks permission to proceed with the reading of the list of the proscribed. He is recognized and begins his startling speech.

"In the lapse of years one is apt to forget the springs from which the wells of human action are fed; it is commonly the lot of man to sink into a state of mind that is at once unreceptive and unretentive." The result is that at the age of thirty he finds himself incapable of grasping new and difficult conceptions. This is the reason why so many injustices are permitted to exist in the world. Men in their youth are thoughtless; in their mature and old age they are neglectful or willingly negligent.

"A degree of success or a degree of failure has a like tendency to blunt the finer qualities of the mind." A man with a competency will not take the troubles of his fellow man to heart. The unfortunate man who has not the wherewithal to support his family is in no position to take the initiative in a labor movement or in a political revolution.

"So the work devolves upon the few men who have the means and the inclination to strive for the betterment of humanity."

"Yet even these men are not always capable of judging events by their true proportions and relations."

"Advancement is the one thing that reformers fear. The ends they would attain are almost always reconstructive; they are never creative." Nevins utters these words with impressive emphasis.

"These remarks I have made by way of prelude to the matter I shall now proceed to discuss directly and earnestly."

"We are each and all convinced that the pernicious system of fostering monopolies that has been instituted in this country can have but one result, the undermining of our popular institutions, and in their place the substitution of moneyed Plutocracy." This result is abhorrent to every true American.

"Now, there is no way to put an end to monopolies except by the people rising in their might and reassuming their own."

"The hypocritical advice of the leaders of the great universities, that the people ostracize the Magnates, has now ceased to satisfy the exigencies of the case." What sort of ostracism would the President of a University endowed by the millions of a Magnate, propose to have enforced against his master?

"Another of the proposals emanating from the hireling counsels of the Trusts, is that the methods of the Trusts be placed under the searchlight of publicity." A pretty programme, indeed, were it not for the fact that the very men who propose this method of dealing with monopolies would be engaged by the Magnates to defend them from exposure.

"To invoke the aid of the courts is to be brought face to face with the servants of the Trusts." Where is the Attorney-General who can successfully prosecute a Trust? The only one who was ever sincere in his attempt met an insurmountable barrier in the courts before which he arraigned the guilty.

"And the votes of the people, do they avail?"

"The executives and legislators whom they elect are false to their pledges."

"The great sin of this country is the worship of gold. Human life is held as secondary to the dollar."

"Who then shall deliver the people from the bondage that has come upon them?"

"Unguided, they are as a flock of sheep without a shepherd. False prophets, mercenary leaders, are an abomination." They have been and are to this day, the clogs in the wheels of progress.

"The work of rejuvenation must be done by an intrepid few." It cannot be entrusted to visionary men, to fanatics, to men who detest government of any form or to men who are willing to suffer present ills rather than face temporary discomfiture.

"To carry on a crusade one must surrender self."

"If our plan did not embrace more than the annihilation of forty of the Transgressors it would not be raised to a higher plane than wholesale homicide."

"But we are to follow the course which the Plutocrats have traversed." They have destroyed individual liberty; they have entrenched themselves in our halls of legislature by bribery; our executives are their puppets; our courts are their final buttress. To reclaim the rights of the people we must reach the powers in control; the actual men who engineer the scheme of public loot. These men have sacrificed human lives to attain their ascendency. We must demand, we must enforce an atonement.

"Because we are to deal with the chief transgressors, who represent a small number, our deed will be regarded in the light of murder."

"Were the magnates in the field as an open foe our assault upon them would be hailed as an act of heroism." Shall we be deterred by consideration of a difference in mere words?

"I propose to vindicate these so-called murders, which we are to commit." The atonement will be frightful. Will it be more so than the conditions which necessitate it?

"Are the lives of forty soulless men to be compared with those

Francis A. Adams

of thousands who are yearly sacrificed to sordid commercialism?"

"Are we to extend our commerce at the price of a life for every dollar of foreign trade?"

"Men prospered in this country before the reign of the Trust Magnates; men grew rich through ordinate profits, and the prosperity of the country was the prosperity of all." To-day men seek to enrich themselves by preying on the necessities of their fellowmen.

"Can the cry of tyrants and sycophants drown the wail of the innocent children and women who have been chained to the wildcat car of Modern Commercialism?"

"In compiling the list of Transgressors," I have selected no man merely because he is possessed of great wealth. There are many millionaires who have earned their fortunes by honest endeavor and in strict conformity with the laws of the land. I have discriminated against those who have prostituted the laws of God and man; not a man whom I shall declare proscribed but he is known to all men as stained with the blood of innocents.

"'The voice of the people is the voice of God.' This voice cries to us from four million mothers' mouths for deliverance from tyrants who compel them to work for a living even in the hours of their pregnancy. The child laborers of this land of freedom raise a piteous plea."

"Do you wait for an actual rain of hell-fire as a sign that God's will is not being done?"

"It is our duty to strike a blow at Plutocracy that shall destroy it for all time." We will act as sovereigns of the land. In us resides the supreme rights of mankind. Our edict cannot be enforced by the courts, so we will act for ourselves.

"The names I read are not given in any fixed order; each man is equally guilty."

Here Nevins takes a slip of paper from his pocket and begins to read:

"By reason of his treasonable act in furnishing the Nation's defenders poisonous food while they were engaged in actual war, and for continued vending of deleterious food to the citizens at large; for his conspicuous participation in the formation of the monopoly of the meat products of the country, for the purpose of extorting tribute from the masses, I name Tingwell Fang as one of the transgressors. This man has a fortune of $200,000,000; more than the life earnings of 2,000 men engaged in ordinary pursuits for a period of thirty years each."

"Judge if God ordained that one man should be possessed of such fabulous wealth when His Son gave as our prayer, 'Give us this day our daily bread.'"

"As the controller of the Wheat Trust, by which the grim hand of famine is laid on the nation, and a tax levied on our subsistence, I name David Leach as another of the transgressors." He has collected $100,000,000, in sums of one and two cents from the millions of men, women and children of this country. He stands between us and our daily bread.

"I need not portray the sufferings that are inflicted on the nation by the presence of the Coal Trust." From the miners to the consumers the tale is one of ever-increasing awfulness. Man to-day, who must live in the northern and temperate regions of our country, cannot endure the cold of winter without artificial heat. He cannot go to the virgin forests, for the land is owned by private individuals; he cannot go to the mines, for they are the property of the coal barons. He must purchase the coal that is needed to heat his home.

"This makes coal not a luxury, but one of the necessities of life."

Francis A. Adams

"In the hands of the Trust the price is raised to the highest possible point. The monopoly is complete; the demand perpetual."

"Every home where coal is consumed is a witness to the rapacity of the Coal Trust." I therefore name as one of the transgressors, Gorman Purdy, President of the Coal Trust, the man who ordered the massacre of the miners at Hazleton; who has driven widows and orphans from the mining towns to let them starve on the highways. He is the possessor of $160,000,000, the equivalent of the earnings of 10,000 miners for forty-five years.

"I name as a transgressor, Ebenezer J. Sloat, President of the Leather Combine." His single fortune is $80,000,000. This man succeeded in effecting a consolidation of all of the leather producers; now the nation pays the Trust a royalty on every pair of shoes that is sold.

"He has driven the cobbler out of existence and has set children and women at the machines which turn out completed shoes, on which not a single part has to be made by skilled labor."

"It is not in the trades alone that the Transgressors are to be found." They have developed in high places.

"I name as one of the proscribed, ex-Supreme Court Justice Elias M. Turner, who, at the demand of the Magnates, recanted his judgment on the question of constitutional taxation, and left the humble citizens to bear the burden of taxes while the Trusts and Monopolies go practically exempt." This act of betrayal to the public weal is the more atrocious as it was done by a man who had been invested with the highest honor that the nation could bestow upon the ermine.

"If the wearer of the robe of justice outrages his garment is it to remain an invulnerable shield against our righteous condemnation?" He who doles justice, must himself be its chief exemplar.

"Another of the high servants of the people who has betrayed his fellow countrymen, is ex-Attorney General Lax." It was his masterful policy of inaction that permitted the trusts and monopolies to intrench themselves during the four years that he stood as their buffer, against all efforts of the several states to curb them.

"Entering the office as a man of moderate means he left it possessed of a fabulous fortune—the bribe money of the Magnates. And not content to retire from office, and cease his nefarious trade, he is to-day the counsel for the Money Trust. It is his mind that conceives the interminable means for forcing the Government to issue bonds for the benefit of the Banking Syndicate?"

"It was Herbert Lax who made me a bankrupt," exclaims one of the committee. "He caused my brother to commit suicide. If ever there was a cold-blooded villain, Lax is the man."

"His acts were those of charity compared to some of the Transgressors," observes Nevins, before he continues to announce the list. "Is the bankrupting of men to be compared with the heinous crime of enslaving children?

"The Cotton King, Herod Butcher of Fall River, who thrives on the life's blood of ten thousand minors—pitiable slaves of his looms, is one of the transgressors who must atone for a life-long career as a merciless infanticide."

"No man is so base that he would stand by and see a child ruthlessly slain." Yet the nation stands supinely in the presence of a system of factory labor which tolerates the inhuman employment of children. The hazy halo of legality is between the transgressor and the people; and men remain unmoved.

"It was for humanity's sake that our countrymen gave their life ungrudgingly on the battle-fields of Cuba. But what of the inhumanity at home? A word spoken against an American manufacturer is a crime in the eyes of the Magnates, and the offender is chastised accordingly."

"I have three sons who grew to manhood, stunted and untutored, who had to work for their daily bread in the mills of Herod Butcher," declares Martin Stark, the Rhode Island committeeman.

"Judas D. Savage is another of the transgressors." A hundred flaming oil wells lit by the torch of the incendiary, hired by his gold, wrote his proscription on the scroll of high heaven.

"And Roger Q. Alger, of the defaulting Savings Bank dynasty comes to you recommended by the cries of anguish that have been uttered by thousands of widows, orphans, struggling husbands and provident wives, who have awakened to find their savings distributed as booty to the Barons."

"But what need have I to recount the misdeeds of this list of men. If the first man or woman whom you meet on the street cannot give you a description of them that will stand as an indictment, then consider the men I name innocent!"

He then completes the reading of the list. There is a painful silence when he ceases to speak. The Forty seem absorbed in deep thought. The chairman finally speaks:

"You have heard the reading of the list," he says. "If it is your desire to substitute names for those mentioned, now is the time to propose the change."

"I move that the list be adopted as read," Carl Metz suggests.

"I second the motion," says Professor Talbot.

Every committeeman votes for the adoption of the list.

The names are written on slips of paper and placed in a hat. As each committeeman passes the table he draws a slip.

"You have all signified your willingness to carry out the terms of the edict of annihilation," the chairman explains. "It now remains for you to redeem your pledges. If there is one of you who regrets the step he has taken it is not too late to withdraw."

There is profound silence, and the men stand immovable.

"Two months from to-day then, October 13th, our Syndicate of Annihilation will declare its dividend; this will require the summary taking off of the Forty Transgressors and our self-immolation." Chadwick pronounces these words slowly, impressively:

"We will separate to-night never to meet again in this life."

"If we are true to our purpose we will not have died in vain." Without formal partings the men leave the store-house.

Nevins is the last to depart; he draws the remaining slip. It bears the name of "James Golding, Bond King; capital, $400,000,000; occupation, United States Treasury Looter."

BOOK III

THE SYNDICATE DECLARES A DIVIDEND

CHAPTER XIV

BIRTH OF A NEW PARTY

"You will soon find that my assertion was based on absolute knowledge, for your nomination will be unanimous," Nevins declares to Trueman as they sit in private conference, on the eve of the Independence Party's convention.

"Then you do not credit the statement that the Eastern delegations have become disaffected?"

"That's only one of the rumors which the Plutocrats have set afloat since they unearthed the fact that you are to be a candidate for the vice-presidential nomination. Gorman Purdy is the instigator of all these adverse stories. He has not forgotten that you were once his most promising pupil."

The President-maker and his intended candidate are in daily communication; they have become firmly attached to each other in the short period of their acquaintanceship. This is not to be wondered at, for there is a striking similarity in their temperaments. Each is endowed with keen perception and wonderful magnetism. Their combined influence has brought to their support the most contumacious of the delegates. On the issue of the following day the hopes of each are centered. Nevins has asked his young champion to visit him at his rooms in an unpretentious hotel on Clark street; there are details for the work of the morrow that have to be carefully planned.

"In your speech you must dwell upon the causes which led to the formation of the new party," Nevins explains. "This must be done briefly; but it will pave the way for your demonstration that a new, a young man must be called upon to make the fight against the intrenched robbers.

"As you know, I have striven for ten years to bring about the present propitious circumstances;" it has been an almost impossible task to get a convention of men who are susceptible of being made to nominate a young and untried man for so exalted an office.

"But all of the political conditions of the hour indicate that the bold proposal will be accepted."

"I have caused a most thorough canvas of the delegates to be made," says Trueman, "and they are almost unanimous in declaring that they will support me for the second place on the ticket. When sounded on the proposition of voting for a young man for the head of the ticket, they demur."

"That is just as I have planned matters should stand before the convening of the delegates," replies Nevins, with a self-complacent smile.

"All of the older men will have spoken before you are called upon." The sharp contrast that will be presented in the staid and uninspiring speeches of your predecessors, and your fervid, fluent and convincing call to action, will lift you to the position of the logical candidate.

"No successful statesman has ever been unmindful of the practical side of politics." A speech may create a whirlwind of enthusiasm for an orator; yet if there is no one to guide the tempest it is soon spent. I shall be on the watch for the moment that must see your name put in nomination.

"When it comes, I shall put you in nomination."

"Day by day I am learning that politics is not a game of chance," observes Trueman, meditatively. "It is a science, with as much to master as the science of war, which it resembles most strikingly."

"A year ago I should have scoffed at the idea that I would be engaged in planning and in carrying out a campaign to capture a convention. Yet it is absolutely necessary to make these preparations."

"How many hours did I spend in convincing you that politics is an exact science?" Nevins inquires, with a faint smile, as he recalls the struggle he has gone through with before he could get Trueman to consent to the methods that had to be adopted to effect his nomination.

"I know that you had an obstinate pupil. I hope that I have not been instructed in vain."

"I have no fear on that score." You will fulfil the mission that is manifestly set for you. Keep the thought of the people uppermost in your mind when you are speaking, and it will give you the needed inspiration.

"Come, we will review the bill of complaint which the people find against the Trusts."

They rapidly name, in chronological order, the events that have been instrumental in bringing about the degradation of labor. There is the primal generator of universal distress—the private corporation—which operates with all the functions of an individual, yet is free from even the most ordinary obligations that are enforced upon the individual; from the private corporation has sprung the Trust, a consolidation of corporate bodies which intensifies the evils that exist under the former institution, and as an inevitable consequence of Trusts comes private Monopolies. These last have been the direct cause of awakening the people to a realization of their condition. For each aggression of corporate wealth the people have been forced from their position as free men to that of servants. The climax is reached when the Monopolies adopt the paternal principle of pensioning their employees, thus making of them retainers in name, as they have long been in fact.

"I shall leave you to your thoughts," says Nevins, in parting. He walks to the entrance of the hotel with Trueman. When his friend departs he returns to his room.

Three of the Committee of Forty are awaiting him. They have come for a short consultation. At the convention they are to be the trusted lieutenants of Nevins.

There is no money to be distributed; no patronage to be pledged for the support of delegates. The preliminary arrangements of battle are strangely dissimilar to those of any preceding convention that has been held in this country for half a century.

The magnitude of the cause that brought forth the Democracy in the days of Jefferson, and the Republican party in the days of Lincoln, is again attracting true patriots; the cry of a people which has long been outraged is demanding to be heard; it has reached the ears of a faithful few who put country above price. It is of such material that the new party is composed.

A young and untried soldier was called by the sage of the Revolution of 1776 to take command of the Continental army. What is to prevent a repetition of our history, now that another crisis has to be faced? Of the committee there are few who do not feel assured that Trueman will be capable of fulfilling the duties of the office to which they seek to elevate him; they are not certain, however, that they can secure the nomination for him.

Trueman is hopeful; yet he cannot drive from his mind the rumors of disloyalty that are constantly brought to him.

In the minds of the Plutocrats it seems utterly impossible for Trueman to even obtain the vice-presidential nomination. It never occurs to them to regard him as a probable candidate for the higher office. Nevins, alone of all men, is confident of the result of the morrow.

CHAPTER XV

CHOOSING A LEADER

Chicago, the city of immeasurable possibilities, the twice risen Phoenix, scene of the fairyland of 1893, when the wonders of the world were assembled for the fleeting admiration of man, is the arena in which a battle is to be waged that shall be remembered when the other events that add to the fame of the municipality shall have passed into oblivion.

To the citizens of Chicago a convention has come to be regarded as an every-day occurrence. If it is not a convention of one of the great parties, then some lesser body is in session; always some band of delegates is reported as either arriving in or departing from the city. There had been little stir when the Plutocratic convention was in progress three weeks before. The result of the proceedings was foreordained.

But with the convening of the delegates of the Independence Party the apathy of the people gives way to intense interest. They realize that at least there will be a lively contest over the choice of a leading candidate.

Political forecasters have been chary of expressing opinions, for the much depended on precedent is lacking. Here is a new party, which is to make its second appeal to the people. Where its strength will lay, whom it will select to be the standard-bearer of its radical platform, these are questions that baffle the most astute observers.

Francis A. Adams

The morning of the opening session of the convention finds the vast auditorium of the Music Hall where the meetings are to be held, crowded with spectators. It is impossible for one-tenth of those present to hear the speakers; they come not to hear so much as to breathe the surcharged air of the political storm which it is known will be fostered. The thin blood of the modern civilian is acted upon by less boisterous and gory scenes than those which sufficed to stir the audiences of the Roman circus; yet the human susceptibilities are the same in all ages, and differ only in expression. In the battle of voices, the audience will shout its approval or hiss its disapproval; at the pleasure of the throng a speaker can be silenced, his victory snatched from his very grasp.

Six thousand people are in their places by ten o'clock. The police have been compelled to shut the doors to exclude the crowds who would be satisfied merely to get inside of the building. A murmur fills the place, although no one is speaking above the normal tone; the combined sound resembles the distant boom of a cataract. Here and there in the galleries a splash of color indicates the presence of a woman. The value of feminine headgear is for once clearly demonstrated; it serves to differentiate the sexes.

On the floor of the auditorium the long avenues of chairs are vacant; a dozen men are busy arranging the location of the state delegations. Guidons bearing the names of the states are put in position. At the press tables, at the foot of the speakers' platform, hundreds of reporters are industriously grinding out "copy" for their papers. A formidable army of messenger boys is lined up along the base of the platform. They are a reserve, to be used in case the telegraph service should break down.

Immediately in the rear of the speaker's table is the indispensable adjunct of American politics, the brass band. At 10.15 o'clock the leader of the band gives a signal, and the "Star Spangled Banner" is played, six thousand voices joining in the best known phases and the chorus.

Now the delegates arrive. The New York contingent walks to its place in the middle of the hall. Ex-Senator Sharp is at their head, followed by the prominent county leaders. Their appearance is the signal for an outburst from the galleries. Cheers and hisses are about evenly divided. The conservatism of the New Yorkers makes them the bone of contention.

"They will try to rule this convention in the interests of Wall Street, as they did in the Democratic convention of '96," observes a man in the West gallery, to the man next to him. "The theory of majority rule that was good enough for the founders of the country, does not seem to hold much force now-a-days."

"No," replies the first speaker. "The rule of the majority has been repudiated. It would have been inimical to monopolies, so the Magnates have nullified it. They did the same thing with silver in '73. There could be no money trust with bi-metalism."

"Do you think the Eastern delegations are strong enough to dominate this convention?"

A tumultuous shout drowns the reply.

"Texas! Texas!" cry a thousand voices.

"California, she's all right!" cry as many more.

Delegates from the above-named states appear at two entrances.

By eleven o'clock the convention is assembled. The chairman rises and pounds on the table with his gavel to quiet the audience.

"We will open this convention with prayer. It is the desire of our party to lift itself out of the mire of partisan politics, and nothing is more fitting than that an invocation to the

Almighty should constitute our initial performance."

An unknown clergyman from Iowa is called to offer prayer. He is listened to in absolute silence; the great horde of men and women hold their breath; religion at least is not extinct in the people. Following the prayer comes the routine work of passing on credentials and appointing committees. This is done with celerity. The men are anxious to begin the real business.

As the last committee is named, a delegate from every one of the States is on his feet clamoring for recognition.

"Illinois has the floor," the chairman announces. This is done as a matter of courtesy to the state in which the convention is being held.

Congressman Blanchard, representing a Chicago district, is the man who receives recognition.

As he steps upon the rostrum the cheering is deafening. He is the favorite son of the state and this is the supreme moment in which he may launch his boom for the presidential nomination.

The power of his oratory is of a high order. He makes the fatal error of being non-committal; his friends see that the chance has passed him.

Favorite sons from a dozen states strive for the prize; yet for one reason or another are unsuccessful in carrying the convention, or of awakening the enthusiasm of the audience.

"No one has spoken from Pennsylvania," remarks the man in the gallery.

"There are few orators of note in that state now," he adds.

"There are very few; but their small number is counterbalanced by the quality of the men. Have you ever heard Trueman?"

"I never heard him speak, but I have read his speeches. He seems to be a true friend of the people."

"Let us call for a speech from Pennsylvania," suggests the observant auditor.

"Pennsylvania! Pennsylvania!" shouts the impulsive man beside him.

"Pennsylvania!" comes the instant response in every quarter of the auditorium. The audience realizes that the great Keystone State has not been heard from.

The uproar increases. Men stand on their chairs and wave their hats, shouting themselves hoarse.

"Pennsylvania, what's the matter with Pennsylvania? She's all right!"

The man in the gallery draws a flag from beneath his coat and waves it frantically.

"Trueman, Trueman! Speech!"

The cry changes instantly.

From his eyrie, Nevins, the omnipresent, flutters his commands. Under his spell the tumult rises. Delegates from Nebraska and Louisiana rush to the Pennsylvania section and seize Trueman. He is borne to the rostrum across a veritable sea of men.

Now Nevins hides the flag, and as though a switch key had cut off the current from a dynamo, the confusion subsides.

Now only fitful shouts can be heard; they come like the final rifle cracks in a battle.

Francis A. Adams

Trueman has gained his feet and stands erect, facing an audience that is already fired to the white heat of spontaneous combustion.

He is saved the necessity of working for a climax; it is prepared.

"Pennsylvania has come to this convention to be heard," he cries.

This happy introduction catches the crowd. They give a long, hearty cheer and then are silent.

"The delegates from the Keystone State are here to aid in producing a platform that shall contain the declaration of the right of mankind to labor."

"The work of this convention is not to be the single effort of one State delegation; it is not to be that of any prescribed body; but must reflect the united opinions of the American people."

"I shall speak, therefore, as a representative of all liberty-loving men, and shall express their hopes and aspirations as I have found them to exist."

"It is the ever constant belief of the people that popular government is the only form that is compatible with Divine ordination; that all men shall be protected in the right to live, to labor and to prosper according to their deeds and deserts."

"These principles are the basis upon which our republic was built; they have served as the inspiration of our lives; for their perpetuation men have given up their lives on the field of battle, on the altar of martyrdom, and for these principles the vast majority of the citizens of this country are to-day ready to make any sacrifice."

A storm of applause momentarily checks the speaker.

"When a man devotes his energy to honest toil it is for the purpose of securing to himself and to his family the blessings of thrift; the safeguard for honorable old age. In his effort he should be protected by every means that a strong government can devise. The 'millstone' should not be pledged or pillaged; the struggle of life should not be made hopeless by compelling a man to slave for mere subsistence."

"Hear, hear!" come shouts from the galleries.

"Our people have seen the Republic dragged from the line of righteous progress and diverted into the unnatural path of Plutocracy." Insidious methods have been resorted to by those who have wrought this transformation. Sophists have told the plain, credulous workers that industrial combination in the form of Corporations and Trusts is the result of a natural law of evolution. But what is the truth? The great consolidations that have been effected during the past few years have resulted from the enactment of statutory laws. These laws have emanated from the brains of men, paid by the Trust magnates to undermine the republic. No more treasonable acts were ever committed than by the men who have sold the rights of a free people to a band of unscrupulous money worshipers.

"The continuance of this country as a Republic depends upon the restoration of the independent citizen." To-day there are fewer men engaged in independent work, as manufacturers and merchants, than there were ten years ago; to-day the great bulk of the wealth of the country is concentrated in the hands of a few thousand men. These men have become the masters of the Nation; on their payrolls are to be found three-fourths of all the working inhabitants of the land, men, women, and children.

"Men, women and children, I repeat, for where is the man who can earn a sufficient wage to provide proper food and raiment for his family by his single effort?"

"As the hope of the people rests on the recovery of the

independence of the individual, the platform of this party must declare unequivocally for the abolition of all forms of private monopoly. This must be the main plank in our platform."

These words, uttered in a voice that reaches the remotest corners of the auditorium, call forth a tumultuous shout.

"With private Monopolies destroyed and the channels they control opened to the people, the billions of revenue that now go to increase the fortunes of the Masters of Commerce, will be enjoyed by the toilers who create our National prosperity."

"The statistics of the future shall record the existence in this land of thousands, hundreds of thousands of independent business men." The columns devoted to enumerating the Child Labor of the land will be dispensed with; there will be an increase in the number of mothers and a decrease in the number of women who are forced to earn a living by manual toil.

"The platform we adopt must contain a plank providing for the imposition of a tax on a man according to his ability to pay." There is no sanction for a law to govern a community, however large, however populous, if this law is in contradiction of the principles that govern a household; for we cannot conceive of a government that is not built on the household as the unit.

"Where is the father so inhuman that he will demand of the stripling, the infirm, the feminine members of his family to procure the means of support, before he has exhausted every other effort that can be made by himself and his stalwart sons?" Even the insatiate Trust Magnates, were they suddenly to be reduced to penury, would shield their wives, their daughters and their indigent.

"Then who shall say that this Republic, a household on a mammoth scale, is not justified in collecting the taxes necessary for its maintenance from the incomes of the rich, and not from the paltry possessions of the wage-earner?" The hundredth part of the income of the rich will more than pay for the legitimate expenses of the Government.

"I am a firm believer in 'vested rights' and carry my adherence back to the dawn of creation." Then it was that God vested mankind with the right to live upon this earth. He endowed man with the ability to earn a living, and gave to each and every man an equal inheritance—opportunity.

"Any laws that man has made which abridge this right of equal opportunity are unconstitutional in the broad sense of being at variance with God's will. Applied to our Constitution, the vested right of the people to the equal opportunity to labor is higher than the right of the few to retain the fruits of the labor of the many."

"I advocate the taxing of the incomes of our citizens before we tax their wages, which is their capital." Cheers interrupt the speaker for a full minute.

"It is my hope, the people's hope, that the bulwark of this country be once more as it was for a century, not a standing army of idle soldiers, but an active army of free men, busied by day in the fields and in the workshops; resting by night under cover of their homes, surrounded by their happy families; an army that is ready at an instant's call to fight for the protection of their Flag and their Homes."

"The united armies of the world would hesitate to face the legions of contented freemen." Our power in the world will be increased more by a fleet of merchant ships than by squadrons of steel battleships.

"We want a National Militia, to be composed of every able bodied man, who in the hours of peace prepares against the possibility of war. We want a Navy strong enough to represent our interest on every sea; a Naval Reserve strong enough to convert our Merchant Marine into the greatest fleet in the world, should need arise."

"We want, and we will succeed in getting the Army of the Unemployed mustered out."

"With us rests the duty of selecting a mustering officer; a man to carry out the wishes of the people; a man who is temperate in his judgment, unswerving in his purpose and unimpeachable in his integrity; a man in whom the people may place full confidence. With such a man as a candidate on the platform we shall adopt, the will of the people cannot be thwarted."

"We can frame the platform. Where is the man?"

"Trueman! Trueman!" comes the cry.

From mouth to mouth the name passes; now it is shrieked by an entire state delegation; now by the entire assemblage. Louder and louder becomes the cry. It is chanted, sung, shouted, shrieked. Men who have shouted themselves hoarse utter it inarticulately.

In the centre of the floor there is a movement; the guidon of New York is moving. It is being borne toward the Pennsylvania delegation.

Another and another state guidon follows in its wake. The convention is in an uproar.

Ten, twenty of the delegations are now swarming about the standard of Pennsylvania. The galleries keep up the incessant shout of "Trueman! Trueman!"

A hundred men are clustered about the speaker as he stands, awed by the outburst of enthusiasm. He is picked up and placed on the shoulders of his friends.

The delegations who have rallied to his support now number forty; they are moving toward the platform. The men carrying

Trueman go to meet them.

The climax is reached. Trueman is carried round and round the hall, the enthusiasm of the delegates reaching the point of frenzy. Every delegation is now in line. Without waiting for the formality of a motion to adjourn, the convention marches from the building; its candidate at its head.

Francis A. Adams

CHAPTER XVI

TWO POINTS OF VIEW

On the way to the hotel after the exciting incidents of the day, which have culminated in his nomination, Trueman has time to reflect. The poise of a man of his sterling character is not easily disturbed; yet he feels misgivings as to the ultimate result of the pending campaign. The odds are so uneven. On the one side the millions of concentrated capital, commanding the servile votes of the dependent operatives; on the other, eternal principles, supported by a few resolute men who will have to inspire the Nation to action.

"If I only had the encouragement of Ethel," Harvey soliloquizes, "it would be nothing to face the foes of my country." But I must make the fight alone. She is separated from me now by a wider barrier than ever. As the champion of the people of Wilkes-Barre I became the antagonist of her father, and she had no choice but to remain with him.

"And yet, at our parting, there was a tremor in her voice which told me that her love for me was not utterly dispelled."

"Sister Martha tells me that Ethel is not happy, that she has ceased to be the social butterfly, the cynosure of the fashionable set in Philadelphia and New York."

"As the inconspicuous leader of the working men of a Pennsylvania mining town I might have won her, even against the opposition of Gorman Purdy. As a candidate for the Presidency, on the Independence party's ticket, my hopes are idle."

He enters his room and finds a telegram on the table.

"VENETIA, L. I.

"As a friend I congratulate you on the honor you have achieved; I wish that circumstances would permit me to aid you in attaining victory.   E. P."

In all the world there is no treasure more precious than the yellow slip of paper which Harvey holds in his hand. It is a proof that Ethel has not forgotten him; it even foretells that if victory were to rest on his standards, he might claim a double prize—the Presidency and a bride.

"What right had I to expect that Ethel could descend from her sphere to share the uncertain fortunes of a social reformer?" he muses.

"The conditions of life that have been fostered in the United States since the era of the multi-millionaire make the problem of marriage more complicated than ever before." How can a woman, born to luxury, hope to find marital felicity with a man dependent on his daily wages for the means of supporting himself and family?

"To say that she may bestow her wealth upon her husband, does not solve the problem; it modifies it by adding a potent deterrent; for a man who will be dependent upon his wife for support, lacks the essential qualifications of a good husband."

"The sharp lines of class distinction now drawn in the country are the cause of most of the unhappiness that attend matrimony. It is the opinion of others, not the needs of self, that engender discontent."

"I must win a position in the world which will demand the respect of all men; then I shall offer Ethel, in place of the ill-gotten millions of her father's fortune, the name and love of an honest and respected man. And I will be honest and respected, even as President."

"What a commentary on human frailty the records of our latter day Chief Magistrates present." Each has been of humble origin. He has risen by virtue of fearless championship of the cause of the masses. Once in the office of the Presidency, all uprightness and independence has left him and he has worshiped at the feet of the Idol of Gold.

"To win the Presidency will be to inaugurate an era of real National prosperity, in which the labor of the people will be insured just remuneration. To win Ethel will be to abolish the distinction of class."

At the very hour Harvey Trueman is pondering over the grave conditions that keep him from making Ethel his wife, she is thinking of the mockery of her riches, which furnish her with every attribute to happiness but one—that eclipses all others—the heart's desire.

From the days that she had first known Harvey as the brilliant counsellor, she has felt that inextinguishable love which thrives on hope, and which will not diminish, even when hope is banished. Harvey and she had been friends. His brains had won him admittance to the social class in which she moved. When their attachment had grown to love, and he had asked her father's consent to their marriage, Gorman Purdy, the man of millions, had not hesitated to sanction the union.

What a joy had filled her heart when Harvey told her of his love! What happiness could have equalled hers when she received the news from Harvey that her father was willing that they should marry?

What has caused their separation?

This is the question that remains as yet unanswered in her mind.

"Is it possible that there can be such a divergence in the views of two men on a question of right and wrong," she asks herself, "that they will sacrifice the happiness of the one woman they profess to love, rather than agree upon a compromise, or one or the other change his views?"

"My father loves me; he lavishes his wealth upon me; I am his only child, his only comfort. He remains a widower so as to give me an undivided love." Yet he will not consent to my speaking of wedding Harvey Trueman. He tells me that Harvey is an enemy of mankind; a man who is seeking to disrupt civilization; that every word he utters is intended to inflame the minds of the people; to incite them to anarchy.

"And Harvey, can his words be false when his actions are so generous?" What prompted him to give the miner's widow a thousand dollars? Was it a desire to do an act of charity, or was it as my father tells me, the act of a demagogue?

"How am I, a woman who knows nothing of politics or the principles of government, to decide a question that divides nations?"

"What does all the advanced civilization of to-day amount to when it stands as a barrier to happy marriages?"

"I cannot exchange places with a woman of the mining districts. My life has been so different that I should be miserable."

As she philosophises Ethel glances about her boudoir. It is midnight. From her open window a refreshing breeze comes from the sea. Venetia, on the Long Island shore, where Gorman Purdy has built his palatial residence, is always fanned by ocean breezes. On this particular night in August the moon shines full and bright. It gives a soft tone to the luxurious apartment in which America's richest heiress lies tossing restlessly on her bed.

"How impossible it would be for a miner's wife to exchange places with me," Ethel sighs.

"I am envied by every woman in the land." And still I am unhappy; O, so unhappy.

"The fetters of wealth are as binding as those of poverty; they are not appreciated by the world, and those who wear them are never pitied. If only Harvey is elected President, and my father's fears are not verified, perhaps—"

Ethel does not dare to express the hope that wells in her heart.

CHAPTER XVII

OPENING THE CAMPAIGN

A National Headquarters at the height of a Presidential election is of all places in the world the busiest. Men there seem to concentrate the pent-up energy of four years in the four months that are devoted to the campaigning; they work day and night, regardless of sleep or food. A few hours rest, taken when a momentary lull will permit, must suffice; a hurried meal must appease their appetite. Meetings have to be arranged; funds distributed to the various committees; literature has to be prepared and distributed; doubtful districts need the attention of the blest spell-binders; the movements of the opposing parties have to be met and counteracted.

Especially is the present campaign an exciting one. The strain on old party lines has at length snapped. The two leading parties in the West and South are disrupted. While not utterly disorganized, the same parties have suffered serious disintegration in the manufacturing districts of the East.

On the virtual ruins of the effete political organizations, the spirit of the people finds utterance through the agency of the new party which chooses as its name the "Independence Party." Vitalized by the infusion in its body of the energetic and patriotic young men of the country, the new party sprang into the lists, as it were, full grown. Its period of adolescence has been as rapid as the transit of a comet. Yesterday it had not existed, even in the minds of dreamers; to-day, in the

Francis A. Adams

convention of one of the great political organizations an attempt was made to throttle the voice of the majority. The voice of a single man rose high and clear above the tumult; it was the voice of a Moses come to lead his people from bondage. And that people were quick to appreciate the importance of the presence of a great leader. The convention cast aside all conservatism and cant; it produced a platform that offered to mankind the direct and constitutional means for the restoration of general prosperity and the re-establishment of the principles of equality.

In the first struggle against the entrenched power of corruption, the new party had been defeated, not by reason of a disinclination on the part of the people to support it, but because of the coercive methods employed by the Trust Magnates. In the momentous campaign of 1900, the vote of the people being divided, the candidate of the Democracy was elected. He was a man of worth and was eager to do the people's bidding. This, however, was not productive of any good to the people, as the President had a House and Senate hostile to him. Thrice his first Congress had attempted to impeach him, and they were deterred from carrying out their partisan measure only by the ominous demonstration of the laboring men in all sections of the land.

Now, the greatest election ever held in this country is on; the forces have met on three occasions and know each other's methods; they know also that the result of the vote at this election will decide the future of the country—it will continue to be a Republic in fact as in name; or, if the Plutocratic party dominates, the dynasty of the first emperor will be established.

The Chicago Auditorium is selected as the quarters of the Plutocratic contingent. The corridors of this magnificent hotel are crowded night and day by throngs of visitors. Men from every state are there to consult with the campaign committee. The grim visaged chairman of the finance committee, Anthony Marcus, is always at his desk in an inner room. Millionaires troop into his presence in a ceaseless stream; they come with their bankbooks in hand and after a short interview with the Powerful One, they depart, reassured that their millions are safe. They pay their tithe to the Protector of American Plunderers.

Anthony Marcus is in many ways a remarkable man; he is exempt from the imputation of being a little man in any sense. His ideas are daring; they can contemplate the debauchery of the Senate; the purchase of the President, and the disruption of the Supreme Court; they cannot stoop to the committal of petty larceny. So every dollar of the funds raised for the expenses of the campaign is spent in purchasing votes or in buying off dangerous leaders of the opposition.

As fast as the funds are received they are distributed, and the method of their final disposal is outlined by the great moving spirit. He seems to possess infinite power of grasping the minutia of politics. None of his lieutenants dares to misappropriate the funds turned over to him. All know that their master has a disagreeable faculty of unexpectedly asking for an accounting.

"We will win by a margin of thirty-one votes in the Electoral College," Chairman Marcus tells every one who inquires as to the probable result. "This figure is based upon the canvass I have had made in the doubtful states; it will not vary from the count by one vote."

It is impossible to get the chairman to give an amplified statement as to which he considers the doubtful states and as to how the canvass has been conducted.

One of the morning papers in Chicago, which takes an impartial stand, and accordingly seeks to publish all of the news, creates a sensation by the publication of a tabulated statement of the contributions paid into the treasury of the Plutocratic party. This table shows a total of forty-seven millions of dollars.

With such a sum to expend, and with the knowledge that the chairman of the finance committee will see that every dollar is properly distributed, it is not unreasonable to suppose that a house to house canvass of the doubtful states has actually been made. The corruption fund provides more than three dollars for each voter in the land.

Did Marcus think that one hundred million dollars will be necessary, he would demand that sum, and it would not be withheld by the prosperous band that derives its wealth from the law-makers whom Marcus elects.

What a contrast is presented by the headquarters of the Independence party. It is in a dilapidated hall in the western part of the city. The only feature of the furnishings in keeping with the times, is the Bureau of Publicity. This provides the campaign committee with telegraphic and telephonic communication with the country at large.

The instruments are arranged on two plain deal tables. In its appearance the room is more like the editorial room of a hustling Western newspaper than the headquarters of a political organization that is aspiring to elect a President of the United States. The floor is bare; obsolete gas fixtures afford the artificial light that is made necessary day and night. The chairs and benches that are scattered about the room, are of the type commonly seen in cheap music halls. There are no ante-rooms, no council chambers and no secret cabinets.

A campaign fund of but two hundred and sixty thousand dollars has been raised through the agency of the labor organizations. This comparatively paltry sum is being doled out in niggardly fashion by a finance committee who feel reluctant to part with a single dollar unless assured that it will have a hundred fold its natural effect on the result.

There are some causes that do not need money to make them successful, and the people's fight against Plutocracy is one of this kind. It needs only the awakening of the people's interest to make victory certain.

The surest way of gaining the public ear is by sending out speakers. There is no dearth in the supply of brilliant orators who offer their services. They foresee that the crucial test is to be given the Institution of Popular Government and they wisely align themselves on the side of the people.

No stream of Millionaires comes to the Independence Party's Headquarters; no line of retainers Stand with open hands to receive the funds of fraud; there is as sharp a contrast between the two headquarters as there is between the platforms and candidates of the parties.

Harvey Trueman is the guiding spirit at Drover's Hall. It is Tuesday, a month before election. He visits the Hall for the last time before the verdict of the people shall be recorded.

"I am going to New York to-night," he tells his friend Maxwell, the Chairman of the Speakers' Committee. "You had better notify the leaders all along the line that I am prepared to make short speeches at every available place."

"Have you made arrangements with the railroads?" asks Maxwell.

"It will not be necessary for me to consult with them; I have outlined my route so that I can make connections on one road or another and go through to New York in sixty hours. This will give me time to make twenty short speeches."

"When do you reach New York city?"

"Friday night. It will be about seven o'clock. I want you to arrange for a meeting in Madison Square Garden. It may cost us two thousand dollars, but it will be money well spent."

"We cannot get the Garden; not if we offered five thousand dollars. It has been leased for three months straight by the

Plutocrats," Maxwell replies.

"Then get the New York Committee to obtain a permit for an out-door meeting. I will speak to twenty thousand people in New York on Friday if I have to address them from a house-top."

"One of the best places for an out-door meeting in New York is on West street, between Cortlandt and Spring streets," suggests an operator who has overheard the conversation. "That's the broadest thoroughfare in the city."

"Yes, that is a splendid place," acquiesces Trueman.

"Have the meeting located there, Maxwell."

Maxwell departs to carry out the order.

A dozen men are soon receiving final instructions from their leader. They hear the plan for the invasion of the East, and all agree that it will be a wise move, and one which the enemy cannot counteract in so short a time as will be left.

The Judas that is present in almost all human conclaves, is among the loudest in his remarks of approval.

"You could do nothing that would give the Plutocrats a harder rub than to speak on the eve, as it were, of election, in the hotbed of Plutocracy," he assures Trueman.

After a few minutes of further conversation on this line, the betrayer departs. He is closeted with Marcus an hour later. The scheme for a counter demonstration in New York is quickly formulated.

Unconscious of the treachery that has been practiced, Trueman prepares for the trip East.

CHAPTER XVIII

ON TO NEW YORK

In all the evening papers the announcement appears that Harvey Trueman is to start on a tour of the East. The fact that he will leave the city by train from the Union Depot is carefully suppressed, except in the two comparatively unimportant journals which advocate the election of the people's candidate.

But the managers of Trueman's campaign have come to know what has to be combatted. Handbills are hurriedly printed and distributed in the late afternoon along State, Clark and Dearborn streets, and on the intersecting streets in the centre of the business locality. These hand-bills announce that Trueman will deliver his farewell speech to Chicagoans that night at seven o'clock at the Adams street Bridge.

At six o'clock the crowds begin congregating; they come from all sections of the city; they are of every type, from the cowboy of the Stock Yards to the Street Railway Magnate. All are intent on hearing the captivating orator.

Ten thousand people huddle in an area of five blocks. They know that they all cannot hear Trueman; yet they hope to catch a glimpse of him, and perhaps hear him make a short speech in their immediate neighborhood.

It is 6.50 when a hansom conveying Trueman hurries down

Adams street from State. The crowds cheer and yell. From a trot the horse attached to the vehicle is forced to proceed at a walk.

"Speech! speech!" cry the excited men as they surge through the narrow thoroughfare.

Trueman stands up in the hansom and leaning forward explains that he cannot stop to make a speech at every corner.

The few words he addresses to the crowd seem to satisfy their demands, and they at once subside.

Slowly the speaker approaches the throng at the Depot steps. In crossing the bridge he twice has to comply with the persistent demand for a speech.

Now he is on the platform.

His voice works a magic spell on the audience. They have been boisterous, fretful, even at times disorderly. Not a dozen words are uttered by Trueman and the silence, save for his ringing voice, is intense.

"I am leaving you that we may be assured of the support of the East," he begins.

"That you are with me and are determined to vote for your rights I do not doubt for a moment. You are men who have learned the lesson of life in the school of experience. A truth once grasped by you is not soon forgotten. You all know who are your enemies."

"Down with the Plutocrats!" howl the people.

"As you stand before me, men of might, one a mechanic, one a laborer, another a tradesman, another a railway employee, is there any one of you who wishes to vote to deprive his fellow-workmen of the right to earn a living?" Is there a single man among you who is striving night and day to corner the food of the land that he may starve his brother-workmen into paying him tribute? Is there a man among you who is living on the distress of his fellows, brought about by his wrecking the bank in which they have hoarded their savings?

"No, there is none such here."

"Then there should not be a voter here who will cast a ballot to put in power men who seek in public office only their personal ends. The Plutocratic ticket has not a man on it who is not an agent of the Trusts. Do not take this assertion on my authority. Investigate the ticket for yourselves."

Here the assembly cheer wildly.

"I want you to roll up a majority in the city of Chicago which shall demonstrate to the world that the citizens of the Star of the West are among the staunchest patriots in the Union."

With the whistling and shrieking of the crowd in his ears, Trueman steps from the platform and makes his way to the train. The trip East is unique. It differs from the ordinary Presidential campaign tour in so much as there is no attempt to have reception committees meet the trains on which the candidate travels; there is no speaking from the rear platform of the trains. The depots are owned by the Plutocrats and no crowds are permitted to congregate to hail Trueman.

At Toledo, Columbus, Philadelphia and Newark, Trueman changes trains and goes to a public square where he addresses the populace. As he nears New York the enthusiasm of the crowds abates. In Newark the Plutocratic missionaries have spread the seeds of falsehood and have made such telling use of coercive threats that the people are actually hostile to Trueman and his party, deeming them Anarchists. The protection of the police is needed to prevent the most violent of the men from attacking the speakers. In the attempt to suppress supposed law-breakers, these misguided citizens become lawless themselves.

At Jersey City there is a great crowd blocking the passageways of the terminal. Trueman is forced to mount one of the mail cars and make a speech. No sooner has he finished, then he is surrounded by the reporters of the New York papers.

"Mr. Trueman, are you aware that the Plutocrats have arranged for a torchlight parade for to-night, as a counter demonstration to your meeting?" one of the reporters asks.

"Yes, I received a telegram at Philadelphia informing me to that effect."

"The line of march is from the Battery north on Broadway to Cortlandt street; west on Cortlandt to Harrison street, and north on that street to Spring," explains another reporter.

"This means that they will run the parade parallel with the river front and one block from West street. It will be timed so as to pass just as you are making your address," he adds.

"You may inform the managers of the parade that I will be delighted to have them send their army of intimidated workmen down to West street, and I may be able to entertain them."

"Those who come within reach of my voice will, I think, hear news that will hold them, as against a brass band and fireworks. If not, then they would be better off in the wake of the procession," exclaims Trueman icily.

"Where do you propose to make your first speech?" asks a youthful reporter.

It is a superfluous question in the minds of all the older newspaper men. They smile inwardly; but the answer this query evokes sends them all flying to telephones.

"I shall make my first speech at the Battery, where the paraders may have the benefit of a little plain truth."

The group of Independents are now on the ferryboat.

Across the river the myriad lights of the metropolis give the scene air appearance as of fairyland. The night is overcast and the clouds act as a reflector to the million lights in the city below; the sky line of Brooklyn is a dull salmon color. A chill October wind sweeps from east to west. It is a bad night to speak out of doors. Upon reaching Cortlandt slip Trueman descends to the lower deck and is among the first to leave the boat. He crosses West street unobserved, and on reaching the Elevated Station at Cortlandt street, boards a down-town train. With him are three of the committee of arrangements. The remainder of the party go to the platform at the foot of Barclay street to address the crowd and announce the cause of Trueman's delay.

When the South Ferry is reached Trueman sees that Battery Park is packed with people. He descends to the street and wedges his way to the music stand in the centre of the park. Without much difficulty he manages to climb upon the stand.

As a piece of good fortune an electric light shines full on his face as he turns to the crowd.

Up to this moment people think that the tall man with the slouch hat is seeking a point of vantage from which to view the formation of the parade.

It does not require two glances, however, to assure the people that the man before them is Harvey Trueman.

"That's Trueman, or I'm a liar!" shouts an Irishman.

"That's who it is," blurts a man beside him.

"What is he doing down here? I thought he was to speak on

West Street?"

Some of the men in the crowd now begin cheering. They cry:

"Trueman! Trueman! Rah! rah! rah! Speech! speech!"

The proper moment has arrived. Trueman takes off his hat and waves it as a sign for silence. The cheering and the rumor that Trueman has suddenly appeared, turns a sea of people in the direction of the music stand. Fully eight thousand men are within the radius of his voice. He speaks at first in a high metallic key; but after the first minute or so he reaches his normal voice, which with its fullness and exquisite modulation makes his oratory remarkable.

Here is an occasion where rhetoric will prove available; the crowd before him is composed for the most part of the better element, so called for reason of its disinclination to change existing conditions. If a sense of justice in this great mass of humanity can be aroused it will impel each and all to yield to the will of the orator. With sharp sarcasm he refers to the precautionary action of the Plutocrats to prevent his addressing a New York audience. Do they fear he may convert it?

Rapidly he pictures the scenes of intimidation he has witnessed in the west and northwest. Is New York chained to the wheels of the Plutocratic chariot?

As the first sign of sympathy answers his appeal, he urges upon his audience the necessity of declaring anew the independence of the people. The fervor of his speech affects the crowd; the indescribable impulse to yield to the will of a fellow-man who commands the power of oratory, asserts itself. At the decalration of a principle of government which is trite in itself, there is a scattered cheer; an apt epigram evokes a storm of applause. Trueman wins the full sympathy of his audience; they are his to command.

"I am expected to address an audience at the foot of Barclay street. It will afford me unbounded pleasure if I may tell them that the meeting will not be disturbed; that you have decided to apply to politics the same spirit of fair play that you would demand in a street brawl."

"We're with you," cries a man. "You're all right." Trueman steps from the music stand. The crowd gather about him, shouting and cheering for him.

"This is an Independence parade," some one shouts.

"Forward, march, for Barclay street!" becomes the general shout. Trueman is pushed on toward the edge of the Battery Park till the line of carriages in which some of the members of the parade were to ride is reached. He is lifted into one of the carriages and the march for the West street stand is begun. The line of march leads along State street to Battery Place; here it turns west to the river, and thence up West street. The traffic which chokes that thoroughfare in the day is absent and the broad expanse of street affords an excellent concourse.

With the clashing strains of three bands, the shouts of thousands of men, the flickering lights of torches and Roman candles, Trueman approaches the audience which has been impatiently awaiting him. Flushed with the pride of his victory he mounts the stand to address ten thousand men in the citadel of Plutocracy. His advent in New York is a signal triumph.

CHAPTER XIX

DEPARTURE OF THE COMMITTEE

By the last election for President a man has been put in office who is the acknowledged tool of the Trusts and Monopolies. He has avowedly sealed his independence by accepting a nomination brought about by the ring leader of a syndicate of Railroad Magnates and Steel and Oil Kings.

The people are in such a depressed condition that it is believed no determined opposition to the dominant party can be conducted. So this man is a candidate for re-election. The few intrepid men who succeed in keeping the people's party in the field are derided and denounced as anarchists. Their very lives are threatened, and in one instance a Governor of the people being elected, he is immediately assassinated. But for the certainty of the Plutocrats that their money will win them a victory, all the leaders of the Independence party would be forcibly done away with.

The prospects of the coming election look dubious for the people. On August thirteenth the Committee of Forty determined to take the step for re-emancipation. The time to strike the telling blow at monopoly is approaching. The men all know what the work outlined will entail, and they have brought themselves to look at the matter in much the same light as the originator of the unparalleled expedient.

"We have been forced into adopting the plan of annihilation,"

Professor Talbort declares to Henry Neilson, a fellow committeeman with whom he is traveling to the Pacific coast.

"I agree with you," replies Neilson, "it is the only course open to us; we have given every other proposal careful consideration. They would only temporarily avert a conflict."

"I have pondered on the question of how our acts will be accepted by the people," the Professor resumes. "I believe they will hail our acts as those of deliverance."

"They will appreciate that we gave our lives for them," Neilson declares unhesitatingly.

All of the Forty act with similar coolness.

Men of action are not as a usual thing great talkers; so it is with the members of this committee. They waive much that would be deemed essential by less resolute and active men. How the several annihilations are to be effected is a matter left for each man to decide for himself. He will have to carry out any plan he devises, and it is considered as the best policy to let his method be known to no one else. This is the surest way of avoiding a possible miscarriage of the plan.

The failure of one of the forty men will not then involve the remaining thirty-nine. Every contingency is weighed. The chance of one or more of the men going insane because of the frightful secret, is taken into account and the idea that each man shall decide the details of the course he is to pursue is adopted.

"I am glad that we parted without formality," Nettinger declares to the group of committeemen who are his companions on a train that leaves Chicago for the South.

"It would have unnerved us to speak of our meeting as '*the last*'" says another of the group. "I have faced danger in my life, but I regard this as the most astounding departure that has ever

Francis A. Adams

been made in the interests of humanity."

"The future of the Republic is at stake," observes a third. "How will it all end?"

This is the question that is uppermost in the minds of all.

"There is no time left to weigh the effects of defeat," Nettinger asserts. "Each of us has but one thing to do, and to do this successfully he has pledged his life. No man can do more."

The eleven disciples, as they separated after the crucifixion, each to pursue a separate course, inaugurated the preaching of a great and potential religion, and their work is the most momentous in history. So it may prove that this Nineteenth Century aggregation of men united for the purpose of benefiting their fellowmen, is of tantamount influence on the human race.

From acting as component parts in a body that exists as a moral protest against the wrongs of the world and the unrelenting hands of the usurpers of the right of the people, these forty men go forth as an army of crusaders.

On the committee of forty there is not a man who has not argued his conscience into a state of appreciation of the worthiness of the action he is to perform.

It is past midnight. Two months from this date, on October thirteenth, the fulfillment of the vows the men have taken, must be made. In the sixty days that are to intervene will any of these intrepid wills bend under the pressure of mental anxiety? Will any of them prove a modern Judas?

Nevins is the last to quit the store-room. He is nervous, almost hysterical; his thin classical features are distorted and tense, as though he were undergoing actual physical pain. And indeed to his sensitive nature, the events of the night are sufficient to unnerve his mind and body.

He is to meet Carl Metz and Hendrick Stahl in the morning, to start for the East.

"The syndicate of annihilation is now incorporated," he observes, half aloud. "I am no longer the promoter; now I assume a place as one of the avengers of the people. God alone knows how repugnant this plan for physical vengeance is to me, yet it is better than to permit a storm of anarchy to come upon us. And the conditions that exist cannot long continue."

Although every man has been called upon to make a personal sacrifice there is none who makes a greater one than he. It is not alone the relinquishment of his position in the world as a patient and industrious worker; his sacrifice of love; the obliteration of his hope for preferment, but the extinction of life itself at an age when all men cherish it most highly.

Nevins is in the heyday of manhood; his forty years and six having been spent in the perfection of his mental and physical forces. He is equipped with a quick, perceptive brain that grasps the intricacies of a problem almost intuitively; his logic is profound. Years of study have made his mind a storehouse of knowledge.

To Nevins, in the allotment of the proscribed, has fallen the head of the money trust, a multi-millionaire banker, a financial Magnate known throughout the civilized world as the most rapacious miser on record. This man has repeatedly shown that he has no regard for honesty of purpose, and his moral appreciation is imperceptible. To recount the deeds of cunning, of fraud, of gigantic robbery that he has committed in his relentless quest for wealth, would be to retell the story of wrecked railroads, enormously profitable bond issues and Wall street panics of the past decade. The obituaries of the hundreds he has ruined afford the best method of arriving at a partial conception of his power for evil.

"What a privilege to rid the world of this genius of evil!" is Nevins's inward comment as he reads the fatal slip and sees that upon him has fallen the lot to execute the sentence of annihilation upon James Golding, the King of Wall street.

CHAPTER XX

IN THE ENEMY'S STRONGHOLD

After an absence of weeks, during which time Harvey Trueman carries the war into the very heart of the Magnates' strongholds, he returns to Chicago. His first mission is to visit Sister Martha. She had been kept in touch with his movements by short notes and aggravatingly brief telegrams, which he sent her as occasion permitted. In the papers she finds but meagre notice of the progress which the Independence party is making, for the censor of the press has effectually silenced all the important mediums. The News Associations, even, are brought under the ban and are given to understand that a violation of the orders of the Plutocratic Party will mean a forfeiture of all privileges of transportation to papers using the offensive news.

The meeting of these two ardent patriots is fraught with emotion. Trueman is the more moved by reason of the knowledge that he is regarded by Martha as the embodiment of all virtue, wisdom and power. He feels his incapacity to fill this exalted role, especially as the unrequited love he bears for Ethel Purdy is still burning in his heart.

"You do not seem yourself to-night," Martha tells him frankly.

"No, that is true; I have so much to think about; so many details to keep in mind that I suffer from abstraction when I am not under the stress of actual labor."

Trueman is seated beside a table in the centre of the Sisters' Home, which has come to be the only haven of rest he knows in the whole world. He is in a communicative mood, and appreciating that the woman before him is an interested listener he is ready to review the events of the campaign.

"I have so many evidences of treachery in my own camp that at times I despair of the result of the struggle," he says, half despondently.

"It is the accursed power of gold that is fighting you," Martha breaks in vehemently. "O, if we could only have a few thousand dollars to fight them with their own weapon."

At the mention of so paltry a sum to be pitted against the unlimited millions of the Magnates, Trueman cannot repress a smile.

"I know it may seem ludicrous for a woman to talk politics," continues his gentle adviser, apologetically. "Yet it would not take as much as you imagine to nullify the effect of the millions of bribe money and tribute money that the Plutocrats are spending."

"What would you have me do with the money?"

"Use it in enlightening the people as to their true condition. It is impossible to conceive of men who would knowingly sell their birthright. The perfidy of the press is the sin of sins in this age of unbridled iniquity," she declares, her face flushing with indignation. "Free speech has not yet been totally interdicted. Speak to the people; tell them to emancipate themselves."

"You make me wish, almost, that your sex was not debarred from the exercise of suffrage," Trueman declares. "If I receive as staunch support from the men of the land as I have already been accorded by the women I shall triumph at the polls.

"Let me recount the events of the past few days that I have only hinted at in my letters." It will make you glad that you were born a woman.

"When I reached Milwaukee, ten days ago," continues Trueman, "I found that the committee of coercion had anticipated my arrival and had issued its edict against the citizens turning out to see me." The police had received their instructions to keep the streets clear, and they were untiring in their efforts to earn the approbation of their masters. The train arrived at one-thirty in the afternoon. Ordinarily there would have been a large crowd at the depot; to our surprise we found the depot and the adjoining streets practically deserted.

"As our party moved in the direction of the hotel, I noticed that a woman was keeping pace with us on the opposite side of the street. She was dressed in a modest gown and would not have attracted attention had she not continually turned her head to look behind her."

"Yielding to an impulse of curiosity I turned my head and saw that at the distance of a block a squad of police was following us." Then it dawned upon me that the woman was endeavoring to give our party the cue. When the steps of the hotel were reached I felt impelled to see where the woman would go. She stood on the corner of the street for half a minute and then disappeared around the corner.

"Half an hour later I was handed the card of a 'Mrs. Walton.' Upon going to the reception room I found that the strange woman had come to see me."

"Her first words, 'Are we alone?' made me feel that I should have a new element to meet." I suspected a trap of the enemy. When I assured her that she was at liberty to speak, Mrs. Walton went directly to the point.

"'I have come to offer you the support of the women of Milwaukee,' she began, 'and that means a great deal at a time when the men are afraid to say their souls are their own."

"The women of this city are not under the yoke and they trust to you to put off the day of their subjugation, if you cannot put them in safety for all time."

"We have realized that the hour for woman to assert her power has come; she cannot vote, nor does she aspire to that questionable right, but she can influence the votes of the men with whom she comes in contact."

"You have come to a city that is as effectually closed to you as if it were walled and the gates were shut in your face." The press, the police, the labor organizations, every power has been subsidized to work against you. I know every move that has been made. For there's not a word uttered that is not brought to the council of women's clubs.

"The moment it was known that you were to visit this city the order went forth that you were not to be permitted to hold a public meeting." You were not to be refused the right to speak; that would have been too bold and brazen an act for even the Plutocrats to carry out. It was decided that the same ends could be accomplished by preventing the army of mercenaries and wage-slaves to parade the streets. The corps of "spotters" were sent out.

"'You are a witness to what end. The streets were deserted. They will remain so during your stay.'"

"I was on the point of interrupting the woman, but she exclaimed, 'Don't interrupt me.'"

"'I was appointed a committee of one to wait upon you and extend you the offices of the Women's League,' she continued. 'While waiting in the depot I overheard the orders of the Captain of Police to the Sergeant. He told his subordinate not to allow you to collect a crowd on the street, and detailed a squad to follow you to your hotel." "'If you have any message to deliver to the men of Milwaukee you may depend upon the seven thousand women who are enrolled in the League to scatter it for you. I can tell you that there is no other way open to you.'"

"I was too surprised to reply for a moment." When I finally formulated a response, I told her that the facts she had just furnished me were of such an extraordinary nature that I should be obliged to give them my most careful consideration, and that if she would call again in an hour I should be able to tell her what use I could make of her offer.

"When I was alone I hastened to rejoin the members of the Committee who had accompanied me on my trip."

"I asked them if they were aware of the conditions that existed in the city. They told me that the Chief of Police had just informed them that we could not hold a meeting outside of a hall. 'Public safety' was given as the cause of this order."

"Then I hastily recounted the incident of the visit of Mrs. Walton." Some of the committeemen were skeptical and advised me not to have any dealings with the woman. I, however, was favorably impressed with her.

"At the expiration of two hours she returned." I had a long talk with her, in which I told her how her League could be of benefit to me if it would impress upon the men the necessity of voting for their rights. She assured me that my messages would be carried into every mill and factory in the city.

"I held a meeting in the hall that the local Independence party had secured." The attendance was made up exclusively of staunch party men. Outside of the hall stood a dozen police-men and a half dozen spotters.

"None of the workmen of the city dared to attend the meeting."

"And this is Free America!" exclaims Martha, under her breath.

"Yes, this is America; but, is it free?" asks Trueman.

"From Milwaukee I went to St. Paul and Minneapolis. The same condition existed in these places. I turned to Detroit; the result was the same."

"I resolved to advance into the one State that the Magnates believe they control absolutely. From Detroit I went to Philadelphia. The reception that awaited me there is one that I shall never forget. My native State is so utterly dominated by the Trust Magnates that the free-born citizens do not dare to attend public meetings."

"What is the use of the secret ballot if men cannot go to the polls and register there the opinion they hold?" Martha asks, with irony in her voice.

"Ah, the secret ballot is but another of the illusive baits which the rich wisely throw out to the poor to keep them in submission. It is secret only in name. The results of an election are what count. The Magnates have so intimidated the masses that they are no longer possessed of the spirit to vote according to their thoughts," Trueman replies sadly.

"The Pharisees have preached the doctrine of the sacredness of 'vested rights' until the people, in many sections of the country, have come to regard the right of property as paramount to the right of mankind to life and liberty."

"Every act that would alleviate the sufferings of the people is at once stigmatized as anarchistic; while the aggressions of the men of money in the legislatures, and through executives, are upheld as justifiable means for the proper protection of property."

"My trip to the West and East has made me doubtful as to the result of the election. In New York City alone is there a tendency to support me."

"Oh, do not say that you have lost hope," expostulates Sister Martha.

"It is not my intention to intimate that I have done so, to any one, other than to you."

"Ah, I cannot believe that a just God will see you defeated!"

"As matters stand now it will take almost a miracle to elect me." I have studied all the elements that enter into this campaign. It will be the last one that can be conducted with the semblance of order. Four years from now, if not before then, the conditions will be ripe for a revolution; the oligarchy of American manufacturers and bankers will have reached its height and will be on the point of dissolution. The perfected mechanism of government that it will have established, will be in readiness to be turned over to the people.

"Socialism of a rational sort will result from the sudden and sharp revolution. History will not be enriched by a new chapter, but be marked by the repetition of its most frequent story—the fall of empire and the establishment of a new government. In the end of all governments at the same point, is the strongest argument in support of the theory of reincarnation; a state, as a being, has its birth, mature age, and decay. None seemingly is endowed with the attribute of immutability. It was the fond hope of our forefathers that the United States should prove the exception. Imperialism was the reef on which the classic empires were wrecked; commercialism is the danger that threatens our ship of state."

"You must take a brighter view of the situation," insists the sensitive woman, to whom these lugubrious words are as dagger thrusts. "You must fight as if there was not the shadow of a doubt but that you will be successful. I have a premonition (woman's intuition, if you prefer), that you will be the victor in this struggle."

With these words of encouragement ringing in his ears, Trueman departs. He has yielded to the human weakness which prompts a man to confide his inmost thoughts to woman. Kingdoms have been destroyed, empires have crumbled in a day; the world's greatest generals have seen their carefully designed campaigns fall flat, all through the treachery of women in failing to keep secret the confessions of their confidants.

The admission that Trueman has made of his misgivings as to the result of the election, if it were made public, would shatter his every chance. The world will not lend its support to a man or a cause that admits its hopelessness. A forlorn hope, however forlorn, has never wanted volunteers.

Fortunately Trueman has made a confidant of a woman unselfishly and devotedly his friend, and who has the good sense to realize that his untrammeled utterances to her are for her alone.

It is eleven o'clock when Trueman reaches his party's headquarters. He finds his supporters working with the feverish energy that attaches to a desperate situation. The soldiers of a beleaguered fortress man the guns with a disregard to fatigue and danger that is inspiring; the men at the pumps, when the word goes forth that the ship is sinking, work with a frenzy that defies nature; so it is with the leaders of the Independence party. They are fighting against appalling odds, yet they do not stop to question the result. "Work, work, work!" is the command they obey.

"The indications from the Southern States are brighter than ever," one of the committeemen tells Trueman.

"Judge for yourself," adds another, and he hands the candidate a telegram. It is from New Orleans. Trueman reads it aloud:

"CHAIRMAN BAILEY, National Headquarters, Independence Party, Chicago, Ill.:

From a canvass of the cotton belt the indications are that our party will carry all the Southern States with the possible exception of Louisiana. This doubtful state can be carried if speakers are sent there.

(Signed) EDWARD B. MASON."

"Is there any way of complying with this request?" Trueman asks.

"We may be able to send three speakers down there the latter part of the week," says the Chairman of the Speakers Committee, after consulting his schedule.

"Have you heard from New York to-day?" Trueman is asked by the Treasurer. "You know we have been expecting to hear the result of the forecast there."

"No, I have had no word. It is barely possible that the message has been intercepted."

As Trueman speaks the telegraph operator approaches and hands him a message.

"Here is the message!" cries Trueman. "It is from Faulkner. He says that the city of New York will be about evenly divided; and that in the state we can rely upon the counties along the canal. He ends up by stating that the result in Greater New York may be assured if I can go there and fight in person."

"Then you will go?" inquires Mr. Bailey.

"Yes, I shall go there at once and try to be there for the close of the campaign."

The routine of the night's work is resumed. Trueman leaves to take a much needed rest.

CHAPTER XXI

THE COMMITTEE REPORTS PROGRESS

As the time approaches for the carrying out of the plan of annihilation, the spirits of the forty vacillate from joyousness to despair at the thought, now of the glorious page they are to give to the history of the world and now, of the terrible means that an inexorable fate compels them to use. Each passes through varying moods. The ever present thought that the day will soon arrive on which each will have to commit two deeds of violence, the one, to take a public enemy out of the world's arena once and forever; the other, the extinction of self, is enough to keep the mental tension at the snapping point.

Yet, not a man weakens. The stolid march of trained men toward inevitable death is the only counterpart to their action. And their unfaltering fulfillment of the work allotted them is the more remarkable as each works independently. It is one thing to be impelled forward by the frenzy and madness of battle; to be nerved to deeds of valor and self-sacrifice in the face of impending disaster, such as shipwreck and fire; but it is quite another thing to deliberately carry out a plan that taxes the will, the heart and the conscience, and that too, totally unaided by the presence or sympathy of others. This is what these forty men have determined it is their duty to perform.

Nevins is in New York to receive reports from the members of the Committee. A month has passed since their departure from Chicago. From most of the men he receives letters in which they tell of their success. No mention is made of the men to whom they are assigned, yet the reports seem to assure Nevins that the plan will not miscarry.

"I have twice been sorely tempted to abandon my mission," writes Horace Turner, the plain, honest Wisconsin farmer. "My heart and not my conscience has been weak. But strength of purpose has come to me." I realize that our undertaking is one that the populace will not sanction at the start; it is not one that we can hope to make acceptable to the public mind until it comes to a successful issue.

"The world does not look with favor upon reforms or revolutions until they are accomplished facts." And this is the reason history records the events of every advance of man in letters of blood. This advance is not to be an exception in this point so far as the spilling of blood is concerned; it is to be exceptional in regard to the quantity that is to be sacrificed.

"The revolutions in politics that have preceded it, the reformations in religion, have necessitated the butchery of thousands of men and women; the overturning of existing conditions and the impediment of the human race for generations."

"This reformation will measure its sacrificial blood in drops. It will have as many martyrs as it had tyrants."

It is the preponderance of reasons in favor of their adhering to their oaths that prevents the members of the Committee of Annihilation from faltering.

At forty points through the world these unheralded crusaders are silently arranging their campaigns against the enemies of the common weal. For the most part the men who have been named on the proscribed list are residents of the chief city of their respective states; they are men who have walked the path of life rough-shod and have stepped to their exalted positions over the prostrate forms of their fellowmen. They are what the world is pleased to call the "Princes of Commerce."

Francis A. Adams

To become acquainted with the habits of his quarry; to fix upon a plan for inflicting death upon him, which will be certain, and to be prepared to carry this programme out at the appointed time, these are matters that each of the forty has to arrange.

They call into requisition all of their talents, all of the skill that has made them men of mark in their respective professions and vocations.

When Hendrick Stahl became sponsor for Nevins he felt that he had not misplaced his confidence, yet it was impossible for him to be unacquainted with the movements of the originator of the Committee of Forty. He so arranges his affairs as to be in New York at the end of the month to meet him. On his visits he seeks Nevins and spends the night with him.

"I have perfected my plans," Stahl tells his friend. "At first it looked as though I could not get acquainted with my man, but I finally struck upon a course that led me directly to him. I perfected the details of a mechanism to do away with manual labor on a machine which he employs in his factory. When I suggested the adoption of it and proved that I could make the improvement, he became interested. I meet him every day. On the thirteenth of October we will examine the model."

Nevins opens a letter bearing a postmark, "Edinburgh, Scotland." The letter simply states:

"I am enjoying the hospitality of one of the Transgressors." He and I are great friends. We are arranging to substitute a counterfeit substance for the new armor plate ordered by the government.

"By our plan the government will be defrauded of thirty million dollars. The armor plate will not stand the test of heavy projectiles. But we can 'fix' the inspectors. My *friend* is delighted at the prospect of giving the United States Government another batch of worthless armor plate."

This particular Transgressor is Ephraim Barnaby, the Pennsylvania iron king. He is the master of the greatest iron and steel concern in the world. His wealth is counted by scores of millions; he has palaces in this country and abroad. His domination over the lives of the thousands who slave in his foundries is kept unshaken by reason of the fact that he coats the bitter acts of oppression of which he is constantly guilty, with ostentatious gifts in the name of benevolence. He presents the cities of the country with public libraries.

This philanthrophic iron master has erected an armory for his private detectives for every library he has established for the people. To make a life of unparalleled achievement as an amasser of money terminate in glory is well within his power, but avarice is the chief occupant of his heart. With sixty and more years on his head and so much wealth that he cannot by any possibility spend one twentieth part of his yearly income, the iron master still has an insatiable thirst for gold. To the Forty who know every detail of his career, this man above all others is the one whom they despise. His hypocrisy makes him the most despicable of the proscribed. Chadwick is proud that to him has fallen the lot of exterminating this Transgressor.

From other letters received by Nevins it develops that not one of the men has failed in locating his man and in laying the net which is to enmesh him.

The proposal of a supposed inventor to create a machine that will reduce cost of manufacture, leads the merchant prince into a trap. He rejoices at the thought of reducing the expense of wage and of maintaining the price of goods to the consumer.

An improved explosive interests the mine owner It will cost him less and can be sold to the operatives at the same price. It is more dangerous to use, but that does not deter him from seeking to utilize it; for it is the operatives who will have to run the risk in the mines.

A substitute for oil is the lure that compels the Oil King to pay respectful attention to another of the committee. The same prospect of a substitute for sugar demands the attention of the Sugar King. To each of the Transgressors there is held out as a bait the needed promise of gain at the public expense.

Thus the details of the pending tragedy are perfected.

CHAPTER XXII

MILLIONAIRES SOWING THE WIND

While the work of the Independence party is being conducted with all the vigor that its scanty financial resources will permit, the opponents of popular government are pushing their campaign in all directions, aided by inexhaustible money, and all the influence that attaches to the party in power. The Plutocratic convention which had been held in Chicago promulgated a platform that pledges the party to institute every form of legislation calculated to appease the demands of the people.

That the pretences of the platform are insincere is a fact that every one is well acquainted with; yet so potential is the power of the party that it is able to persuade men against their best judgment, and those whom it cannot bring to its support by argument are forced to align themselves on the side of phitocratic government by the force of coercion.

Where in 1900 the Trusts employed four million men, they now have on their pay rolls more than ten millions. This represents seventy-five per cent. of all the able-bodied men in the country. The tradesmen in every city are as effectually dominated by the Trust magnates as if they were on their payrolls. Through the general establishment of the system of "consignment," by which goods are placed on sale in small shops, under covenants with the Trusts, the retailers are made to sell at the prices dictated by the manufacturers. It is useless

Francis A. Adams

for a retailer to rebel; he has either to handle the goods of the Trusts or go out of business altogether.

To realize how far-reaching this system is, it will suffice to cite the case of the retail grocers. Their staple articles, such as sugar, flour, salt, coffee, tea, spices and canned meats are all controlled by Trusts. If the retailer attempts to sell any article not manufactured by the Trusts, his contumacy is taken as a cause for all the staples he has "on sale" to be reclaimed by the Trusts. This leaves him with practically nothing to sell.

Where a man, more pugnacious than the majority, attempts to fight the Trusts, his stand is made futile by the Trust immediately establishing a rival store in his neighborhood, where goods are sold at an actual loss until ruin comes upon the recalcitrant tradesman.

This is the story of all trades. It is the condition that exists in all lines of manufacture as well, and the system reaches even to the farmers. They have either to sell their products at the prices offered by the Trusts or run themselves into inevitable bankruptcy. They may dispose of one year's crop, but the next year they are doomed to find themselves without a purchaser. Failing to intimidate the farmer, the Trust will bring its influence to bear upon the purchaser—he will either be absorbed or annihilated.

From being a nation of independent producers, the people of the United States have been slowly and insidiously pushed back to a position where more than nine-tenths of the people are the servants of the remaining few. With the changed condition has come a deterioration in the spirit of the masses. They are apathetic, and take the scant wage that the Trusts condescend to pay them. The efforts to regain a place of honorable independence are becoming weaker and weaker.

The enervating effects of urban life have told on the millions who live in the great cities. The number of men who can stand the rigor of out-door life, and the exigencies of labor afield, grows smaller year by year.

Adulterated food, sedentary work at machines which require practically no skill to operate, and dispiriting home surroundings have brought millions of men to a mental and physical condition which makes them little better than slaves.

These truths Trueman and his co-workers endeavor to impress upon the people. In some districts the audiences evince interest in the arguments. In others the speakers are met with open derision.

"We are content to work in our present places," some of the laborers assert. "Are we not sure of getting our bread as it is? If we were to bring on a revolution where would our next day's wage come from?"

To this argument, which exhibits to what a debased position the wage-earner has sunk, the Independence party leaders who have formed the party of the fragment of free-minded men that still remains, marshal all the arguments of logic and political economy. They appeal to the pride, the decency of the men, to drag themselves from the slough into which they have fallen. The appeals are fervent, yet their effect seems uncertain.

The terror of "lock-outs," of massacres done under the seal of the law, is vividly recalled.

In 1900 the people had made a desperate effort to throw off the yoke of the Trusts. They had failed and been made to feel the lash of their victors. Eight years have passed, during which the Trusts have become impregnable, the people impotent.

Trueman is in St. Louis on a flying trip. This city of two millions is the great centre of the labor organizations.

It is Friday night, and the local headquarters is the scene of wild excitement. It resembles nothing more closely than a camp on the eve of battle. Leaders from all districts of the city are on hand to receive final instructions, as in a camp they would be given ammunition, rations and assignment of positions. The determined expression that marks the face of a man who is set at a task which involves his entire future, is upon every man who enters the headquarters. The fountain of their inspiration is Trueman, who has a word for everyone. He seems to be everywhere and to be able to do all things.

From the hour of his triumph at Chicago he has won the support of the rural districts. Mass meetings have been held in villages, hamlets and cross-roads in all the States. In the smaller towns the people have likewise hailed Trueman as their deliverer. It is the good fortune of those dwelling outside of the cities to be still in possession of the dormant spirit of independence. They have been crushed, yet not cowed by the Trusts.

The fact that they are self-supporting in so far as procuring the actual necessities of food and shelter, make them capable of retaining a hope for emancipation from Trust domination.

The wage-slaves of the cities are in a condition actually appalling. It is part of Trueman's campaign to go amongst the shops and factories in the environs of the cities to talk with the men, and to picture to them the results that will follow their voting in their own interests. He has seen poverty in its most direful forms.

The evening has worn on until it is within an hour of midnight. Reporters come and go; the last of the committee-men has said good night. Trueman is alone with his secretary, Herbert Benson.

Benson, a young newspaperman, volunteered his services at the opening of the campaign. He is a brilliant writer, and what is of more consequence, he is beyond doubt an ardent supporter of popular government. There are few men in the journalistic field who are free thinkers. The universities, colleges and academies in which the higher branches of study can be pursued, have all been brought under the power of the Magnates. Endowments are only to be obtained by observing the commands of the donors. The chief offence which an institution of learning can commit is to tell the truth regarding social conditions. For this reason the men who enter journalism from college, are unfitted to grasp the social problem; or if, in the case of a few, the true conditions are realized, they find it expedient to remain silent. Excommunication from the craft is sure to follow any radical expression in favor of socialism. The press is free only in name.

A strong friendship exists between Trueman and Benson.

"Tell me candidly, Benson," Trueman inquires, "do you think there is a chance of my carrying New York City and St. Louis?"

"I am satisfied that you will have a clean majority in both. My belief is based on personal observations. I have been in all quarters of the cities, and have questioned workmen in every industry. They seem of one mind. Your Convention speech converted them."

"What do they say about it?"

"Why, it makes it clear to them that with a fearless and noble leader, the masses can express their will. You showed to the world that reason *can* rule passion. It needed but a word from you to have precipitated a revolt in the party which would have spread through every state. To most men in your position it would have appeared that out of the tumult and confusion, they would have come out with a decided advantage. But you gave no thought to a personal advantage; it was the good of the people that actuated you. And now you are to reap your reward. What was plain to the inhabitants of the rural districts from the start, is now manifest to the toilers in the cities, especially in this city and Chicago."

"This condition must be known at the Plutocratic Headquarters. What is being done by the managers there, to overcome the sudden change in the public mind? I hear so many stories that I am at a loss to tell which is true and which false."

"The local committee of the Plutocrats has abandoned all hope of coercing the people. This evening it sent out a letter of instruction to the manufacturers calling upon them to exercise drastic measures to prevent their operatives from voting; but this is only a blind," replies Benson.

"The Chairman of the National executive committee at the same time held a conference with the chief labor leaders." These leaders were offered a flat bribe if they prevent the men whom they represented from voting. Eight out of the ten who were present accepted the bribe, which was $50,000, in cash. Two declined. One of these afterwards went to the local treasurer and agreed to deliver his people into bondage for $100,000. His terms were acceded to.

"The one who spurned the bribe has been given to understand that if he divulges the nature of the meeting, his life will be the penalty. Notwithstanding this, he has just informed me of the matter. I had to pledge not to make public the information he gave me. But we can counteract the influence of the labor leaders."

"In what way?" Trueman asks, with deep interest.

"You have made a great mistake," he continues, before Benson has time to reply. "You never should promise to keep a secret. Publicity would have been our sure means of thwarting their design."

"If I had not promised to keep the secret I should not have learned of the plot," protests Benson. "I have an idea that we can bring the labor leaders to terms. We are driven to the wall by the Trust Magnates, who will stop at nothing. We must do what instinct would suggest. The labor leaders shall receive notice that if they attempt to prevent the people from voting, their blow at public suffrage will bring on a revolution. It will be on treacherous leaders of the people that the vengeance will fall."

"No, no, that will never do. I cannot consent to the use of a threat of violence," declares Trueman, with emphasis.

"But this is not a question of what you may or may not consent to," replies Benson. "It is what I will do. I know what I say is certain to be true. To avert an uprising I shall warn the labor leaders myself. You will have no part in this matter. I am determined that the vote of the people shall be recorded at this election." Benson hurries from the room.

He is soon in secret conference with the leaders at Liberty Hall. They are inclined to scoff at his assertion that the people will resort to violence if they discover that they have again been betrayed; but when Benson repeats the circumstances of the compact between the Magnates and the Labor leaders, with every detail and word, they realize that their positions as leaders are endangered.

With threat and bribe they seek to win Benson to silence. He withstands their blandishments; at the suggestion of a bribe he flies into a passion.

These men are cowards at heart; they have taken the gifts of the Magnates for years, and have contrived to pacify their followers. Now that they are brought face to face with the possibility of exposure, they tremble at the thought of the popular denouncement that will come upon them. They even weigh the chances of physical harm that may befall them. Secretly planning to get the bribe money, they agree to make no attempt to coerce the vote of the people.

"The first word of intimidation or coercion which is spoken will be my signal to expose you," Benson tells them at parting.

The Trust Magnates remain ignorant that they are sowing the wind. They receive daily reports from the leaders telling of their success in intimidating the masses. To every demand for money the Magnates willingly respond. It is an election where money is not to be spared. Benson and his faithful corps of workers keep a vigilant watch over the Labor leaders.

When the Magnates arrange for a great parade, Benson warns the Labor leaders not to attempt to force any workingman to march. This causes the parade to turn out a dismal failure.

"We must have more money," the leaders assert.

Two millions of dollars is set aside for use in St. Louis alone. Against such odds can the Independence party win?

CHAPTER XXIII

A DAY AHEAD OF SCHEDULE

It is two o'clock P. M., on October twelfth. In sixty minutes the New York Stock 'Change will close. The day has been exceedingly quiet; brokers are standing in groups discussing the whys and wherefores of this and that stock scheme; all are of little consequence. Indeed, there has been nothing done on the floor since the abrupt departure of James Golding, the Head of the Banking Syndicate for Europe, three weeks before this pleasant twelfth day of October.

Golding's mission abroad is vaguely guessed to be the floating of a bond issue for the government, as there has been an alarming shrinkage in the money market, and the Secretary of the Treasury has called upon the Banking interests to relieve the strain on the Treasury.

The slightest indication of weakness in the money market has its instant effect on stocks. New York quotations are looked upon as the criterion of the country, and for that reason the brokers are disposed to be cautious. Wall street traditions make it seem proper for the brokers to wait the result of the European trip.

Since the inauguration of the system of bank favoritism, which, was one of the strong features of the previous Plutocratic Platform, and on which the Party was able to raise an enormous Campaign fund, the secrets of the Government and its favorite bankers are not shared with the brokers in ordinary stocks and industrials. For this reason the timidity of the brokers is more pronounced than ever before.

To them it seems inexplicable that the Government should seek to float a bond issue on the eve of an election. They do not grasp the full import of this scheme to force the people to support the Plutocratic candidates as the preservers of the country's credit.

A broker, running the tape through his fingers listlessly, reads this sentence: "London, Oct. 12,—James Golding announces his intention to float $245,000,000 three per cent. U.S. gold bonds in London."

In an instant he realizes that the confidence of the market will be restored. Rushing to the pit he begins to buy everything that is offered. Half a hundred tickers in the Exchange convey the same news to as many brokerage firms.

A wild scramble is started; everyone is anxious to go "long" on stocks which they have been cautiously selling for days past. Point by point the listed stocks advance.

The clock strikes half-past two. Will half an hour suffice to readjust the market?

An exceptional, an unprecedented bull panic is in progress. Brokers, messengers, clerks, every one connected with the Stock Exchange is in a flurry. Tickers are for the time being utterly forgotten.

In a corner of the Exchange sits the operator who has to send the doings of the day to the Press Association. He is unmoved by any excitement that may occur on the floor; it is an every-day experience with him. Stolidly he reads the tape, and jots down the advance in the stocks as a matter of course.

He has sent word to his office that Golding is to float the bond issue; but he knows that this news has reached the office through another channel before his belated report. He sends the message because it is a part of his routine.

"Calais, Oct. 12th," are the words that now appear on the slip of paper he is scanning. "James Golding, accompanied by M. Tabort, French banking magnate, entered rear car Paris Express from London to cross the Channel. Car uncoupled in tunnel; explosion; both men instantly killed; submarine tunnel wrecked."

Here *is* news. The instinct of the broker is awakened in the operator. He leaves his desk and walks rapidly to the pit. He places his hand on the shoulder of a prominent broker. In a few words he tells this man the news, and asks that the broker make him a "little something" for the tip.

With the news of Golding's death this broker enters the pit as a seller. There are now but twenty minutes left before the closing of 'Change, yet by cautious work he will be able to sell out his holdings at the inflated prices that prevail. He alone of all the members of the Exchange knows that the greatest American financier is dead. On the morrow every stock on the list will depreciate. Now is the time for him to unload.

A hundred bidders are eager to buy the stock he offers. He reaps a fortune in the quarter of an hour before the 'Change closes; the rest of the brokers heap up trouble for the morrow. Five minutes before three the news of Golding's death is brought to the brokers. It is too late. In their frenzy the men fear either to buy or sell. The floor is a veritable bear pit. Men swear and rage in impotent grief as they realize that they have brought ruin upon themselves by their rash speculation.

While this scene is in progress the world is being told of the death of the great Financier.

It will be recalled that to William Nevins was assigned the task of ending the career of James Golding. He has worked secretly, as have all the other members of the Committee of Forty. Now his role as shadow of the financier leads him to New York, while some banking scheme is being consummated; now he is rushing across the continent to be near the Magnate in San Francisco; the last trip takes him to Europe.

At the time he began to study the movements of Golding, the Magnate was in London and thither Nevins went; he was detained there, on that occasion, but three days. On the voyage back to the United States he was afforded an excellent opportunity to observe Golding. Nevins became acquainted with the man whose life he was to take, through a business proposition in regard to an investment. He professed to represent a syndicate of French investors which was negotiating to purchase and work a gold mine in Lower California. According to his story, he had secured the necessary privileges from the Mexican government. Golding was invited to be a participant in the enterprise, which was destined to prove a bonanza.

Plausible, suave, intelligent, Nevins has impressed the Magnate most favorably. So when Nevins proposes that he accompany Golding to Europe to introduce him to the French capitalists, the financier readily agrees.

As traveling companions on the millionaire's yacht, the two men leave New York on September twentieth. Golding is bent on the successful launching of the big bond issue, with the gold mining scheme as a secondary consideration; Nevins has only the awful work before him to consider. London becomes the permanent abode of the two, their trips to France being short and frequent.

The newly constructed Channel tunnel connecting England with the continent is a transportation improvement which makes it possible for one to leave London, at ten o'clock in the morning and be in Paris at one in the afternoon. The Air line to Paris enters the sub-marine tunnel at a point twelve miles north of Dover and emerges on the plains eight miles south of

Calais. As an engineering feat the construction of the tunnel has been heralded as unparalleled.

It is by this speedy route that Golding and Nevins make three trips to Paris. The Committeeman contrives to interest several French bankers in his supposititious mine, and by artful manipulation he brings these bankers and the American Money King together in preliminary negotiations.

On October twelfth the two are to effect a final understanding with the members of the French syndicate. The newspapers have given an inkling of the transactions, and have run stories to the effect that Golding is negotiating with a French banker for rich gold lands in Mexico.

Independently of Nevins, the bond issue plan has been developed by Golding and the time for announcing the fact is this same twelfth day of October.

Knowing the result that will be produced on American securities, he delays the announcement until the London Exchange closes for the day. He knows that immediately after making the news public, he is to leave London, for Paris to be gone until the twentieth. Thus he will avoid being interviewed.

Golding has calculated that the difference in time of five hours between London, and New York will result in the announcement being cabled for the opening of the New York Exchange. This would be the result did not a number of large London speculators, who hold American securities, determine to hold back the messages until they apprise their New York representatives of the matter and advise them how to act.

The monopoly of the cable is obtainable by an easy means. All four of the lines which communicated with the United States are leased. Messages rumoring important developments in the China alliance question are transmitted and suffice to explain the cessation of other news—the Government is supposed to be using the cables.

Despite the efforts of the speculators, an enterprising correspondent of a New York News Association succeeds in sending the news of the bond issue announcement, so that it is received on 'Change at two o'clock. From another source the message of death is cabled fifteen minutes before the closing of the market.

Golding and Nevins lunch together before starting for Paris.

"I have closed a deal to-day that will net me twenty-five million dollars within six weeks," Golding confides to Nevins with an air of satisfaction. He might be a retail merchant discussing trade with a neighbor and relating the result of a barter which will net him a profit of a hundred dollars, for there is no stronger emotion in his speech or manner than would be evoked by such a commonplace transaction. Yet this man has just arranged a financial deal which is to maintain the stability of the currency of a Nation of a hundred millions of people.

"Then it is true that you are to shoulder the responsibility of disposing of the United States bond issue?" Nevins inquires with a semblance of interest. "What would that Republic do if it were not for its public spirited men of wealth? Republics are all right when they are curbed by the conservative elements, but when the riff-raff gets the reins in hand, then there is always trouble."

"The days of mob rule in America are over," Golding declares. "It was no easy matter to wean the people of the fallacious idea that a proletariat could manage the finances of the country."

"When our mine is in operation you will not have to seek the aid of England in taking bonds off the hands of the Treasurer of the United States, will we?" Nevins asks.

"That's just the point," exclaims Golding. They talk on in this strain until the meal is finished.

"We have ten minutes to get to the terminal," says Nevins, consulting his watch.

"O, that will be ample time. It only takes five minutes to ride there."

When the train is reached, Golding looks at his watch. "There, I told you we could make it in five minutes. I am always just on time. Never a minute too soon or a minute too late. Time is money. Perhaps I am the wealthiest man in America, if not in the world, because I know the value of time."

"That certainly is the secret of your success," Nevins declares blandly.

The Special Paris Express is composed of six coaches and the motor; this train runs at an average speed of sixty-two miles an hour. It is the fastest train on the continent. So that they may not be disturbed, the mine promoters have arranged to occupy a private car attached to the rear of the train. This car they enter. Nevins carries a small hand-satchel which he declines to give over to the willing porter.

The superintendent of the road is on hand to see that the influential patrons are properly cared for; he has received his instructions from the president, who is an intimate friend of James Golding.

The signal is given and the express starts.

In an incredibly short time the tunnel is reached. As the train rushes into the darkness, Golding notices that the electric lights have not been turned on.

"Ring for the porter, will you, Mr. Tabort," he asks of Nevins, whom he knows only as M. Emile Tabort.

"But where is the button? Ah, I have an idea," replies Nevins. "I shall go into the forward car and find the porter; it will not take a minute."

The car is engulfed in pitchy darkness, save for a glimmer of diffused light that comes from the cars ahead.

"Hurry, won't you; I hate to be in darkness," says Golding, uneasily.

"I won't keep you waiting long," calls back Nevins, who is half way to the door.

He turns to look at the Magnate. A vague shadowy form is all that he can discern in the gloom.

"So here is where you are to end a life of mammon-worship," Nevins mutters as he steps upon the platform of the forward car.

He bends down, and with a strong, quick jerk uncouples the rear car.

For a few seconds the detached car keeps up with the train, then as its momentum is exhausted, a rapidly widening gap is made.

"In five minutes you will have light," Nevins calls grimly, as he looks at the fading car.

The train rushes ahead with speed that is imperceptibly increased. Nevins climbs to the top of the car and crawls toward the front of the train. He works his way to the coach immediately behind the motor. Standing on the platform he removes his coat and trousers and reappears arrayed in the common suit of a train hand. A soft cap completes the disguise.

A faint rumble reaches his ears.

"*The first Magnate has fallen*" he whispers, as if confiding

The Transgressors 207

a secret.

"Yes; I have carried out my plan. James Golding is buried at the bottom of the Channel. The time-fuse worked."

When the train emerges from the tunnel it is stopped by the signals of the Block station. The operator inquires if anything has gone wrong. He has been unable to communicate with the English station for more than fifteen minutes, and supposes that the wires have been deranged. Then it is that the loss of the rear car is discovered.

While the trainmen and passengers discuss the matter, a sound from the tunnel reaches their ears; a roar resembling a series of dynamite explosions.

"The tunnel has caved in!" exclaimed the conductor. "Get aboard, for your lives!"

A rush is made for the train, and in half a minute it pulls away from the mouth of the tunnel at top speed.

From the rear car the tunnel is visible. The train is five hundred yards away when the waters burst from the mouth of the tunnel.

Loosed from the confining walls, the gigantic column subsides in height, spreading on either side of the tracks. It inundates a vast area of the low country surrounding the station.

Through the employment of the block system, but one train in each direction is permitted to enter the tunnel at the same time.

A partition wall bisects the tunnel into 'parallel sections, each containing a single track. The left-hand section, on which are east-bound tracks, is the one in which the telegraph wires run. The explosion wrecks the walls of the tunnel and breaks the wires.

Francis A. Adams

The only explanation that can be offered is that the compressed air cylinder on the car exploded. On each of the tunnel cars a compressed air apparatus is attached, to insure against the trains being stalled in the tunnel in the event of the electric motor giving out.

Nevins experiences no difficulty in losing himself in the crowd when the train reaches Calais. He goes at once to a cheap furnished room which he has previously engaged. He still wears the attire of a train hand. Once in his room he sinks upon the bed, his mind and body thoroughly fatigued by the strain that has been placed upon them.

For more than an hour he is motionless; then his reserve gradually returns.

"I have fulfilled my pledge," he says to himself. "It had to be done to-day, for otherwise I should have been compelled to die with Golding. I have started the execution of the edict of proscription a day in advance of the schedule.

"This will be the signal for the thirty-nine to do their duty." They must hear of Golding's death to-day. I shall cable the news to New York; once there it will be heralded through the country.

"And they will suppose that Golding and a French financier met death accidentally." Yes, the people will accept this view; but the Committee! ah! it will know the truth. To the Thirty-nine it will mean that one of their brothers has gone to his fate with one of the Transgressors. It will dispel any symptom of hesitancy on their part.

"Two men are supposed to have died in the explosion. The tunnel is destroyed. Who can say that one of the occupants of the car escaped?"

He sits on the edge of the bed bending forward, and rests his head in his hands. In this attitude he remains for several minutes.

"Good God, forgive me!" he cries, fervently. "I cannot die in ignorance of to-morrow! I must hear that my plan is faithfully carried out; that the Transgressors are annihilated, and the committee have kept their pledge. Is it false in me to wait? No; for I do not fear death; I would have faced it forty times could I have done so. The Transgressors would all have fallen by my hand had such a thing been possible. I shall keep my pledge, to-morrow."

A few minutes later Nevins leaves the house dressed in a plain suit. He enters the cable office and writes the following message:

"James Golding, accompanied by M. Tabort, French Banking Magnate, entered rear car, Paris express for London, to cross the channel. Car uncoupled in tunnel. Explosion. Both men instantly killed. Sub-marine tunnel wrecked."

"Send this message to the New York Javelin," are his instructions to the operator. "Rush it, and I will give you a hundred francs."

"Cable is engaged," is the reply. "Orders from London."

"What news is London sending over this cable?"

"None. It seems strange to keep the cable tied up, when there is such important news to be sent. But the instructions are, 'Send no messages to the United States.' I'm sending an unimportant House of Commons speech."

"Your wire is free, then? I'll give you a thousand francs if you will send this one message through," Nevins urges persuasively. "I want to get the news to my paper. They will pay royally for it."

The operator hesitates. A thousand francs is a tempting offer.

"When will you pay?" he asks.

"I will pay you now, on the very spot."

As he speaks Nevins counts out the bills.

It is twenty minutes of eight by the local clock in the cable office. The clock indicating New York time registers two-forty P. M.

A glance at the Bank of France notes decides the question in the operator's mind. He takes the money and transmits the message.

Nevins returns to his room to await the developments of the thirteenth of October.

BOOK IV

IN FREEDOM'S NAME

CHAPTER XXIV

THE SYNDICATE IN LIQUIDATION

The crisis has arrived. On the bulletins in front of the leading newspaper offices in New York crowds congregate. Men discuss the startling tidings that come from all points of the compass and ask themselves what the next report will be. Golding's death is the forerunner of a long list of fatalities.

JAVELIN BULLETIN.

United States Senator Warwick,
of California, was assassinated at
his villa in San Diego.

The murderer, after shooting
the Senator, turned the smoking
pistol upon himself and died with
his victim.

This bulletin is posted on the board in front of the Javelin office.

"What's happening?" asks one of the crowd of the man at his side. "Is this a wholesale butchery planned by Anarchists, or is it a plot of the Mafia?"

"God only knows," is the reply.

And to the thousands who stand waiting with breathless excitement for the next announcement the inability to locate the source of the outburst of violence is quite as complete as this man's. They realize that a series of appalling crimes has been committed; yet none can ascribe the least pretext for them.

The name of one after another of the leading magnates of the land is posted as the victim of a simultaneous homicide, and the notion that it is the work of anarchists begins to prevail.

JAVELIN BULLETIN.

Robert Drew, the Sugar King,
while riding in Central Park, was
stabbed to death by an assassin.

The man jumped into his carriage
as it was descending the hill
leading to the One Hundred and
Tenth Street entrance at Seventh
Avenue.

No sooner had the dagger been
buried in the heart of Mr. Drew
than the fanatic withdrew it and
plunged it into his own heart.

The murderer fell forward and
died even before his victim.

When this notice is displayed it causes a shudder to run through the crowd. This is the first of the deaths to be inflicted in New York.

With the apprehension of men who feel that danger is imminent, the crowd in front of the bulletin shifts uneasily. There is the thought in all minds that some awful calamity may come upon them as they stand there. Then, too, there is the thought that they may not be safe elsewhere. In such a state of mind men become susceptible to emotion. A word can then sway a multitude.

From five o'clock, when the first bulletin appeared, until the announcement of the killing of Mr. Drew, a period of two hours and a half, the list has grown to frightful proportions.

From Chicago comes the report that Tingwell Fang, the Beef King, has been killed in his private office by the explosion of a dynamite bomb or some other infernal machine brought there by a man who for weeks had been transacting important business with Mr. Fang. The explosion entirely demolished the office, and when the police succeeded in getting at the bodies it was found that the bomb-thrower had paid for his deed with his life.

In a bundle of papers which the man left in the outer office a note is found which gives his address as the Palmer House. At his room in the hotel a card is found addressed to the public: It read as follows:

I have fulfilled my oath; my self-destruction
is proof that I am sincere in the belief that I
have acted for the good of mankind.

BENTON S. MARVIN.

Almost as soon as the papers are on the street announcing the tragedy, another message comes from Chicago telling of the strange death of Senator Gold. His body and that of a man who had been with him at the Auditorium are found in the Senator's room. Death has been caused by an unknown agency. There are no signs of violence on either. The money and jewelry of both are undisturbed. Neither man appears to have been the victim of the other's hand, for the apparel of each is unruffled. One is found lying on the floor near the window; the other is found stretched across the table in the room.

Following these early bulletins come others from Philadelphia, St. Louis and Boston, successively announcing the mysterious deaths of President Vosbeck of the National Transportation Trust, Captain Blood of the St. Louis Steamship Association, and of ex-U.S. Supreme Court Justice Elias M. Turner of Massachusetts.

"President Vosbeck met his death while on a tour of inspection in the new power house of his company in the western part of the city. With him were his private secretary and a stranger from New York whom he was taking on a tour of inspection. The secretary was sent to find the superintendent of the power house. He returned to find both President Vosbeck and the stranger in the throes of death on the floor near the great dynamo. In the stranger's hand a cane was clutched. This cane was one of those that are commonly made at penitentiaries. It was of leather rings strung on a steel rod."

The above dispatch is spread on the bulletin board, followed by these details:

"As soon as the hospital surgeons and the electrical experts arrived they decided that the cane must have come in contact with the deadly current; and that at that instant Steel and the stranger were standing upon the metal flooring which made a perfect conductor." The death of Captain Blood was even more astounding than that of President Vosbeck.

"In company with the newly appointed Superintendent of the grain elevators, of which the Captain had a monopoly, he descended into the hold of the steamboat that was taking on a cargo of wheat at the Big Three Elevator. The two men were hardly below deck when, by some inexplicable error the engineer received the signal to open the shoot. An avalanche of golden grain rushed upon the two captives. There was a cry of dismay from the hold, and then only the sound of the rushing stream of grain."

"The engine was reversed and the bucket chain began to take

up the grain; but it was too late. When the bodies of the men were reached they were contorted in the agony of death. Suffocation had come as a tardy relief to them."

This bulletin adds to the excitement of the crowd. While the people are reading the extras that tell of the series of strange deaths of men of such national importance as Vosbeck and Captain Blood, the news comes from Boston that a double murder has been committed in Brookline, a suburb of that city.

Ex-Chief Justice Turner of the United States Supreme Court and a friend who was visiting him at his country house, were set upon by highwaymen as they were strolling through a strip of woodland, and had been hanged to trees. It was not known how much money the road agents got. The Justice had never been in the habit of carrying any large sums. As to what money Mr. Burton, his friend, might have had on his person, there was no way of ascertaining.

"The Supreme Court, the Senate, and three of the leading-men in the country, this is pretty big game," remarks one of the crowd.

"It will be well if it ends there," says another.

"This will cause 'Industrials' to take a slump," observes a stout, sleek, well dressed man.

"Yes," replies a voice at his elbow, "and it may be that a slump of the market is at the bottom of most of this. I wouldn't trust these brokers. They'd kill a regiment to get a flurry on the market if they were short."

The stout man, who happens to be a stock broker, says no more.

"Get yer extra, all about six millionaires killed; get yer extra!" cry the newsboys.

"Make it seven," shouts a coarse voice from the very heart of the mass of humanity.

And seven it is to be.

The bulletin is being cleared for a fresh notice.

"Bet you it's a Banker this time," a book-keeper, who had deserted his desk to get the latest news, says jestingly.

"Ah, it'll be a dead shoemaker next," laughingly exclaims a messenger boy who has heard the book-keeper's remark.

By a strange coincidence the name that appears the following instant is that of Henry Hide, the head of the leather Trust. The ribald jest of the boy proves to be all too true.

CHAPTER XXV

BIG NEWS IN THE JAVELIN OFFICE

Inside the newspaper offices there is even greater excitement than on the streets. The editors are non-plussed at the appalling news that comes pouring in from every section of the laud.

How is the news to be conveyed to the people? is the question that the oldest journalist is unable to answer.

In selecting the leading feature of the day's terrible news, what is to be considered? The fact that an astounding number of murders or accidents have simultaneously stricken with death a score of the leading men of the country, is in itself a matter of unprecedented importance. But the end is not in sight. Every half hour brings tidings of still other deaths and murders.

The peculiar feature of the news is, however, that in every instance where a banker, mine owner or financier is murdered, the evil-doer has committed suicide. What does this indicate? Is it a concerted move on the part of some society; or is it the result of an inexplicable fatalistic phenomenon?

Just as a decision on these points is arrived at, and the editors have given their orders for the make-up of the extras, some account, either of the death of a railroad magnate or the head of some one of the great trusts, is received. The necessity of a change in the form of the paper is made imperative. For the thought that a rival sheet may feature the news forces a change.

Extras of the evening papers are being issued every half hour. The excitement on the streets exceeds even that of the days when the reports of our wars was the all absorbing topic.

In the present calamity men know not what to think. To some it is apparent that a modern juggernaut is abroad; others hold the belief that a conspiracy is being carried to its bloody fulfillment.

No more accurate idea of the confused condition of the public mind can be gathered than from a study of the action in the editorial rooms of the great New York newspaper, the Javelin.

The editorial staff of this paper is composed of the brainiest men in journalism; men who have won distinction in their profession by reason of their ability to handle the news of the day in a manner that will satisfy the demands of the public.

On the large reportorial staff are men who have been brought from various cities; each is competent to gather news and present it in the most interesting fashion.

In the composing room sixty of the most skilled linotypists sit at their machines ready to set the words as they fall from the pencils of the writers.

Still other men are at the presses, awaiting to put the great mechanisms in motion, to pour out a stream of a hundred thousand papers an hour.

All is in readiness to turn out the news with unerring accuracy and incredible speed.

Year in and year out the routine of publication has been gone through with. Now one man who is advanced or discharged vacates a position, which is immediately filled by the man next in line for promotion. The machinery of the office never clogs.

Francis A. Adams

But on this night, turmoil takes the place of system.

A crisis in the history of the paper is being reached. The heads of departments are all present, having been summoned by telegram or telephone. They are ready to act. Yet the signal for action is delayed.

To run off the edition of a morning paper is a far different thing from getting out an edition of an evening paper.

The morning newspaper must contain the "*news*" in its first edition if it is to reach distant points; if it is even to reach the suburban towns. In these towns, by far the largest percentage of the readers are located. They will be anxious for the latest and most complete news. The evening papers give hurried accounts of the events that are stirring the country. For the full details the readers depend upon the morning papers. The newspaper which fails to satisfy their demands will lose its popularity.

So the editor-in-chief and the proprietor of the Javelin are in a quandary.

"It is now 1.30," says the editor-in-chief, as he consults the clock. "If we are to get out a paper we must start the presses."
"What is the leader?" inquires the proprietor anxiously.

"A general review of the casualties; the summary of the result of the announcements of the sudden deaths of so many leading men. This is followed by the story of the deaths of six Senators. The head runs across the page. The head-line reads 'Death's Harvest, Thirty-Six!' The banks tell of the sudden deaths that have come upon Senators, Judges, Manufacturers, Railroad Magnates, and a score of multi-millionaires."

"We can't tell everything in a line, or in one edition," observes the proprietor, "so I think it is safe to 'go to press.' Is there nothing of importance left out?"

Before an answer can be given to this query the telegraph editor rushes from his desk waving a slip of paper.

"Hold the press!" he exclaims. "Here's the biggest news yet. Attorney General Bradley of the United States has been assassinated as he was leaving his office."

"The man who killed him made no attempt to escape, but, waiting to see that the three shots he had fired point-blank at the Attorney General had done their work, he deliberately turned the pistol on himself. He placed it at his right temple and fired, dropping dead in his tracks."

"Wait a minute; wait!" cries the editor-in-chief. "Don't say another word."

Turning to the night editor he says, "It will be necessary to change the first page. A new head will have to be run, and the leading story will have to tell of the murder of the Attorney General. This news is national. I think I had better go to the press room and do this work myself. The press will start in twenty minutes, if you give me the word 'Go ahead!'"

"Go ahead," is the laconic reply.

Down the winding staircase that leads to the composing room, and then to the basement where the presses are located, the chief runs. He sets about his work with a calmness and speed that is remarkable. The first page is put on the composing table and the form opened. The head lines are removed and the copy that the editor is turning out a dozen words at a time on a page, are instantly set up and put in place.

In eight minutes the form is keyed up and the stereotypers have it in their hands. Three minutes later the pressman has the stereotype plate. A minute later the press is in motion.

With the first half dozen copies of the edition wet from the press, the editor rushes back to his office.

In his absence there has been nothing startling reported. He breathes a sigh of relief and sinks exhausted into his chair.

At a score of desks men are writing special portions of the news. One is telling of the startling murders, another of the unusual accidents that have claimed a dozen prominent men as victims.

The strange story of the hanging of an Ex-Justice of the Supreme Court Judge is being written by one of the sporting reporters; the assassination of six Senators is the theme of another special writer. Every one is busy.

The chance that always comes to the young reporter is at hand. He is entrusted with the important work of writing the story of the deaths of five railroad magnates. His face is a study. It is scarlet and beads of perspiration run down his cheeks.

Even the copy-boys are alive to the fact that a night of unusual import is passing, and they carry copy without being called. A boy stands at the side of every reporter and runs with the pages to the desks where the copy readers scan it and write the head lines; it is not a night when copy is carefully read and "cut." Everything is news, and the responsibility for the accuracy of the writing is upon the heads of the reporters.

Surrounding the bulletin board in the City Hall square, a crowd of from one hundred and fifty to two hundred thousand has gathered.

The lateness of the hour is forgotten. Men and women stand through the chill hours of the late night and early morning waiting for news. There is an ever varying stream passing in front of the *Javelin* office. Early in the afternoon the police have taken control of the streets and compelled the people to keep moving. There is fear that the disorderly element will start a riot.

Fortunately the first of the calamitous telegrams of the day has been received after the close of the Exchanges. This has prevented a panic. Brokers and bankers receive the tidings with consternation; they dread the opening on the morrow. Many of them are in the crowd anxiously waiting for further details of the deaths of the controllers of railroad and industrial stocks.

At midnight a bulletin announces that Senator Barker, who had been the staunch advocate of Bi-metallism until the recent session, and who had then voted with the Gold element, has been found murdered in his palatial home at Lakewood, N. J. His private secretary has also been killed, evidently because he had attempted to rescue his employer. Both have been stabbed.

After this the only news that is posted is of a confirmatory nature. It tells of the development of the national wave of death. Then, too, it begins to give the first positive information that the majority of the deaths have been the result of a plot.

Either on the body of each of the assassins or in his effects have been found papers that show conclusively that the men acted in concert. While the phraseology of each of the letters differ, there is a similarity which is very apparent when they are compared.

"I have kept my word. The world will judge if I was justified," is found on one of the suicides.

"If thy right eye offend thee, pluck it out," is all that the card on another bears.

"A part is not greater than the whole," is the inscription on the card that is found in the breast-pocket of the man who has killed the Sugar King.

When the news of the assassination of the Attorney General is given to the people, there is a reaction in the spirit of the multitude immediately surrounding the *Javelin* bulletin. They have previously received the notices with expressions of wonderment. Now all realize that the Nation itself is imperilled.

"This is another Suratt conspiracy," says one man to another.

"Will it reach the President?" is the question that men do not dare ask, though they think it.

"This is not the work of cranks, you may depend upon it," observes a Central office detective, who has a reputation for sagacity. His fellow-officer, who stands a pace in advance of him, turns and inquires if the detective thinks he could run the gang down.

"If I am set on the case I shall not waste much time in looking for ordinary crooks," replies the detective. "It will be my aim to unearth a society of malcontents."

At another point a party of club men, who have come down town from their Fifth avenue haunt, stand discussing the terrible events.

"Do you remember the night that the news was received here that Lincoln has been shot?" asks a patriarchal New Yorker of an equally ancient citizen.

"Indeed I do. You and I were at the Niblo's Garden, weren't we?"

"That's right. It's strange that history should repeat itself; and that we should be together to-night?"

"There is quite a difference between the murder of Lincoln and this series of crimes," observes one of the younger men. "This night's, or rather day's, work is aimed at all classes of wealth. It is evident that it is an attack on capital. And the inexplicable part of the news is, that in every instance the murderers have cheated the gallows."

"Come, move on there," gruffly shouts a policeman.

"Hallo, Mason," cries one of the club men as he pushes his way to the side of the policeman.

"O! How do you do, Mr. Castor," says the blue-coat, in deferential tone.

"Mason, these are my friends; we want to stand here for a few minutes. It's all right, isn't it?"

"Certainly, it's all right. I thought that you were a lot of the idle crowd, sir, and we have had orders to keep everyone on the move. But you're all right."

Mason had been appointed to the force by the Clubman's influence.

Turning from his patron the policeman roughs his way through the crowd and makes the men and women "move on."

"Nothing like having a friend at court, eh?" laughingly cries one of Mr. Castor's friends.

"It is this custom of privilege that has brought on this calamity," soberly observes the philosopher of the group.

A riot breaks out at this moment at the foot of the Franklin statue; and the shouts and curses of the men who are being beaten by the police send a thrill through the multitude.

The people on the fringe of the swaying thousands begin a retreat. Their action is quickly imitated.

The Clubmen decide that they have seen all that they want of the crowd. But the matter of getting out is not easy of accomplishment.

"What are you plug hats looking for?" sneers a rough from the slums. And his arm swings out and hits the foremost man in the face. This seems to be the cue for a dozen ruffians to fall upon the party of well dressed men.

Two policemen who stand nearby come to the rescue of the party and conduct them to a place of safety. From thence the sightseers are glad to make their way up-town.

The ambulances from the Hudson Street Hospital take four of the rioters who have been beaten with the night sticks of the police, to the station house. Under ordinary circumstances the prisoners would be taken to the hospital; but the Inspector of Police, who is on the scene, deems it advisible to take them to the Station house.

A sullen crowd of young men from the neighboring streets follow the ambulances, shouting execrations at the policemen who have made the arrests.

The hands on the clock in the cupola of the City Hall point to 2.15 A. M.

The news wagons are wedging their way through the sea of humanity. Morning papers are being sold by the ever vigilant newsboys. Still the people linger.

An event of graver nature than any that has preceded is what the crowd craves. The appetite of a man, or of a collection of men, is the same; if it is fed to repletion, it cannot resist the desire for an excess.

"Let's wait for one more bulletin," an engineer suggests to his fireman.

"All right; we can stay until 2.30. That will give us time to get to the building."

Before the fifteen minutes elapse all thoughts of tending in the engine room are driven from their minds.

The first bulletin announcing the tidings of the Wilkes-Barre uprising is posted by the *Javelin* at 2.35 o'clock. From this moment the crowds in City Hall increase. No one who can get within range of the blackboard thinks of leaving. There is a subtle fascination in waiting for the details of the momentous events.

At daybreak the evening edition of the day's papers containing news of the transcendent occurrences of the hour are on the street. In these papers the first intimation of the full scope of the blow that has been dealt the Magnates is given to the public. Link by link the chain of evidence that the accidents and murders are each part of a general and concerted movement is built.

"Martyrs or Murderers?" This is the interrogatory headline that appears in every paper.

The events of the past twenty-four hours have been so unparalleled that men dare not jump at conclusions. To proclaim the forty agents of the Syndicate of Annihilation martyrs, may lead to an instant uprising of the anarchistic element. To denounce them as murderers may have the same effect. Fear prompts the people to take a conservative stand, they wait for full evidence before pronouncing a verdict.

They do not know that Harvey Trueman is pleading the cause of justice and right to a mob at Wilkes-Barre.

The case is now in the hands of the great public as a jury.

A verdict that will shake the world is about to be tendered.

This verdict is to be entered at Wilkes-Barre.

CHAPTER XXVI

ON TO WILKES-BARRE

When the first news of the Act of Annihilation reaches the Independence Party's Headquarters, Trueman is out on an important mission, a conference with the American Mothers' League for the Abolition of Child Labor. This League, it is believed, can influence scores of thousands of voters.

A telephone call from Benson brings Trueman back to the headquarters. On the way down town he hears loud cries in the street.

"Get y'er Extra! All about the big murders!" the newsboys are calling in front of the headquarters. Trueman buys a paper. He reads about the murder in Central Park. "This is an unfortunate occurrence," he says, half aloud. "The people will put more credence in the assertions of the Magnates, that there are anarchists working to disrupt the Government."

Once in the rooms of the Campaign Committee he receives the messages direct from the *Javelin* office over a special wire.

He is as ignorant of the true condition of affairs as any of the public. What to think of the wholesale destruction of the leading magnates, is a riddle to him.

"WILKES-BARRE, PA., Oct. 13th.

Gorman Purdy was murdered in his house at 2 o'clock this afternoon, by Carl Metz. After shooting Purdy, Metz committed suicide. Come to Wilkes-Barre at once. Miners are threatening to sack the palaces on the esplanade. Ethel is in great danger.   MARTHA."

This telegram is handed to Trueman. He reads it; re-reads it. The full import flashes upon him. He knows the character of the miners; knows that there is an element which will take advantage of every opportunity to commit acts of violence. He pictures Ethel at her home, besieged by the mob of miners.

"I must get to Wilkes-Barre immediately," he declares.

"Mr. Benson, will you telephone to the Inter-State Railroad and ask when the next train leaves for Wilkes-Barre?" If there is not one within an hour, ask if it is possible to engage a special. I must reach Wilkes-Barre as quickly as possible.

"Here, read this," and he hands his secretary the telegram.

"Send this message to Martha Densmore. Address it, 'Sister Martha, Care of the Mount Hope Seminary, Wilkes-Barre, Pa., I leave for Wilkes-Barre at once.' If you can find out the time the train will leave, state it in the message to Martha."

In five minutes Benson returns to inform Trueman that the Keystone Express will leave at 3.30 P.M. This gives Trueman thirty minutes to catch the train. He hurries to the street and jumps into a cab.

"Drive to the Twenty-third street ferry as fast as you can. I'll give you an extra dollar if you make the four o'clock boat," he tells the cab driver.

"All right Mr. Trueman," replies the man, who recognizes the people's candidate. "You'll get the boat. Don't worry about that."

From Twenty-third street and Broadway the cab starts. It turns west on Twenty-fourth street. Then the driver whips up his horse. At Eleventh Avenue a freight train is passing. It will delay Trueman for five minutes. He jumps from the cab.

"Mr. Benson will pay you," he calls to the cab-man. The train moves down the street at a slow rate of speed.

Trueman jumps on a car, climbs across it and jumps to the street. At a run he makes for the ferry house.

As he passes the gateman he throws down a silver piece for ferry fare and rushes toward the boat. Half a minute later the boat draws out of the slip. When he enters the train, Trueman seats himself in the smoking-car. The man next to him is reading a late extra which he has bought at Cortlandt street.

Glancing over the man's shoulder, Trueman reads of the deaths of financiers, statesmen, manufacturers. All have met sudden and violent deaths, and in each instance there is announced the suicide or accidental death of an unknown companion.

Under a seven-column head, printed in red, is a suggestive paragraph. It asks if the wave of annihilation can have any connection with the Committee of Forty. And as if to answer the interrogation affirmatively, the paragraph concludes in these words:

"On the cards of six of the men whose bodies have been found with the murdered multi-millionaires, reference to the Committee of Forty is made point-blank. One asserts: 'In the future, arrogant capitalists will not sneer at the protestations of a committee of the people. As a deliberative body the Committee of Forty was impotent; as the avenger of the down-trodden, it will never be forgotten.' Another bears this strange inscription: 'When anarchy seems imminent, take courage, for an honest leader will deliver you from harm.'"

"There are two cards which quote direct from the Scriptures: 'The wicked in his pride doth persecute the poor: let them be taken in the devices that they have imagined.' This gives the motive which supplied the assassin of the Sugar King with courage to commit a double crime. He was a religious fanatic. The name George M. Watson was scribbled on the back of the card. This is the name of one of the Committee of Forty."

"The other card reads: 'And the destruction of the transgressors and of the sinners *shall* be together, and they that forsake the Lord shall be consumed.'"

Here is a matter which sets Trueman thinking. He knows every member of the Committee of Forty; they are men who would not take part in a dastardly crime.

But is this terrible annihilation to be looked at in the light of an ordinary crime?

"Metz is a member of the committee." Trueman resolves this thought for several minutes.

The train rolls on at a rapid rate; the towns of Jersey are entered and passed so quickly that no idea of the excitement that is stirring them can be formed. It is not until Trenton is reached that Trueman hears the news of the deaths of still other prominent men.

He buys a paper and returns to his seat. This extra contains the details of the threatened uprising in Wilkes-Barre, and the statement that the Committee of Forty has converted itself into a Syndicate of Annihilation.

When the train reaches Philadelphia a battalion of the State Militia goes on board. The Major in command has instructions to report to the Sheriff of Luzerne County. This means that the militia is to be handed over to the Magnates.

As the train is about to leave the depot a telegram is received at the dispatcher's office, which causes a delay. A freight on the Wilkes-Barre division has jumped the track. The wrecking train is called for. After the departure of the wrecking train the express pulls out. The accident has occurred thirty miles east of Wilkes-Barre. It causes the Keystone to be two hours late.

During his enforced wait, Trueman improves the time by telegraphing to New York. He gets from Benson the latest details of the news; the full import of the terrible atonement dawns upon him. The Committee of Forty had come to the conclusion that it must meet force with force. This was a step which Trueman would never have sanctioned. He realizes that the opprobrium for the act of the committee will be placed on him. He has been associated with the committee; has been the one candidate which it indorsed. And for all that he has known absolutely nothing of its intention to carry out a wholesale annihilation.

"Who will believe that I am not an accomplice?" he asks himself.

"I have but one way to clear my name of such an imputation. I must stand out as the advocate for rational action. I must bring the people, those who know me and who will obey my wishes, to unite to suppress anarchy."

As this thought shapes itself, the words on the card of one of the committee obtrude themselves on Trueman: "When anarchy seems imminent, take courage, for an honest leader will deliver you from harm." Is there something prophetic in these words?

Reinforcements are arriving on trains that are obliged to stop in the rear of the express. One of the new arrivals is a part of the infamous Coal and Iron Police. As these men are familiar with the mining district, the Sheriff of Luzerne requests that they be placed on the Keystone and rushed through first. This request is complied with. When the train starts, after the track is cleared, the three hundred and fifty members of the Coal and Iron Police have exchanged places with the militia.

From the intemperate speech of the men, Trueman foresees that the conflict between the miners and the police will be sanguinary. He resolves to keep the two bodies of men apart, if anything in his power can effect this result.

As the twilight deepens the train reaches the ten-mile grade that leads to Wilkes-Barre. The powerful engine responds to the utmost of its capacity and begins the ascent at a speed of fifty miles an hour.

"We shall be doing business in fifteen minutes," remarks one of the Coal and Iron Police, as he pulls his rifle from under the seat.

"Thank God, we don't have to stand up and receive a shower of sticks and stones, as the militia did in the old days. We have the right on our side now, and we can shoot without waiting to be shot," asserts a dyspeptic clerk, who has quit his desk for "*a day's shooting.*"

CHAPTER XXVII

SISTER MARTHA AVERTS A CALAMITY

When the tidings of the murder of Gorman Purdy reach the mines, the rejoicing of the miners and their families is undisguised. They feel that an avenging hand has been raised against the man who has caused them so many days of suffering.

"The devil has a new recruit," says a brawny miner.

"Hell is too good for a man like Purdy," another declares.

In all of Wilkes-Barre not a man or a woman except those who live under the Coal King's roof has a word of pity to express.

Sister Martha is silent; she feels shocked at the news; yet even in her heart there is no room for sympathy for the Magnate. The thought comes to her that Ethel will need comforting. Ethel Purdy is the woman who eclipsed Sister Martha in Harvey's mind. It is not to be supposed that Martha has forgotten this; yet it does not deter her from hastening to the place. She finds Ethel on the verge of hysteria.

Under the soothing influence of the Sister of Charity, Ethel's composure is restored.

"What is to become of me?" she asks, despairingly. "How am I to face the world? I have wealth; but will it restore my father?"

"Have faith, my dear, and you will find your troubles lightened."

Martha prays with the late Magnate's daughter. They are on their knees in the sumptuous bed-room of Ethel's suite when a servant abruptly enters.

"O, Miss Purdy, run for your life," cries the maid. "The miners are coming to burn the house."

Ethel utters a cry of terror.

"Leave the room!" sister Martha orders. And the frightened servant retires.

"Do not feel alarmed. I shall stay here and the miners will do you no injury. They love me and will obey me."

Ethel clasps the hand of her defender and crouches at her feet. A knock at the door startles the two women. Sister Martha remains in possession of her faculties; Ethel swoons.

"Come in," calls Sister Martha.

The butler enters.

"I have come to inform you that the miners are on their way to the house. They have sworn to sack it. What shall we do?"

"Who told you that the miners intend to come here?"

"I have just received the warning from the office; one of the clerks telephoned. He says the Superintendent is on his way here, but will probably be cut off."

Fear has anticipated the actual trend which events are to take. The miners are parading the streets but have not formulated any definite plan to attack the Purdy palace.

Francis A. Adams

Superintendent Judson arrives and assumes charge of the house. He brings definite news of the intention of the miners. They are bent on claiming the body of Carl Metz to give it a public funeral. "We shall never be able to prevent violence," he declares.

"The police and the militia have been summoned; but it will be hours before they arrive."

"If there was some one here who could pacify the mob until the troops come; there is no one they will heed."

"Perhaps I can pacify them," suggests Sister Martha.

"You can try," says the Superintendent, scrutinizing her closely. "You are known as the friend of the miners; they may respect your wishes."

Inwardly he doubts her ability to check the mob; he feels, even, that she may meet with physical violence at their hands. Yet his nature is so small that he is eager to sacrifice her if it will keep the miners at bay for an hour.

"I shall try to keep them in the town," Sister Martha assures him as she departs. On reaching the centre of the town Sister Martha meets some of the miner folk. A woman comes up to her and whispers:

"They have sent for the police. The work will be done before they get here."

"What work?"

"Why, we are going to give Metz a decent funeral. He died for us. He said in a letter,—died to set us free from Purdy."

"When are you going to demand the body?"

"This evening when the mines and shops close. We will all get together and then the sheriff can't stop us."

An inspiration comes to Martha. She hurries to a telegraph station, and sends the message to Trueman calling him to Wilkes-Barre.

"If he only gets here before the police or the troops, he can prevent trouble," is the thought that consoles her. The hour that passes before she receives word that he will arrive on the Keystone Express, seems an eternity.

With the knowledge that Trueman will arrive at five o'clock she breathes a sigh of relief. Again she mingles with the crowds which fill the streets. Here and there she goes, begging of the men and women to refrain from doing anything that they will regret later.

The afternoon wears on, and as rumors float through the town that the Governor has called out the State Guard, the excitement increases.

At four o'clock Sister Martha hears that the miners have determined to wreck the express, as it is bringing the Coal and Iron Police.

This news appalls her. Can she tell them that Trueman is on this train, and hope to have his arrival effective? No. He must come unexpectedly.

The plot to wreck the train must be defeated.

She hurries to the house of one of the miners who she knows will be in sympathy with any movement that has for its object the destruction of the Police. His two sons were shot at the Massacre of Hazleton. One of the young men died from the effects of his wounds. The other is a confirmed invalid.

On reaching the miner's cottage, Sister Martha finds that her intuition is correct. Henry Osling is telling his son the plan of vengeance.

"We will wipe out the old score to-night," he is saying. "When the express starts up the grade, we will send a ton of Paradise Powder down to meet it."

"How will it explode?" asks the son.

"How? Why, by the collision with the engine."

"But it may not go off," suggests the invalid. "You had better make sure by using dynamite. No! that won't do either."

"Use nitro. You can get it from the Horton shaft. They have to use it there to blast the slate."

"That's what we'll do, 'sonny.' Just lie still 'til you hear the bang, then you can get up and dance, for the Police will be blown to pieces."

Sister Martha waits for no further details. Her plan of action is decided upon. She knows every foot of ground in the mountains. A short cut will bring her to the home of Widow Braun. This woman will do anything in the world for Harvey Trueman. She will help Sister Martha to save the train; for by so doing she will save Trueman's life.

The widow is at home. In a few words Martha tells her what she must do if she would save the life of the men who rescued her boy and herself from the sheriff.

"Do you have to ask me twice to help you?" cries the woman. "I would lie down on the track and let the cars run over me if it would protect Mr. Trueman."

Martha and her ally start for the long grade. On the way they discuss the manner in which they may derail the car with the nitro-glycerine.

"We will put rocks on the track," suggests Sister Martha. "But the miners will see us;" objects the widow, "it won't be dark when the train arrives."

"I heard the miners say the train would be late. A freight was off the track east of Mathews and the wrecking crew was at work," Martha goes on to explain.

When the rescuers arrive at the track they realize that in their haste they have neglected to bring a lantern, the one thing that may be needed to signal the train, for now a dilemma confronts them. If they place a pile of rocks on the track, the train may reach that point before the car of destruction, and in this event the obstruction will cause the wrecking of the train.

The roadway is along the side of the mountain.

On one side of the tracks the rocks rise in a sheer wall; on the other is a steep embankment that in places is almost as precipitous as the crags above.

"We will have to separate," Martha advises. "You go up the track. No, I will go up and you down. If it is possible, you must stop the train. I will wait till the last moment and then put rocks on the track. When you see Mr. Trueman, tell him to hasten to the Purdy house, for Ethel is in great danger. Tell him I will be there to aid him in pacifying the miners."

"But you can never pile rocks enough on the track to stop the car," Widow Braun says compassionately, glancing at the frail form before her.

"Have no fear. I can do my part of the work. God will give me strength. And you, He will guide you, as well. Come, let us set about our work."

With a parting blessing from Sister Martha, the widow hurries down the track. She can discern the station five miles below at the beginning of the ten-mile grade. This station is her objective. If she can reach it before the arrival of the express, the life of Harvey Trueman and those of all the passengers will be saved.

The nature of her mission gives her strength to travel over the rough roadbed with incredible speed. Her eyes are upon the station, which momentarily becomes more and more indistinct; she knows that if the train starts up the grade she can see the headlight. Her lips move in an articulate prayer that she may not see the light. So absorbed is she in the thought of how to stop the train in the event of its passing the station that she fails to see a culvert bridge. At the bridge the roadbed terminates and a trestle carries the tracks for a distance of fifteen yards. The culvert is dry nine mouths in the year, and is a raging mountain torrent only in the spring.

Widow Braun rushes upon the trestle. Her steps are not regulated by the ties, and almost instantly she falls between them. Her hands grasp the rails on either side; but she has not sufficient strength to support herself. With an agonizing cry she drops twenty feet upon the jagged rocks below. Her head strikes a rock and she lies motionless.

Several minutes pass; then she regains consciousness. On attempting to rise she finds that her ankle is sprained. Despite the agony it causes her, the brave woman struggles to climb back to the track. It is now quite dark and she realizes that the train must be along in a few minutes. She cannot reach the station. But she may yet stop the train at the culvert bridge.

A long shrill whistle sounds. It is the familiar signal of the Keystone Express.

Regardless of the acute pain which every step causes her, the widow scrambles over the rocks.

As she reaches the roadbed the express rumbles over the trestle. With a cry of despair she sinks to the ground.

Sister Martha is acting her role of heroine at a point a mile and a half further up the grade. She has posted herself where she can observe the station and the summit of the grade.

At the side of the track she collects a dozen boulders, the heaviest she can move. These she determines to put on the track to derail the car which the miners are to send down the grade to wreck the train.

"Will the widow Braun stop the express?" Martha asks herself again and again, as the terrible minutes of suspense pass. "Perhaps I should have gone down the track instead of sending her."

Through the darkness a glimmer of light shines from the summit of the mountain.

"The miners are in readiness. What shall I do?"

For an answer, the whistle of the train falls upon her ears.

She hesitates, then with an energy born of desperation she begins to pile the rocks on the track. The ragged edges cut her tender fingers. She works on unmindful of cuts and bruises.

Higher and higher the pyramid rises.

Only once does she glance down the track to see the train. Its great headlight looks like a beacon. It is approaching nearer and nearer.

"Have they started the car?" Martha wonders. She can hear the rumble of the train, but not a sound from the road above.

"The train will reach this spot first," she cries aloud. "The miners are waiting for it to get nearer to them."

Acting upon a sudden impulse, she runs up the track a distance of a hundred yards. There are rocks lying on the side of the track nearest the mountain.

One, two, three big rocks she places on the track.

A faint cheer reaches her.

"They have started the car," she laughs hysterically.

"It will not harm the Keystone. No, it will stop here."

Another and another rock is placed on the rails.

She knows that these boulders are a poor impediment to a wildcat car; but they are the only things available.

A whirring sound rings in her ears. It is the car rolling down the grade with the velocity of a thunder-bolt.

In a minute or two at the most, the car will be upon her.

Still she does not falter. The second pyramid must be completed.

Again she turns to look down the track. The headlight of the engine seems to be upon her. It is, in fact, just crossing the culvert.

A glance at the pile of rocks makes them appear insignificant.

"They will never be able to stop the car," she moans.

Then with a final effort she tugs at a boulder larger than any of the others. She has it on the rail when the whistling of the engine startles her.

The engineer has seen the lower pyramid of rocks on the track and has whistled "down brakes."

The train is stopping; it will be saved, for one of the two

obstructions will derail the motor-car.

Sister Martha starts to run down the track. She has not taken a dozen steps when the juggernaut dashes into the pyramid of rocks.

Instantly there is a flash and an explosion, that shakes the mountain. Great ledges of rock slide from the overhanging crags.

In a shower of splintered stone, Martha is literally entombed. Her life is sacrificed on the altar of devotion. She has lived a Christian and dies a martyr.

But the Keystone Express is saved.

Its passengers and crew, when they recover from the fright occasioned by the explosion, hasten from the cars. Trainmen are sent up the track to investigate. Brakemen are also sent down the track to carry the news to the station.

One of these men stumbles across Widow Braun. He returns to the train carrying her.

From her, Trueman and the other passengers, including the Coal and Iron Police, learn of the plot to wreck the train and of the heroic effort made by Sister Martha and the widow herself, to avert the calamity.

Trueman starts in quest of Sister Martha. Accompanied by one of the trainmen with a lamp, he reaches the scene of the explosion.

The trainman discovers the body of Martha.

Bending over the prostrate body Harvey Trueman weeps. It is the manly expression of deep emotion.

"She died to save my life and the lives of the hundreds on the train. Was there ever a more noble sacrifice? It cannot be that she has given her life in vain. I must do the work she has begun. If I can prevent the miners from committing acts of violence it will atone for the loss of Sister Martha."

From the top of the mountain, Trueman catches a glimpse of the torches and miners' lamps. The miners are moving toward the town. Trueman is familiar with every inch of ground about Wilkes-Barre. He has played on the mountain as a boy. He now recollects a by-path which will bring him to the town in advance of the miners who are on the wagon road.

"Have the body of Sister Martha taken to the Mount Hope Seminary," he says to the trainman, and away he speeds for Wilkes-Barre.

The Coal and Iron Police are thrown into utter consternation. They dare not advance upon the town in the darkness for fear that there is another plot to destroy them.

The captain orders them to march across the mountain so as to enter the town from a direction opposite to that by which they are expected. To affect this detour will delay their arrival several hours, but their own safety is more to be considered than that of the townspeople.

And the miners? They have heard the explosion and believe that the Coal and Iron Police have been sent to their doom.

With the police out of their way there is nothing to check the miners in the accomplishment of their design to recover the body of Carl Metz.

It is the radical element that has conceived the idea of wrecking the train. They take full control of the miners and lead the way to join their comrades on the Esplanade. As they pass through the streets hundreds of men and women who have known nothing of the plot to wreck the train, fall in line and march on in the procession. The number of miners and townspeople soon reaches the thousands. By the time they arrive at the Esplanade there are ten thousand in line.

Francis A. Adams

CHAPTER XXVIII

AT THE DEAD COAL KING'S MANSION

Along the Esplanade the hurrying thousands begin to move in the direction of the Terrace; miners who have been in the shafts for eighteen hours; yard-hands from the railroads; iron founders, naked save for their breeches, have quit their furnaces; townspeople whom fear impels to see what the night will bring forth; this heterogeneous horde presses on to the scene of the murder.

It is a night that lends an appropriate setting to so strange and uncanny an event. The sky is leaden except for a streak on the western horizon where the fading, sinister light of the sun gives token of a stormy morrow. Through the walled banks, the river rushes turbulently, swollen by recent rains; its waters tinged by the dyes and other refuse from the city above.

On the further bank, the groups of breakers and foundries loom up as vague shadow creations. From fifty chimney mouths thick black smoke curls unceasingly; now soaring to a considerable height, now driven down to earth by fitful gusts of wind. In their sinuous course these smoke-clouds resemble the genii of fable, who spread over the earth carrying death and devastation.

In sharp contrast to this picture is the Avenue of Opulence on the side of the river which boasts of the Esplanade. Here is a line of fifty palatial residences; the homes of the owners of a hundred mines and factories and the task-masters of fifty thousand men, their wives and their progeny.

Clustered about the breakers and furnaces are the squalid huts and ramshackle cottages of the operatives; there too, a little removed from the river are the caves in which the Huns and Scandinavians dwell, even as their prehistoric ancestors dwelt before the light of civilization dawned.

Nero thrumming his violin from the vantage point of the crowning hill of Rome, had no such portraiture of the degradation of humanity as that which the Magnates nightly view from their balconies. A stranger would be struck with surprise that the thousands should be huddled in dens that wild animals would find uninhabitable, while the sons of greed and avarice flaunt their trappings of mammon from the hilltops.

This is the arena in which is to be enacted a scene of this great drama. The actors, the audience are gathering.

Mingled sounds of strange nature are on the air. The murmur always present where multitudes are assembled runs as an undertone; the sharp notes of frightened women and terrified children rise as the tones of an oratorio; steady, full, vibrant are the sounds of the men's voices.

On the countenances of the men can be read the exultation of their hearts, that at least one of their tyrants has encountered his Nemesis. Faces here and there are wreathed in smiles, as though their possessors were hastening to a fete. Some are grave, for the thought of the retribution that the Magnates will demand, and which they knew so well how to secure, is enough to bring a pallor to the cheek. There are men in the eddying thousands who have felt the hot lead of Latimer and Hazleton burn into their backs and the recollection makes them shudder. They are again upon a highway, but is this a protection against the violence of their masters? They are now, as then, unarmed, but is this a safeguard against the rifles of

Francis A. Adams

the hirelings?

From the bridge that connects the shores of the river, to the mansion of the Coal King, is a distance of two miles. The broad avenue affords an excellent concourse and down it the throng fairly runs. They traverse the distance in twenty minutes.

An army advancing into an enemy's country could not preserve better order. Far in advance of the main body of the toilers is the vanguard, a group of twenty of the acknowledged leaders of the men. It is at their suggestion that the cowed wretches have mustered up courage enough to cross the bridge and enter upon the interdicted boulevard. So it is incumbent upon them to show no trepidation.

Immediately behind them are the more adventurous ones, followed by the women and children, who, like angels, tread where men fear to go. The great mass of the crowd is composed of the workmen of the town. The faint-hearted and the cowardly bring up the rear. When the marble steps that lead up to the mansion are reached, the vanguard halts. The impetus of the entire line is arrested as if by magic. An unheard, invisible signal is obeyed, the signal of fear. Then the men in advance beckon to the people to come forward.

A score of young men respond as if to a summons for volunteers, and in their wake press the multitude.

The tumult ceases. The moment for action is approaching and men concentrate their attention on what is being done by the leaders.

"I have come for the body of Carl Metz," shouts Foreman O'Neil, from the foot of the terrace; his voice ringing with a tone of defiance.

"I have come for the body, and if you do not bring it out we will go in after it."

This ultimatum is addressed to the private detective who stands on the piazza of the Coal Magnate's palace, as a sentinel.

He does not seem disconcerted at the sight of so great a number of people. On the contrary his mouth curls in a derisive smile.

"O, you had better all go back to the breakers," he retorts. "We will see that Metz's body is buried."

Then he pauses, waiting to see the effect his words will produce. On and on comes the tidal wave of humanity. If it is not checked soon it will deluge the palace.

"I will shoot the first man who sets a foot on this piazza," defiantly cries the detective, at the same time drawing his revolver. "Get back to your breakers. If the superintendent sees you on this side of the river, you'll all get *sacked*," he adds as a threat more terrible than the shooting of one of them.

"We don't want to make trouble," explains O'Neil. "All that we ask is that we may take the body of Metz and give it decent burial. Has the superintendent said we could not have it?"

Mr. Judson, the superintendent of the Giant Breakers, appears at the door. He steps out on the piazza.

A sullen roar greets him.

"Until the coroner has disposed of the case," he begins, "no one will be permitted to touch the body. You have heard my decision. Now go back to your work."

The recollection of the treachery practiced on them in the riot of 1900, when their dead fellow-workmen were put in crates and buried by the police at night, without religious rites, comes to the minds of all. They have sworn then that never again would they be cheated of the right to bury their martyred brothers.

"Give us the body," cry a hundred voices in chorus.

"Go on, go on," shout the pressing thousands. "Go in and get it."

The forces for a storm have been gathering since the first tidings of the tragedy reached the people.

When they heard that Carl Metz, the foreman of the Keystone furnace, had killed Gorman Purdy and had then ended his own life, they were dumbfounded. Then as a lightning flash the information had spread that Metz had left a note explaining that he had killed the tyrannical Coal Magnate for the good of mankind. This word of explanation had clarified the confused thoughts in the minds of all. They read in that message their emancipation. The hour to strike a blow for their long lost rights had come.

The opposition offered by the detective and Judson, proves to be the shock needed to precipitate the storm.

By a single impulse the crowd rushes up the terrace. Its advance is irresistible. Both Judson and his hireling see the futility of attempting to resist the mob. They, therefore, withdraw within the house. As they enter they close the massive oak doors. Even as the doors swing to, the weight of a dozen powerful shoulders is thrown against them.

For a moment the advance is checked.

Turning to the windows, the infuriated men shatter them one by one, and like the sea pouring into a breach in a ship, they enter the house. One of the first to enter runs to the doors and flings them open. "Come in!" he shouts. "This is ours for to-day."

A marble staircase leads from the first floor to the one above.

This marvellous masterpiece had been made in Europe and imported. It cost two hundred thousand dollars—more than the appraised value of the two thousand hovels of the crowd that now trample upon its polished steps.

Up this staircase the impetuous leaders run. At the head of the stairs is the library, the room in which the tragedy has been enacted.

On the floor in this room is the body of Metz. It has not been disturbed.

The body of the Magnate has been removed to his bed-room to be prepared for burial.

O'Neil and two members of the Committee of Labor take up the prostrate form of their friend and make their way toward the door. It is not their intention to commit any violence in the house. Yet, as is always the case when men are under high mental tension, there is an element that cannot resist the instinctive craving of the animal spirit for blood.

"The sewer was good enough for Metz," exclaims an iron-worker, ferociously. It's good enough for Purdy."

"Where is Purdy's body?"

This question now presents itself to the invaders. It serves as the keynote for future action.

"Let's find it," suggests the ironworker. And the search of the mansion is begun.

Anticipating that the crowd might demand the body of the multi-millionaire, his faithful attendants have hurriedly removed it to the top of the building. It is concealed in the apartments of the chief butler. A superficial hunt fails to reveal its place of concealment. This intensifies the eagerness of the people to find it. They are positive it was on the premises, for the crowd without completely surrounds the palace.

Again are the gorgeous furnishings of the forty rooms thrown helter-skelter. Costly cabinets that refuse to yield to first pressure, are wrenched open. The frightened butler and the corps of other servants are impressed into the search. They are compelled to give up the keys to all closets and rooms. As case after case of silver and gold service are disclosed, the vulture element pounces upon them. For every piece there are fifty contestants, and the result is a wild scrimmage which prevents any one getting so much as a spoon without paying dearly for it.

Half an hour of vain search heats the tempers of the men to the fever point. Those with the butler finally threaten him with instant death if he does not disclose the whereabouts of the body, and reluctantly he obeys. Hounds falling upon their quarry could not exhibit more ferocity than the mob as it pounces upon the corpse.

Gorman Purdy had been seated in his library when his last summons came. He was attired in full evening dress. On his shirt bosom, over the heart, is a spot of blood. It shows where the bullet had found its mark.

A hurried consultation is held. It is decided that the body be carried to the Potter's field and thrown into the open grave that is kept for paupers.

Three men pick up the body and start to leave the house.

All this while the impatience of the throng outside has found vent in ribald jests.

"One dead millionaire is better than an army of workmen," jeers one man.

"He has come to life and has offered to arbitrate," sneers another.

"Bring him out!" is the incessant cry of the thousands.

And now the cortege appears. O'Neil and three committeemen carry the body of Metz. They pass between an avenue of men, who give way deferentially.

On reaching the Esplanade the pall-bearers pause. They face toward the bridge and wait for the procession to form. Then the trio who carry—or to be precise, drag the body of Purdy—emerge.

A great shout is given as the masses catch a glimpse of the body of the man who in his lifetime was their unmerciful master.

Darkness has supplanted the twilight. Now the contrast between light and shade is sharp. At intervals of fifty feet along the Esplanade, wrought iron gothic flambeaux support powerful electric lights. Objects beyond the immediate radius of the lights are indistinguishable. The windows of all the palaces are all closed and barricaded. From across the river the accustomed flare of the furnaces is missing. The fires are extinguished.

The uncouth countenances of the men and women can be studied in intermittent flashes as they pass under the strong glare of the lights. The utter absence of men and women of gentility makes the procession seem like the invasion of the Huns into the Empire. Among the thousands there are descendants of those very men who made the legions of Rome flee in terror. The torch of progress is again in the hands of the uncultured, and as history proves the race is to undergo another evolution.

That it is to be effected by internecine revolution none doubts. The march of carnage is on. Whither will it tend?

A leader of genius is wanted. The plastic emotions of the multitude will yield to his command.

Already the peaceable character of the visitation of the humble to the habitation of the haughty, has changed to one of violence.

O'Neil has been able to create the storm, but he lacks the capacity to direct it. The man of might has stepped forward and has been hailed as chief.

Just as the body of Purdy is to be brought down the terrace the sound of distant cheering is heard. It comes from the direction of the bridge. The men who have hold of the millionaire's body, drop it.

Do the shouts come from the militia?

With ever-increasing magnitude the cheering continues. Whatever the object may be, it is approaching the palace.

A reflex movement in the crowds indicates that danger is upon them.

"It's the Pinkertons!" is the terror-stricken cry that arises.

CHAPTER XXIX

PEACE HATH HER VICTORIES

Now the shouting swells into a general outburst of enthusiasm. "Trueman! Trueman!" are the words that reach the ears of the men at the foot of the terrace.

It is not the militia then, that is swooping down upon the people to crush them for demanding the body of their dead; it is not the Pinkertons. It is the champion of the people come to their aid!

Breathless from the three miles he has traversed at a run, Trueman sinks exhausted on the stone steps in front of Purdy's house.

The excited leaders cluster about him and tell him of the events that have transpired during the afternoon and early evening. "It was four o'clock when we first heard that Metz had shot and killed Purdy. The news spread to all the mills and furnaces," explains Chester, one of the yard hands of the local depot.

"Some one started the story that the police had been instructed to bury Metz secretly for fear there would be trouble if he was given a public funeral. You know there was a note found on him which said he had killed Purdy for the good of the workingmen."

"Yes," breaks in O'Neil, "the folks all over town said they were bound to see Metz given decent burial." A committee came to me and asked if I would head a procession to come here and demand the body. We came and were refused it. Then we broke into the house and got Metz's body.

"Some one started the cry, 'Find Purdy's body and bury it in Potter's field!' This set the crowd crazy. I could not prevent their seizing it."

Harvey Trueman listens to the stories of the men. He realizes that no half-measure can be proposed. It will either be necessary for him to acquiesce to their plan to throw the multi-millionaire's body into the Potter's field or else oppose them to the last point.

With the knowledge of the various events that have occurred he can estimate the effect that such an act of violence will have upon the country. Should the people of the other mining districts hear that the miners of Wilkes-Barre have risen in revolt against their masters it may precipitate a general uprising.

The deaths of the leading financiers and manufacturers throughout the country have made a panic inevitable. If to this is added rioting, the country will be plunged into a state of veritable anarchy. Why should not Wilkes-Barre be the centre of this national movement for a peaceable solution of the question of the rights of labor? One clear note of confidence sounded amid the general babel may serve as the signal for rational action.

Reasoning thus, he determines to make a grand effort to convert the crowd to moderation.

As he passed through the larger cities on his way to the town he heard that the people of Wilkes-Barre were up in arms. The militia have been ordered out and will arrive at any moment. The Coal and Iron Police are crossing the mountain and will show no mercy to the miners. If they find the people engaged in mischief, the story of past massacres will be repeated.

"Come with me," says Trueman to his lieutenants. They move quickly up the steps to the piazza of the magnate's palace.

Here Trueman turns to the crowd.

The cheering and shouting has been kept up during the two or three minutes that he has been resting. The people have again massed themselves about the grounds surrounding the house.

"Speech! speech!" they cry.

Trueman raises his hands before his face and lowers them in a sign for silence. The buzz of the thousands is instantly hushed. In a clear full voice that increases in volume as he proceeds, he begins his never-to-be-forgotten oration.

"Women and men of Wilkes-Barre:"

"That you are; testified in claiming the body of the man who sacrificed his life that you might live as freemen in this land of equal rights none can deny; that you should be moved to seek revenge upon the body of the man who has of all men been the most intolerant, tyrannical and merciless to you and the hundreds whom death has claimed, during the past twenty years, is nothing more than human."

"I believe, as have the philosophers and statesmen of all ages, that the people can do no wrong; for the voice of the people is, in fact, the voice of God."

As these words fall upon the ears of the multitude a great shout is given. Men wave their hats; women flutter their vari-colored shawls, which serve them as headgear; the sense of righteousness is awakened in them.

"With an abiding faith in the justice of the Almighty, you have bided your time; tolerance has ever been your actuating principle; reason has dictated every appeal that you have made to your masters."

"To-day you feel that the hour for your deliverance has come; that the fetters have fallen from your wrists." You stand here as emancipated men of a great nation. That your hearts should be filled with rejoicing, shows that you are alive to the importance of the occasion.

"Metz, who this day sacrificed his life for you, is worthy of your admiration." He is one of the world's heroes, one of its martyrs. It is for you to say if he shall have a monument worthy of his memorable act.

"The peoples of all ages have had their heroes and their martyrs." The progress of the world is marked by the monuments that have commemorated the deeds of these men.

"It remains for you to erect a monument for the martyr of the Twentieth Century."

"Shall it be of brass or of enduring granite?"

"Either of these would be a prey to the long lapse of time."

"You may choose as a monument, a mound that shall endure as long as the world rolls through space; you may convert those piles of brick and iron on the further side of the river into a mass of ruins; you may set the indignant torch to this fine line of palaces."

"Whatever you do you may be sure that your example will be the signal for your fellow workmen throughout the land."

"Burn down the breakers!" cries a thousand voices.

"Those breakers as they stand to-day are fit only to be destroyed," continues Trueman.

"They have consumed a pound of human flesh for every ton of coal that fed them. They have afforded money to a few Plutocrats, with which to satisfy the rapacious desires of greed; they have been the source of revenue that made these palaces possible. Those breakers have given you in return for your long days of toil, only enough to keep life in your bodies; they have bound you to this spot with fetters stronger than those of steel. If you should flee from this bondage you would find starvation awaiting you on the roads."

These sentences have an electrical effect upon the audience. The passive temperaments of the men and women are being quickened.

"Should you destroy the breakers and furnaces, and these homes of your oppressors, your own losses would outweigh those of the millionaires."

"Yet your acts would be justifiable."

"Do not move till I have delivered the message I bear."

"I come to you with tidings that will make the blood in your veins flow faster in a delirium of joy."

"I come to tell you that your fellow workmen in every state in this Republic are to-day emancipated, even as you yourselves have been. The sword has been wrested from the hands of tyrants, and has been placed in the hands of the people."

"The centuries that have come and gone since Christianity was first preached have seen the sword turned upon the humble, the meek, the worthy. Now it is to be turned upon the craven few who have fattened at the expense of the many."

"At the very hour when Melz sent Gorman Purdy to his doom, avenging angels, disguised as men, were abroad in our land weeding out the seed of iniquity."

"In San Diego, California, Senator Warwick was killed by the hand of a man who, when he had rid the earth of the most avaricious man who ever worked a mine, completed the chapter by taking his own life."

"Henceforth men will not slave in the mines of California or elsewhere for the sole benefit of misers. The miner will enjoy the fruits of his labor. He will make significant the words 'The laborer is worthy of his hire.'"

"In St. Louis at the same hour, the owner of the grain elevators, in which is stored the crops of the great plains, there to be kept until the needs of the people shall place an exorbitant price upon every bushel, was smothered to death in the hold of one of his own ships." With him died the martyr who had succeeded in bringing a just retribution upon the head of an insatiate oppressor.

"Henceforth bread shall not be made a product of speculation. The hungry mouths of women and children shall not go unfed that the stock broker and the grain speculator may amass fortunes."

"The Cotton King of Massachusetts, who has kept men and women out of employment, and in their stead has worked children in his mills, was killed in his office as he refused the fifth appeal for an advance of three cents a day in the pay of the six thousand half-grown children, most of them girls, who tended his looms and spindles for pauper wages."

"The man who thus abolished for all time the further slaughter of innocents, went to eternity with the dragon he had slain. The mill owner went to expiate his sins; the martyr to receive his reward."

"And in New York, the city which I have just left, the ruler of the Nation's money, the President of the Consolidated Banker's Exchange, died in a pot of molten lead which he had been brought to hope would be turned into gold under the touch of an alchemist. The lust of gold that in life had been his only incentive, proved the means of his undoing."

"Bond syndicates will no longer be formed to corner the people's money, that millions may be squeezed from the public treasury."

"My fellow-countrymen, this is indeed a great day."

"The full story cannot be told you at a single meeting."

"Know that you are once again free men, not in name only, but in reality; that your children will never suffer the degradation through which you have passed."

"The story of your deliverance you will soon know in its entirety. To-night I can only give you a summary."

"Tell us all! Tell us everything!" thunder the astonished masses. They forget Metz and Purdy in the presence of this greater news.

"I have only just learned the true facts of this remarkable movement." The representatives of the people who met in Chicago six months ago to formulate plans for the protection of labor, found that little could be accomplished against the combined wealth of the Trusts.

"A permanent committee of forty was elected to carry out the purposes of the convention." For several weeks the committee occupied itself in routine work. Its sub-committees reported that they could make no headway.

"Then at one of the meetings a committeeman named Nevins proposed that inasmuch as the committee had to deal with a wily and unscrupulous foe, it constitute itself into a secret body."

"At the first secret meeting he submitted the plan which was

Francis A. Adams

carried into effect to-day."

"It required that every one of the forty men should pledge himself to rid the world of one of its chief tyrants." He proved to the satisfaction of the men that by so doing they would be securing the blessings of liberty and happiness to mankind.

"He counselled them to strip their acts of any semblance of selfishness by sacrificing themselves with their vanquished enemies."

"At this moment the news is being flashed around the world that the forty tyrants and the forty martyrs have been gathered to their Maker in a single day."

"Again is the message that was first uttered in the Garden of Eden sent to the world: 'Labor is the God-given heritage of man.' Nor shall anyone keep man from his inheritance."

"To you, men and women of this Trust-ridden community, is given the opportunity to reap the full benefit of to-day's atonement."

"That you should waste your efforts on the mere gratification of revenge, was but natural when you did but know of the result of one deed in the plan of emancipation. Then it might have been enough that you should destroy the breakers and tear down these palaces."

"But now that you have heard of the National blow that has been struck for you, all thoughts of violence must be swept from your minds." Now you must realize that a greater triumph awaits you than to watch the flames lick up the property of your tormentors.

"That property is now yours!"

"These breakers, furnaces, factories; these houses, the mines beneath the earth's surface, the lands above them, all, all, are yours. It needs but for you to take possession of your own; for you to enjoy the full measure of the profit of your labor."

"Return to your homes, filled with rejoicing that you have not been called upon to stain your hands with blood; that your rights have been restored through the sacrifice of forty men to whom you and your posterity shall give immortal fame."

"You will have to work as hirelings only until you yourselves place your government in the hands of trusted men of your own selection."

"Fraud will no longer seek for public office; avarice will no longer scheme to gain possession of the world's wealth for the satisfaction of inordinate desires; inhumanity will no longer vaunt itself in our mills, our mines, our fields, for to-day the edict has been sent to the world that death awaits those who shall again seek to enslave labor." There will be forty martyrs ready for another sacrifice. Who will dare to be their foe?

"Choose your leaders with care; see that they are sincere in their determination to work your will."

"When this is done the hovels you now live in will be supplanted by decent homes; the poor food you now eat will be kept for your swine; your children will grow up to manhood and womanhood without having had their minds and bodies stunted by premature toil."

"A Republic of universal happiness and comfort will be yours."

"Such a Republic will be a monument to endure for all time to the memory of Carl Metz and his thirty-nine co-workers, to the honor of yourselves and to the security to future generations of the liberty that this Republic will afford all men."

"Pick up the body of Metz, and I shall help you bury it. I leave the body of Purdy for whomsoever may be inclined to care for it."

"Men of Wilkes-Barre, again I tell you, to-day you have been delivered from serfdom. Act as men, not as brutes."

"Choose some one to be your leader and let him direct you until to each of you is given the opportunity to vote for the laws that you may desire."

"With blare of trumpet and with tap of drum
Barbaric nations pay to Mars his due,
When victory crowns their arms. To him they sue
For privilege to war, though Mercy's thumb
Bids them as victors, rather to be mum,
And show a noble spirit to the foe;
To vaunt not at their fellow-creature's woe:
O'er victory only doth the savage thrum!
They conquer twice who from excess abstain;
The gentle nation that is forced to war,
In triumph seeks to hide, and put afar
All vestiges of carnage, and restore
Peace in the land, that men may turn again
To worthy toil, as they were wont before."

"Labour is your heritage; return to it."

He ends in a tumult of enthusiasm.

The multitude has been led from one emotion to another with such rapidity that they are fairly bewildered.

Two things only are clear in all minds. Trueman, the man who has become their most faithful champion, assures them that now they are to be free; that they are to be made the sharers in the wealth they create; he also tells them to select a leader.

By a spontaneous decision Trueman is the name that comes to every lip.

"Trueman! Trueman! You are the man to lead us."

The cry "Trueman!" sweeps through the crowd. It rises in an acclaim the like of which has never been heard before.

Men rush toward the orator and pick him off his feet. He is placed on the shoulders of the stalwart miners whom his eloquence and logic has won, and is borne in triumph at the head of the procession that goes to bury Carl Metz.

The millionaire's corpse lies on the steps of his late mansion. Clinging to it in the desperation of outraged womanhood, is Ethel. She had crept from the house while the eloquence of Trueman's words held the mob enraptured.

As Trueman is being borne in triumph down the steps his eyes rest on the terrible picture presented by the dead magnate and his daughter. In an instant the champion of justice forms a resolve. His heart and mind have a common impulse—Purdy's body must be saved from desecration; it must be buried with that of Metz.

"Pick up that body," he orders of the men who surround him. "It must be buried with Metz."

In his voice there is a ring of command that none dares to question. As the miners stoop to lift the corpse Ethel utters a cry of anguish that pierces the hearts of even the most hardened men. It is the wail of humanity protesting against anarchy.

By a vigorous effort Trueman frees himself from the miners who are carrying him on their shoulders. He is at the side of Ethel in a moment.

"Do not be frightened. I am here and will protect you and your father's remains."

His words are spoken in a loud decisive tone and reach the ears of the crowd that press around the corpse.

Yielding to his indomitable will Ethel arises. She wavers an instant; then stretches out her arms toward her protector.

Trueman seizes the delicate hands and draws her to his side.

"You are safe in my charge," he whispers to her soothingly. "Come with me and you shall witness your father's burial. If it is done now the mob will be pacified and will cease to clamor for vengeance."

Ethel walks by his side in silence.

The magnate's body is picked up and placed on the improvised litter of boards which serves to support the body of Metz. In silence the procession moves on toward the town.

The battle for moderation is won.

CHAPTER XXX

A DOUBLE FUNERAL

It is in an utterly hopeless frame of mind that Ethel walks beside Harvey Trueman. She cannot conceive that one man will have sufficient power over the passions of the multitude to prevent a violent demonstration when the graveyard is reached.

"They will tear my father's body to pieces," she sobs.

"Take my word for it, there will be no disorder," Trueman assures her. He walks with Ethel at the head of the motley crowd that only an hour ago was clamoring for the body of Purdy; this same crowd is now transformed into an orderly procession. The absence of music, or of any sound other than the tramp of feet on the smooth hard roadway, makes the procession unusual. There is deep silence, save for the occasional words that are spoken by the principal actors.

"This is a sad reunion, Ethel; one that could never have been predicted. When we parted that afternoon, two years ago, you said you never wished to see me again. I have remained away, until now. You are not sorry that I have come to protect you. Tell me that you are not." Harvey's words are spoken earnestly; he has kept the love of all the months of separation pent up in his heart. Now he is in the presence of the one woman in all the world, he adores. Her imperfections are not unknown to him; he has felt the sting of her long silence, broken only by her telegram sent at the hour of his triumph in

Francis A. Adams

Chicago; yet for all this be feels his heart throb as quickly as in the old days.

"O, Harvey, can you forgive me for my heartlessness?" she asks in a faint whisper.

"I could not decide against my father that horrid day, when you and he parted enemies. And after you had departed I was urged by all my family and friends to put you out of my thoughts; I was told that you had sworn to be an enemy to all men and women of wealth; that if I were to communicate with you it would necessitate my disowning all my home ties. I am only a woman—a woman born to wealth. How could I foretell that you are not an enemy to the rich, but a true friend of humanity?"

"Then you know me by my true character and not as I am depicted by the Plutocrats?" Trueman asks, joyfully.

He has heard the word "Harvey," and feels the exultation of the lover who hears his name pronounced in endearing tones by the woman he loves.

"Yes, I know you as you really are and I have felt the power of your words; it was not to the mob alone that you spoke. I stood in the shadow of my father's palace and heard your words. Harvey, you made me feel a deep pang of sympathy for my fellowmen and women."

The events of the day have been of such a momentous nature that it is not strange that Ethel should collapse. She has sustained the shock of her father's murder; the visitation of the citizens, bent on vengeance; then the unexpected appearance of Harvey Trueman.

She clings to her companion's arm, struggling to control her emotions. When she ceases to speak a great sob escapes her; then she begins to cry hysterically.

Trueman cannot bear to hear her heartbreaking sobs. With the impulse of a father soothing a child he lifts her from the ground, and holding her in his strong embrace, strides on at the head of the cortege.

When the town is reached the perfect order of the procession is preserved. It winds through unfrequented streets to the bridge; crossing the river it continues until checked by the closed gates of the cemetery.

At the sight of so vast an assemblage and at such an unheard of hour, the gate-keeper flees in terror. Two or three men enter the house to emerge with the keys of the great gates and a lamp.

By the fitful rays of this single lamp the movements of the burial party are conducted.

"Where shall we bury the bodies?" O'Connor asks Trueman.

"As near the gates as possible. I should suggest that the grave be dug in the circle of the main driveway. The grave of Metz and Purdy will become one of the most famous in Pennsylvania; it should not be put in an obscure place."

So the circle is decided upon as the proper place for the common grave of the millionaire transgressor and the martyr.

As the throng passes through the gates many of the men seize spades and picks, implements which they know only too well how to use.

It does not take twenty minutes to dig the grave.

When the work is completed, the fact dawns upon the minds of the leaders that they have neglected to provide a coffin for the bodies.

"What shall we do for coffins?" one of the grave-diggers asks, as he smooths over the edges of the grave.

"Give them soldiers' burial," suggests one of the bystanders.

"Here, take my shawl," says a shivering woman, as she pulls a thin faded gray shawl from her shoulders.

Her suggestion is followed by a score of other trembling wretches. The strangest shroud that ever wrapped mortal remains is used in the interment.

The bodies of Metz and Purdy are still being carried by the miners. Now a priest who has accompanied the funeral from the time it crossed the bridge, is escorted through the crowd to the edge of the grave.

"Will you conduct the burial service over these two bodies?" Trueman asks of the man of God.

"Neither was prepared for death," protests the priest.

"That is all the more reason for your offering up prayers for their souls."

"Were they of my faith?" inquires the priest.

"They are dead now and faith has nothing to do with the matter. We want you as a Christian to pronounce the words of the burial service over these bodies."

"One of these men was a murderer," further protests the priest.

"Which one?" demands Trueman.

"They say Mete killed German Purdy," is the response.

"And a hundred men within call of us will tell you that Gorman Purdy killed fifty men in his time," retorts a bystander. These words, so bitter yet so just, would be cruel indeed for the ears of Ethel Purdy; but she has lapsed into semi-consciousness. Harvey still holds her in his arms; he seems oblivious of the burden he has borne for more than a mile and a half.

"I cannot go through the forms of the church over the grave of these men," the priest declares emphatically. "It would be a sacrilege. But I will say a prayer for their departed spirits."

On the tombs that range in a wide semi-circle from the entrance, the crowd has taken points of vantage. Those who cannot force their way to the inner circle about the grave, stand aloof, yet where they can observe the simple, impressive ceremonies.

In a thin, querulous voice the prayer is asked. It is such an invocation as might have been uttered over the remains of two gladiators. Blood is upon the head of each; the prayer craves forgiveness. As the priest concludes, the bodies are wrapped in the shawls and lowered into the grave.

While the earth is being replaced, Trueman speaks to Ethel. She partially revives, and seems to understand that her father's body is being interred. When this thought has been fully grasped she realizes that she is being supported in Harvey's arms. She makes an instinctive effort to escape from his clasp; an instant later she looks up into his face and asks: "You will not leave me?" She pauses. "Give my millions to the people. I hate the thought of money. Only tell me that you will not desert me!"

"No, my darling," comes the whisper, "I shall never be parted from you again, so long as we live. The priest could not perform the burial service; he can, however, make us man and wife."

As he speaks, Harvey places Ethel gently on her feet.

Standing side by side at the grave which holds victor and

vanquished in the great war for the recovery of the rights of man, Harvey Trueman and Ethel Purdy present a strange contrast. He is the acknowledged leader of the plain people; she is the richest woman in America. For him, every one within reach of his voice has the deepest love and admiration; for the hapless woman beside him, there is not a man or woman who would turn a hand to keep her from starving.

If the men and women of Wilkes-Barre can be made to sanction the union of Trueman and Ethel Purdy, is there any reason to doubt that the question of social inequalities can be settled without bloodshed? Trueman determines to venture his election, his future, his life, to win the greatest triumph of his career, a wife whom the world despises as the favorite of fatuous fortune.

With a voice vibrant with emotion he addresses the multitude. Now by subtle argument, now by impassioned appeal he pictures the conditions that made Ethel's life so utterly different from theirs; how it was impossible for her to sympathize with them when she had known no sorrow, when her every wish had always been gratified. He pictures her as she appears before them; a daughter whose father has been stricken, as if by a blow from Heaven; a woman left friendless; for the friends of prosperity are never those of adversity. Thus he awakens a feeling of pity in the hearts of the people for the woman they have so recently reviled. Pity gives place to love as he tells them that Ethel Purdy wishes to give to the citizens of Wilkes-Barre the millions that her father has hoarded; when he concludes by telling them that she is to become his wife, an acclaim of rejoicing is given.

The priest, this time without reluctance, pronounces Harvey Trueman and Ethel Purdy man and wife.

"Go to your homes, my good brothers and sisters," Trueman counsels, "for to-morrow you enter upon your inheritance through the speedy channel of voluntary restoration; you are blessed of all men and women, perhaps, because you have long been the most grievously sinned against."

"Let no one commit an act of violence. It is from you that the country is to take its signal; you have curbed the hand of anarchy. What you have done will strengthen others to be patient. No one will have to wait longer than the next election to have wrongs set right."

The silence that awe induces takes possession of the people. They disperse quietly to their homes. At two o'clock there is no one on the streets.

The Coal and Iron Police, who have been lost in the mountains, enter the town at that hour to find it, to all appearances, deserted.

Harvey and Ethel accompany the priest to the parish house, where they remain for the night.

All the events of the afternoon and night have been telegraphed abroad. When morning dawns the people of the country and the world at large read of the uprising of the miners of Wilkes-Barre, of the attempt to wreck the train bearing the militia; of the rescue by Sister Martha at the sacrifice of her life; the stirring scene at the palace and the final obsequies and marriage ceremonial. All are known to the world. In the chaotic state of the public mind, this example of reasonable action is needed. Spread by the power of the pen, it wins man's greatest victory, a victory of peace.

CHAPTER XXXI

THE NEW ERA

From every section of the country the news of the pending election gives promise of a victory for the Independence party. The people have accepted the assurances of Harvey Trueman that he will not countenance violence on the part of the radical element of either the people or the Plutocrats. His conspicuous action at Wilkes-Barre is an incontestable proof of his sincerity, and also demonstrates that the masses are not desirous of reverting to an appeal to force in order to regain their rights. If the man whom the public hails as a deliverer can be elected, all the evils of the Trusts and monopolies, it is believed, can be settled amicably.

So strong has the sentiment in favor of the Independence party become, that for days before the election great parades of the workingmen in the principal cities celebrate the coming victory of the people.

Yet the subsidized press maintains a defiant position, and gloomily predicts that anarchy will prevail upon the announcement of the election of the Independence party's candidates.

This foreboding has little or no effect on the minds of the earnest workers; they are ready to trust their interests to men who have proven themselves honest champions of right, rather than suffer the bondage imposed by the Magnates.

Trueman, since the hour of his marriage, has spent much of his time in Wilkes-Barre. He decides that it is better for him to guide the closing days of the campaign from his home.

After settling the estate of Gorman Purdy, and turning over to the workingmen the mines, furnaces and breakers that were owned by the late Coal King, Harvey and his wife go to live in a comfortable villa in the suburbs.

By her voluntary surrender of the $160,000,000 which the criminal practices of Gorman Purdy had amassed, Ethel becomes the idol of the people, not only of Wilkes-Barre, but of the entire country. She gives substantial proof of the sincerity of her promise made at the grave of her father. This act of altruism does much to avert any reaction of the turbulent elements of the large cities.

The prospect of regaining the public utilities by purchase and the establishment of governmental departments to control them in the interests of the people as a whole, is made bright by the magnificent example that is furnished by the towns of Pennsylvania.

Harvey Trueman establishes the leaders of the Unions as the managers of the mines and breakers. Under his direction the profits of the business are divided proportionately among all the inhabitants of the town in which the works are located; those who work receive as their wage one-half of the net proceeds from the sale of their products. The remaining fifty per cent, is turned into the public treasury.

Had the millions of the Purdy fortune been distributed to the people by a per capita allotment, each man and woman of Wilkes-Barre might have been made independently rich. But this would defeat the ends which Ethel and Harvey wish to attain. They desire to see every citizen prosper according to his or her personal effort. So when every one in Wilkes-Barre is set to work at a profitable trade or occupation, the residue of the fortune, some $125,000,000, is used to establish a similar system of co-operation in neighboring mining districts.

In the thirty days that intervenes between the acts of annihilation and the election, two hundred and fifty thousand miners and other operatives in Pennsylvania are benefiting by the disbursement of the Purdy millions. This army of prosperous men makes the state certain of going to the Independents. The electoral votes of the Keystone state, it is certain, will decide the election.

As an object lesson which speaks more eloquently than words, Harvey adopts a suggestion which Sister Martha had made at the opening of the campaign and which had not been used because of lack of funds.

Biograph pictures of happy and contented miners in Pennsylvania, under the co-operative system, showing them at their work and at their decent homes, surrounded by their families, well fed, and clothed, are obtained in manifold sets. To contrast with these, there are pictures taken from the actual scenes in other parts of the country, showing women harnessed to the plow with oxen; women at work in the shoe factories, the tobacco factories, the sweat-shops. Pictures of the children who operate the looms in the cotton mills and the carpet factories are obtained to be contrasted with those which exhibit children at their proper places in the school room and on the lawns of the city parks.

The pomp of the Plutocrats and the destitution of the masses is portrayed by these striking contrasts.

With this terrible evidence the Independents carry their crusade into every city. The principal public squares of the cities are used to exhibit the biograph pictures. Night after night the crowds congregate to view the pictorial history of the Plutocratic National Prosperity. That which arguments cannot do in the way of weaning men from party prejudice the picture crusade accomplishes.

One of the side lights of the great drama that is being enacted is the sentiment that develops for the Committee of Forty. Memorial societies in the states from which the several committeemen hailed, are formed to give the martyrs, as the forty are now called, a decent burial. Thirty-nine of the martyrs are thus honored by public interment.

The one missing committeeman is William Nevins. He is supposed to be buried in the wrecked tunnel under the English channel. It is impossible to repair the damage done by the explosion; futile efforts are made by sub-marine divers to locate the exact point at which the break in the tunnel was made. The action of the water has totally obliterated the breach. So to the public this watery grave must remain the resting place of the genius who conceived the plan for the restoration of the rights of man.

All of the details of the committee come to light through the papers found on the body of Hendrick Stahl, secretary of the committee. The fact that Nevins was alone responsible for the plan of annihilation and that Trueman knew absolutely nothing of it, is incontestably established.

This takes away the last argument of the Plutocrats who seek to connect Trueman with the act of Proscription.

And Nevins? What of him?

He has not kept his pledge to the committee by dying with the Transgressor who was assigned to him. His pledge to God, to follow the committee the day after the atonement, has not been kept.

When October fourteenth dawned, the news of the uprising of the people of Wilkes-Barre and of the part played by Trueman and Ethel, were read by Nevins from the cable dispatches at Calais.

A fear arose in his heart that the plan for the election of

Trueman might fail. He delayed ending his life and hastened to New York. Upon his arrival he went as a lodger to a room in a lofty Bowery hotel. From this watch-tower he reviewed the political field. "I shall redeem my pledge to-morrow," he said to himself each day.

The night would find him irresolute, not for his fear of death, but for the dread that some unexpected occurrence might arise to thwart the people in their effort to carry the election by the peaceable use of the ballot.

On the flight before the election Nevins hastens to Chicago. In the crowd at the Independence Headquarters he mingles unobserved. "What news have you from California?" he asks of one of the press committee. This is thought to be the pivotal State. At least this is the claim made by the Plutocrats.

"The indications are that the State will go against us."

"And why so?"

"Because we have not been able to send speakers there, and the Plutocrats wrecked the train which was conveying the biograph pictures. You know the Press of the slope, with but few exceptions, are owned by the Magnates and suppress every bit of news that would be detrimental to them. They have distorted the acts of the Committee of Forty. Out in California the great mass of the people look upon the Independents as a party of Anarchists."

"Trueman can be elected without California, can he not?"

"Elected! Why, he will carry forty States."

"You really believe it?" asks Nevins, earnestly.

"I would wager my life on it," is the instant reply.

Nevins hurries from the headquarters and goes to his room.

He writes a letter to Trueman, setting forth his hopes that the interests of the people will ever remain Trueman's actuating principle. With absolute fidelity he tells of the struggle he has undergone since the day he sent Golding to his death, and his reason for procrastinating in ending his life.

When the letter is finished Nevins reads it with evident satisfaction.

"Now I will go to the committee," is his resolve.

A pistol lies on the table. He picks up the weapon. There is no hesitancy in his manner. Death has been a matter which he has contemplated for months, and it holds no terror for him.

"If I have sinned against Thee, O, God," he murmurs, "death would be too mild a punishment for me. I would deserve to be everlastingly damned, to live on this earth and bear the denunciation of my fellowmen."

"My death, like those of the committee who have already fulfilled their pledge, is not suicide, but part of the inevitable price of liberty."

The pistol is raised to his temple. Then a thought flashes upon him. "Your death will come as an ante-climax to the election. It may be the means of defeating the Independents."

This thought causes him to lower the pistol.

"To-morrow," he mutters.

At daybreak Nevins is at the headquarters and remains near the chief operator, eager for every detail of the election.

"What is the weather prediction?" he inquires.

"Generally clear; light local rains on Pacific seaboard."

"I am most intensely interested in the result of the election," Nevins confided to the operator, to explain his presence at headquarters. "I have come all the way from San Francisco to congratulate Trueman on his election."

"I'm afraid you'll be disappointed. Mr. Trueman is at his home in Wilkes-Barre."

"Well, I shall telegraph him my congratulations. I want to be the first man in the United States to send him an authoritative message confirming his election. If you can arrange to let me have the news first, when it comes in, and will send my message, I shall be glad to pay you for the service."

"I have the wire that will send him the news," the operator states as he pats a transmitter on the desk before him. "What do you call a fair payment for the message?"

"Twenty-five dollars."

"I'll send your message."

Nevins gives the required sum, and sits at the elbow of the man who is to flash the news of victory to Trueman.

In Wilkes-Barre the day has dawned auspiciously. Trueman is among the first to perform his duty as a citizen. After voting he returns to his home.

With his wife at his side he reads the dispatches that come in by a private wire from headquarters.

"I am happier to-day than I ever was in my life before," Ethel tells him. "And I know that you will be elected."

"I hope your words come true. But whether I am President or not my campaign has not been in vain. I have won the fairest bride in the world, and she and I are doing a real good with a fortune that might have been a curse."

"Now I can understand the words that are a mystery to so many of the rich: 'It is more blessed to give than to receive,'" Ethel says, as she places her hand on her husband's shoulder. "Now I can appreciate the emotion that impelled you to give the one thousand dollar check to the miner's widow." As they sit together, through the long day, they discuss what they will do for the improvement of the people, there is no provision for the repayment of anti-election promises to the managers of trusts; no talk of rewarding henchmen with high offices.

By five in the afternoon the messages begin to announce the forecast in the extreme Eastern states.

"Rhode Island has polled the largest vote in its history. The Independence Party claims the state by fifteen thousand." Harvey reads this with an incredulous smile.

"We can hardly hope to carry Rhode Island," he declares frankly.

"You told me only yesterday that Fall River is going wild over the biograph pictures," Ethel protests.

"The rural vote in Maine is believed to have caused the state to go to the Independents," is the next message that causes Harvey to doubt his senses.

"New Jersey washes its hands of trusts. Trueman carries Newark, Trenton, and Jersey City by overwhelming majorities."

Thus the story of state after state is wired to Wilkes-Barre.

"Pennsylvania, New York, Ohio are claimed to have voted for the people's candidate. The Plutocrats ridicule the assertion, yet have no figures to quote."

At nine o'clock the returns by election districts in the populous cities, begin to arrive.

Francis A. Adams

"In 1238 districts, Greater New York, Trueman leads by a clear majority of 75,000." Harvey reads without comment.

Ten minutes later, this message is received: "Total of 2200 election districts, Greater New York, Trueman's majority 180,000. This makes the state Independent by a safe margin of 100,000."

Harvey Trueman feels for the first time since his nomination that he will be elected. Joy is written on his face.

"Pennsylvania casts its vote for Trueman and co-operation."

It is eleven-thirty. The proverbial "landslide" of politics has occurred. Already the townspeople of Wilkes-Barre are surging about the villa, cheering their champion.

A dozen times Harvey goes to the window to bow his acknowledgments.

Ethel is excited, almost hysterical. With a woman's quick perception she realizes that her husband has triumphed.

Again they stand at the elbow of the telegraph operator who is receiving the messages.

"Chicago—" then there was a break.

"Trueman, have Trueman come to the instrument. Answer. Is Trueman at your elbow?" This message is sent by the operator at headquarters. He has indicated that it is a private message and only the word Chicago is written.

"What's the matter?" asks Trueman, who has noticed the pause.

"It's all right, sir; the operator want's you to get this message immediately." There is another pause.

CHICAGO, ILLINOIS,
INDEPENDENCE PARTY HEADQUARTERS.

To HARVEY TRUEMAN, Greeting:

"You are elected President of the United States by popular acclamation of forty States. I congratulate you. Keep your faith with the people; place them always above the dollar; remember that your office was bought by the blood of patriots, as true as the founders of the Republic; that you owe it to the majority to keep their rights inviolate. I go to inform the Committee of Forty that the Revolution of Reason is victorious.

WILLIAM NEVINS."

As Trueman reads these words and grasps their meaning, Nevins, at the other end of the wire, in distant Chicago, redeems his pledge and drops dead.

The curtain falls on the Tragedy of Life. The struggle for mere existence that has retarded mankind from creation, is at an end. Man enters into possession of his God-given inheritance, *equal opportunity*, with a valiant leader, and the fairest land in the world in which to begin the building up of a Republic that insures to all men Life, Liberty, and the Pursuit of Happiness.

Choose from Thousands of 1stWorldLibrary Classics By

A. M. Barnard
Ada Leverson
Adolphus William Ward
Aesop
Agatha Christie
Alexander Aaronsohn
Alexander Kielland
Alexandre Dumas
Alfred Gatty
Alfred Ollivant
Alice Duer Miller
Alice Turner Curtis
Alice Dunbar
Allen Chapman
Alleyne Ireland
Ambrose Bierce
Amelia E. Barr
Amory H. Bradford
Andrew Lang
Andrew McFarland Davis
Andy Adams
Angela Brazil
Anna Alice Chapin
Anna Sewell
Annie Besant
Annie Hamilton Donnell
Annie Payson Call
Annie Roe Carr
Annonaymous
Anton Chekhov
Archibald Lee Fletcher
Arnold Bennett
Arthur C. Benson
Arthur Conan Doyle
Arthur M. Winfield
Arthur Ransome
Arthur Schnitzler
Arthur Train
Atticus
B.H. Baden-Powell
B. M. Bower
B. C. Chatterjee
Baroness Emmuska Orczy
Baroness Orczy
Basil King
Bayard Taylor
Ben Macomber
Bertha Muzzy Bower
Bjornstjerne Bjornson

Booth Tarkington
Boyd Cable
Bram Stoker
C. Collodi
C. E. Orr
C. M. Ingleby
Carolyn Wells
Catherine Parr Traill
Charles A. Eastman
Charles Amory Beach
Charles Dickens
Charles Dudley Warner
Charles Farrar Browne
Charles Ives
Charles Kingsley
Charles Klein
Charles Hanson Towne
Charles Lathrop Pack
Charles Romyn Dake
Charles Whibley
Charles Willing Beale
Charlotte M. Braeme
Charlotte M. Yonge
Charlotte Perkins Stetson
Clair W. Hayes
Clarence Day Jr.
Clarence E. Mulford
Clemence Housman
Confucius
Coningsby Dawson
Cornelis DeWitt Wilcox
Cyril Burleigh
D. H. Lawrence
Daniel Defoe
David Garnett
Dinah Craik
Don Carlos Janes
Donald Keyhoe
Dorothy Kilner
Dougan Clark
Douglas Fairbanks
E. Nesbit
E. P. Roe
E. Phillips Oppenheim
E. S. Brooks
Earl Barnes
Edgar Rice Burroughs
Edith Van Dyne
Edith Wharton

Edward Everett Hale
Edward J. O'Biren
Edward S. Ellis
Edwin L. Arnold
Eleanor Atkins
Eleanor Hallowell Abbott
Eliot Gregory
Elizabeth Gaskell
Elizabeth McCracken
Elizabeth Von Arnim
Ellem Key
Emerson Hough
Emilie F. Carlen
Emily Bronte
Emily Dickinson
Enid Bagnold
Enilor Macartney Lane
Erasmus W. Jones
Ernie Howard Pie
Ethel May Dell
Ethel Turner
Ethel Watts Mumford
Eugene Sue
Eugenie Foa
Eugene Wood
Eustace Hale Ball
Evelyn Everett-green
Everard Cotes
F. H. Cheley
F. J. Cross
F. Marion Crawford
Fannie E. Newberry
Federick Austin Ogg
Ferdinand Ossendowski
Fergus Hume
Florence A. Kilpatrick
Fremont B. Deering
Francis Bacon
Francis Darwin
Frances Hodgson Burnett
Frances Parkinson Keyes
Frank Gee Patchin
Frank Harris
Frank Jewett Mather
Frank L. Packard
Frank V. Webster
Frederic Stewart Isham
Frederick Trevor Hill
Frederick Winslow Taylor

Friedrich Kerst
Friedrich Nietzsche
Fyodor Dostoyevsky
G.A. Henty
G.K. Chesterton
Gabrielle E. Jackson
Garrett P. Serviss
Gaston Leroux
George A. Warren
George Ade
Geroge Bernard Shaw
George Cary Eggleston
George Durston
George Ebers
George Eliot
George Gissing
George MacDonald
George Meredith
George Orwell
George Sylvester Viereck
George Tucker
George W. Cable
George Wharton James
Gertrude Atherton
Gordon Casserly
Grace E. King
Grace Gallatin
Grace Greenwood
Grant Allen
Guillermo A. Sherwell
Gulielma Zollinger
Gustav Flaubert
H. A. Cody
H. B. Irving
H.C. Bailey
H. G. Wells
H. H. Munro
H. Irving Hancock
H. R. Naylor
H. Rider Haggard
H. W. C. Davis
Haldeman Julius
Hall Caine
Hamilton Wright Mabie
Hans Christian Andersen
Harold Avery
Harold McGrath
Harriet Beecher Stowe
Harry Castlemon
Harry Coghill
Harry Houidini

Hayden Carruth
Helent Hunt Jackson
Helen Nicolay
Hendrik Conscience
Hendy David Thoreau
Henri Barbusse
Henrik Ibsen
Henry Adams
Henry Ford
Henry Frost
Henry James
Henry Jones Ford
Henry Seton Merriman
Henry W Longfellow
Herbert A. Giles
Herbert Carter
Herbert N. Casson
Herman Hesse
Hildegard G. Frey
Homer
Honore De Balzac
Horace B. Day
Horace Walpole
Horatio Alger Jr.
Howard Pyle
Howard R. Garis
Hugh Lofting
Hugh Walpole
Humphry Ward
Ian Maclaren
Inez Haynes Gillmore
Irving Bacheller
Isabel Cecilia Williams
Isabel Hornibrook
Israel Abrahams
Ivan Turgenev
J.G.Austin
J. Henri Fabre
J. M. Barrie
J. M. Walsh
J. Macdonald Oxley
J. R. Miller
J. S. Fletcher
J. S. Knowles
J. Storer Clouston
J. W. Duffield
Jack London
Jacob Abbott
James Allen
James Andrews
James Baldwin

James Branch Cabell
James DeMille
James Joyce
James Lane Allen
James Lane Allen
James Oliver Curwood
James Oppenheim
James Otis
James R. Driscoll
Jane Abbott
Jane Austen
Jane L. Stewart
Janet Aldridge
Jens Peter Jacobsen
Jerome K. Jerome
Jessie Graham Flower
John Buchan
John Burroughs
John Cournos
John F. Kennedy
John Gay
John Glasworthy
John Habberton
John Joy Bell
John Kendrick Bangs
John Milton
John Philip Sousa
John Taintor Foote
Jonas Lauritz Idemil Lie
Jonathan Swift
Joseph A. Altsheler
Joseph Carey
Joseph Conrad
Joseph E. Badger Jr
Joseph Hergesheimer
Joseph Jacobs
Jules Vernes
Julian Hawthrone
Julie A Lippmann
Justin Huntly McCarthy
Kakuzo Okakura
Karle Wilson Baker
Kate Chopin
Kenneth Grahame
Kenneth McGaffey
Kate Langley Bosher
Kate Langley Bosher
Katherine Cecil Thurston
Katherine Stokes
L. A. Abbot
L. T. Meade

L. Frank Baum
Latta Griswold
Laura Dent Crane
Laura Lee Hope
Laurence Housman
Lawrence Beasley
Leo Tolstoy
Leonid Andreyev
Lewis Carroll
Lewis Sperry Chafer
Lilian Bell
Lloyd Osbourne
Louis Hughes
Louis Joseph Vance
Louis Tracy
Louisa May Alcott
Lucy Fitch Perkins
Lucy Maud Montgomery
Luther Benson
Lydia Miller Middleton
Lyndon Orr
M. Corvus
M. H. Adams
Margaret E. Sangster
Margret Howth
Margaret Vandercook
Margaret W. Hungerford
Margret Penrose
Maria Edgeworth
Maria Thompson Daviess
Mariano Azuela
Marion Polk Angellotti
Mark Overton
Mark Twain
Mary Austin
Mary Catherine Crowley
Mary Cole
Mary Hastings Bradley
Mary Roberts Rinehart
Mary Rowlandson
M. Wollstonecraft Shelley
Maud Lindsay
Max Beerbohm
Myra Kelly
Nathaniel Hawthrone
Nicolo Machiavelli
O. F. Walton
Oscar Wilde
Owen Johnson
P.G. Wodehouse
Paul and Mabel Thorne

Paul G. Tomlinson
Paul Severing
Percy Brebner
Percy Keese Fitzhugh
Peter B. Kyne
Plato
Quincy Allen
R. Derby Holmes
R. L. Stevenson
R. S. Ball
Rabindranath Tagore
Rahul Alvares
Ralph Bonehill
Ralph Henry Barbour
Ralph Victor
Ralph Waldo Emmerson
Rene Descartes
Ray Cummings
Rex Beach
Rex E. Beach
Richard Harding Davis
Richard Jefferies
Richard Le Gallienne
Robert Barr
Robert Frost
Robert Gordon Anderson
Robert L. Drake
Robert Lansing
Robert Lynd
Robert Michael Ballantyne
Robert W. Chambers
Rosa Nouchette Carey
Rudyard Kipling
Saint Augustine
Samuel B. Allison
Samuel Hopkins Adams
Sarah Bernhardt
Sarah C. Hallowell
Selma Lagerlof
Sherwood Anderson
Sigmund Freud
Standish O'Grady
Stanley Weyman
Stella Benson
Stella M. Francis
Stephen Crane
Stewart Edward White
Stijn Streuvels
Swami Abhedananda
Swami Parmananda
T. S. Ackland

T. S. Arthur
The Princess Der Ling
Thomas A. Janvier
Thomas A Kempis
Thomas Anderton
Thomas Bailey Aldrich
Thomas Bulfinch
Thomas De Quincey
Thomas Dixon
Thomas H. Huxley
Thomas Hardy
Thomas More
Thornton W. Burgess
U. S. Grant
Upton Sinclair
Valentine Williams
Various Authors
Vaughan Kester
Victor Appleton
Victor G. Durham
Victoria Cross
Virginia Woolf
Wadsworth Camp
Walter Camp
Walter Scott
Washington Irving
Wilbur Lawton
Wilkie Collins
Willa Cather
Willard F. Baker
William Dean Howells
William le Queux
W. Makepeace Thackeray
William W. Walter
William Shakespeare
Winston Churchill
Yei Theodora Ozaki
Yogi Ramacharaka
Young E. Allison
Zane Grey